The suspense was killing her

She gazed upward quizzically, trying to gauge his mood. A moment ago, he'd been playful as a puppy when she'd honestly believed he would take his revenge. Then suddenly his arms had tightened around her and he'd backed down. She had no idea why.

That was the problem with Malone. He didn't make anything simple. Not only that, nothing in her experience had prepared her for what she felt when she was with him. She'd enjoyed the calm balance of her life, the symmetry of knowing what would happen and when. It was certainly easier than this tumultuous sensation of rushing headlong into the unknown.

Then again, Dani mused, a little excitement wasn't all bad. Especially when it came wrapped in a package like Malone. It was time to press him a little; with any luck, she might find out just how complicated her life was about to become.

ABOUT THE AUTHOR

According to Laurien Berenson, there's no greater thrill in the world than seeing your own words published between the covers of a book. Laurien began writing at the age of five but admits that her first published work came much later. After spending most of her childhood on the back of a horse, she decided to write her first American Romance around the milieu of polo. Laurien makes her home in Connecticut with her husband and young son.

Winner Take All
Laurien Berenson

Harlequin Books

TORONTO • NEW YORK • LONDON
AMSTERDAM • PARIS • SYDNEY • HAMBURG
STOCKHOLM • ATHENS • TOKYO • MILAN

For Chase.

Published August 1987

First printing June 1987

ISBN 0-373-16210-3

Chapter One

Dani Hawthorne drove a car the same way she rode a horse: quickly, deliberately and without a single wasted motion. The sleek Porsche 944 Turbo was agile and responsive beneath her hands. Pushing the speed limit in third gear, it clung to the tight curves like an amorous suitor. Dani respected that. She appreciated high performance, good horseflesh and winning, and she was intimately familiar with all three.

The narrow road twisted like a cow path through the verdant Connecticut countryside. Coming into a turn, Dani checked, downshifted, then accelerated out the other side, leaving a fine spray of gravel in her wake. Her brow lifted briefly as she glanced into the rearview mirror, then settled back down in a frown. She knew she was driving too fast, and knew too that it wouldn't work. She couldn't escape the events of the past hour merely by leaving them behind.

God, how she hated making a scene. Even more than that, she hated losing control. This morning she had done both.

I wouldn't marry you if you were the last man on earth! The angry words reverberated inside her head like a Greek chorus gone mad. She'd shouted them at Spence earlier, and she'd meant every word. Now, however, she was beginning to wonder how she could have ever done such a thing.

Not that Spence didn't deserve to be turned down, Dani told herself quickly. It was just that she could have found a way to deliver the message more kindly. Of course, at the time, kindness had been the last thing on her mind. If only he hadn't made her so mad!

Dani sighed and settled back in the bucket seat, her irritation finally beginning to ebb. Warm, moist summer air blew in the car's open window, swirling the long strands of golden blond hair that lay on her shoulders. Absently she reached up, pulling the heavy hair back and twisting it into a coil at her nape.

Here and there wisps escaped, forming tiny curls that framed an oval face with pale, almost translucent skin. Clear sea-blue eyes gazed out at the quiet back country road with cool determination and a calm sense of purpose. In five minutes she'd be at the hunt club, and ten minutes after that, on the back of a horse. The prospect cheered her, as it always had.

The sun filtered through the leafy canopy above, forming a kaleidoscope pattern on the tree-lined lane. Dani breathed in deeply, savoring the sweet scent of the heavy air. Her lips curved with the beginnings of a smile as she pondered the ride ahead. Then, finally, she would be able to put Spencer Hamilton III out of her mind once and for all.

Really, Dani mused, the whole fiasco that morning never should have been allowed to happen in the first place. It was inconceivable that by the age of twenty-six she hadn't learned how to control her temper better. Then again, she decided in her own defense, she'd have thought that Spence would have more sense than to think she might consent to marry him!

Dani did smile then, remembering how his jaw had dropped open quite comically in response to her unexpected answer. In the space of just a few short seconds, he'd managed to look first shocked, then chagrined, then finally furious—none of which was surprising when she stopped to consider that this was probably the first time in his entire overprivileged life that anyone had ever told Spencer Hamilton III that he wasn't going to get something he'd gone after.

Of course, Dani was the first to acknowledge that it wasn't actually *her* that Spence had wanted. No, this was one rejection that had hit him where it mattered most—right in the bank book. And if he'd been livid, his response was nothing compared to what her mother was going to say when she came home from the Far East and found that Dani had turned down yet another eligible, meaning wealthy, suitor.

But then, Dani mused, Amelie Ford Hawthorne Nelson Abbott Shearson Barazini had always viewed marriage as a vast wonderland of opportunity—a game of wits and wiles to be played to full advantage and milked for everything it was worth. Amelie may have been born with a silver spoon, but she'd since acquired the keys to the entire vault, and it was clear that she expected Dani to carry on in the same tradition.

Dani shook her head irritably. Already the yearly income from the trust fund her father had set up was enough to feed the inhabitants of a small South American nation. How could she possibly ever need more?

It wasn't that she was ungrateful, thought Dani. It was just that having the vast resources of Hawthorne Enterprises standing behind her tended to be a bit overshadowing. Take men, for example. The ones she met were always either wildly impressed, or else wildly intimidated. But either way, she herself had little to do with it.

Not that Dani had any doubts about her own appeal. After all, she wasn't her mother's daughter for nothing. She knew that she had style and flair, and an innate sense of dignity and grace, all of which contributed to her strong, uncommon sort of beauty. At an early age, however, she'd learned that beside the seductive allure of a multimillion-dollar fortune, her own assets only paled by comparison.

Still, Dani realized, there were worse things in life. Her work with the Pegasus Program had certainly shown her that. The children she worked with were so brave, and so full of hope, in spite of the obstacles stacked against them. And if they could still manage to face the world with a smile, what right could she possibly have to complain?

None at all, Dani decided firmly. She eased her foot off the gas pedal, and the Porsche slowed to a more sedate pace. Only two more minutes to the hunt club. Then she would be free.

THE ENGINE ONLY had to buck twice before Rick Malone knew he was in trouble. In the past three days, he'd nursed the ailing horse van all the way from Arizona, a trip, he mused now, that would probably be its last. But with only another mile or so to go until he reached the Silverbrook Hunt Club, he had every hope of completing the journey. Until he saw the smoke.

Quickly he nosed the van over onto the road's narrow shoulder. It bumped over a section of rocky ground before coming to rest in a small rut. There was a sharp clatter from inside as a horse lashed out in protest, catching the side of the truck with its hooves.

With a muttered curse, Rick hopped out of the cab. He brushed his fingers across the hood, testing for heat. It was there. As he weighed his options, a high-pitched whinny rang out impatiently.

"Keep your shirt on," he called. "I'm coming."

Snatching up a rag from inside the cab, he wrapped his hand, then threw open the hood. More smoke billowed out. Smoke but no flames, Rick noted. It was a good sign.

He waited for the smoke to clear, then leaned in to assess the situation. The electrical tape he'd used to patch the engine in Pittsburgh had melted into a sticky mass of black goo. The van wasn't going any farther today, and perhaps, from the look of things, not ever.

Shrugging philosophically, Rick slammed the hood and dusted off his hands against the worn seat of his jeans. He'd get the horses out and delivered to Silverbrook. They were the most important thing. Once they were bedded down, there'd be plenty of time to worry about the rest.

ROUNDING THE LAST TURN, Dani saw up ahead a small three-horse van that had pulled over to the side of the road. Automatically her foot lifted from the gas pedal, slowing the car as she approached. The van was painted a weathered shade of green with gray trim. Though she knew most of the stables in the area, Dani didn't recognize the colors. The horses must have been on their way to the hunt club, she decided. But why on earth were they being unloaded here?

She heard a familiar clanking sound as the ramp on the far side was lowered to the ground. Dani stared curiously, wondering what had made the driver stop just short of his goal. Then, as she passed the van, she saw the small spiral of smoke curling out from beneath its hood. All at once things made perfect sense.

Without stopping to think, Dani pulled over to the side of the road. She was out of her car before it had even stopped rolling. As she hurried around the side of the van, she heard someone crooning quietly, his soft voice soothing the animals whose nervous fidgeting was making the van rock on its unsteady perch.

"Hello?" Dani called. She stuck her head around the side of the ramp and looked up into the truck. "Do you need any help?"

"Lots," the driver replied without bothering to turn around. Dani could see why. With one horse already unfastened and two others straining against their chains, he had his hands full. "How are you with engines?"

"Terrible. Though I do know enough to tell you that yours is on fire."

"It is?" That got his attention in a hurry. Dropping the lead rope that he held in his hands, Rick spun around to lean out the door and see for himself. Still no flames.

She'd never seen him before, thought Dani, squinting upward as he paused in the doorway. If he was from the area, she'd have known about him. Dani was sure of it.

His eyes were a dark, sooty shade of brown. They were, at the moment, distinctly troubled, a sentiment echoed by his mouth, which was drawn in a frown that sharpened the planes of an already angular face. Smooth waves of brown-black hair softened the effect somewhat, but not enough to erase the impression of strength. At another time, Dani decided, she might have called him handsome; now he merely looked harried.

When her eyes slipped lower, they saw a well-toned physique that was lean yet muscular, its latent power displayed to perfection in a tight navy blue T-shirt and a pair of worn jeans. Abruptly then, her perusal ended. The bay gelding, who'd been freed, loomed suddenly in the opening, using the man's momentary distraction to muscle his way past and out the door.

Rick snatched for the lead rope and came up with a handful of air. "Grab him, will you?"

Dani did, snagging the rope as the horse scrambled down the unsteady ramp then bounded onto the grass with a playful buck. "Lucky for you I'm better with horses than I am with engines," she said dryly, bringing the gelding under control with a sharp snap.

"It certainly is," Rick agreed, grinning down at her. "Think you can hold on to him? He's usually a perfect gentleman, but this trip has been enough to undermine anyone's good manners."

Including yours, Dani thought. She glared up into the empty doorway as the man disappeared once more. Maybe she was a bit spoiled, but she certainly wasn't used to being taken for granted!

Beside her, the bay snorted suddenly, tossing his head high in the air as a car whipped around the turn and bore down upon them. Though they were standing safely on the shoulder of the road, the driver hit his horn anyway. At the sound of the loud blast, the bay shied violently to one side, dragging Dani several feet before she was able to bring him under control.

"Damn!" Quickly Dani threaded the lead shank through the halter and over the gelding's nose.

"What's the matter?" The man reappeared, holding a gray mare with a dished face.

Dani's reply came through gritted teeth. "Your perfect gentleman just bit me."

"Sorry about that." He led the mare down the ramp. "But you did say you knew how to handle a horse." Before Dani could shape a reply, he thrust the second lead rope into her hands. "Just one more trip and I'll be all set."

Dani did know her way around horses. She'd started riding when she was three, jumping when she was six, and she'd been playing low-goal polo since graduating from college. Now she needed every bit of expertise she had gleaned over the years. Obviously the horses had been cooped up in the van for a long time. Add that to the way the smoke from the still-smoldering engine filled the air, teasing their sensitive nostrils, and the combination was a volatile one.

Speaking to them softly under her breath, Dani led the pair away from the van as the driver unloaded the third horse, a wiry chestnut with white-splashed legs. She watched the driver fold down the sides of the ramp, then push it back into place and close the door.

"Thanks for the help, Miss, er..." The man filled in the blank with a broad grin.

Dani took measure of his confident stance. It was obvious this was one man who was used to having things his own way. And from the looks of him, no wonder! Then she remembered Spence and frowned. She wasn't in the mood to be pushed around by anybody, much less a cocky delivery man with gorgeous brown eyes.

"My name's Dani," she said shortly.

Rick's eyes skimmed the trim but definitely feminine figure before him. "That's a boy's name," he pointed out affably.

"I know that." Dani frowned. "My father wanted a son. He got me instead. He had to make do." Belatedly she heard the underlying bitterness that had crept into her voice and sought to mitigate its effect. "It's really Danielle," she added indifferently. "Danielle Winslow Hawthorne."

Rick nodded to himself. It all fitted. He'd had her pegged the moment she'd appeared at the bottom of his ramp, and the Porsche he could now see parked up ahead only confirmed his suspicions. Sure she'd caught his eye, but unless he missed his guess, this one was trouble—daddy's darling, and mummy's little girl. The small blue stones that glittered in her ears were, no doubt, sapphires. They didn't call Fairfield County the gold coast of Connecticut for nothing.

Then again, Rick conceded, she was due some credit. When Trigger had slipped by him, he'd expected a shriek and a hasty retreat. Instead, she'd nabbed the gelding's shank with authority, controlling the horse as though she'd been doing it all her life.

Rick's eyes narrowed thoughtfully. He could see the angry red welt on her arm where Trigger must have nailed her. But after her initial response, he hadn't heard a word of complaint. That alone shot her up several notches in his estimation. Perhaps, he decided, there was more to Danielle Winslow Hawthorne than met the eye.

Rick walked over to where she stood. "Pleased to meet you," he said, holding out his hand.

Dani glanced down at his hand balefully. "Do you want the one with the gelding?" she asked, one brow raised. "Or the mare?"

"Sorry," Rick said easily. "I didn't think. But now that you mention it, you may as well hand them both over. I guess I should be on my way."

"Do you really think you can manage all three?"

"Do I have a choice?"

"That depends. Are you delivering them to the hunt club?"

Rick nodded. "Is it far?"

"About a mile," Dani replied. She couldn't resist a grin. "Uphill all the way."

Rick's chuckle was resigned. "I should have known."

Dani considered only briefly before making a choice. She wasn't in any particular hurry, after all. Besides, she'd done this much, so she might as well finish it. "Would you like some help?"

Her offer was a pleasant surprise. His day, Rick decided, was turning out to be full of them. "I don't want to take you out of your way."

"Don't worry about it. I'm headed there, too."

"But your car . . ."

Dani shrugged. "I'll send someone back for it."

The mare chose that moment to pull back on the rope, so Dani missed the way Rick's brow rose at her imperious tone. When he spoke, however, there was no mistaking the amusement in his voice. "I'll bet the other girls at prep school called you Winnie, didn't they?" he asked.

"Only if they wanted a black eye," Dani retorted, wondering what it was he found so funny.

"You must have been quite the tomboy."

"Quite," she agreed. Then she frowned. "How did you know I went away to school?"

"Danielle Winslow Hawthorne?" he said, enunciating each syllable of her name slowly and carefully. "No matter how you slice it, that simply isn't a public school name."

"Oh, no? Then suppose you tell me what you think a public school name ought to sound like."

"Rick Malone," he answered quickly. "At your service."

"Or vice versa," Dani pointed out, smiling.

Rick Malone, she thought, turning the name over in her mind. It sounded vaguely familiar, though she couldn't imagine why. He couldn't be anyone Amelie had mentioned, could he? Quickly she dismissed the notion. Of course not. Anyone her mother considered worth knowing wouldn't have been caught dead driving a van, much less one that looked like that.

She might not know him, Dani mused, but he certainly seemed to have latched on to her name quickly enough—probably, she thought disgustedly, for all the usual reasons. Especially after the experience she'd just had with Spence, the last thing she needed right now was another man who thought of her as nothing more than a branch office of Hawthorne Enterprises.

"Now that you mention it," said Rick, breaking into her thoughts, "having another set of hands along would make this whole thing a lot easier."

Dani shrugged. What difference did it make? She could handle him, and would. "All right then, let's go. I'll take Mr. Personality here, if you can manage those two."

"Fine by me." Rick nodded. "By the way, his name is Trigger."

"Trigger?" Dani choked on an unexpected laugh. "You're kidding, aren't you?"

Rick's look was wounded. "Of course not. What's the matter with that?"

"Let's just say that it lacks something in the way of originality."

"If that's the way you feel," he said, starting away down the road, "then I guess it's no use introducing you to Silver and Scout."

"What?" Dani called after him as she hurried to catch up. "No Buttermilk?"

Rick shook his head. "But I once had a dog named Bullet," he offered hopefully.

Dani's giggles began anew. "And a best friend named Tonto?"

"Not yet," said Rick. "But you never know."

They looked at each other and smiled. She'd needed a good laugh, Dani decided. And Rick Malone, with his horses' names pulled straight from a bevy of old Westerns, had given it to her. Suddenly she felt much better.

The steady clip-clop of the horses' hooves echoed hollowly on the hard-packed dirt on the edge of the road as Dani matched her strides to the man beside her. He was taller than she was, she realized suddenly. It was something that didn't often happen for a woman who stood five foot ten in stocking feet.

A big, strapping girl, that's what her mother called her. "Peasant stock," petite Amelie had sniffed. "Must come from your father's side of the family." Her mother's objections aside, however, Dani liked being tall. Playing as she did on a men's polo team, she needed every advantage she could get.

Men, she knew, often found her strength intimidating. Rick, she decided, didn't look like the sort of man who would be intimidated by much. Idly she wondered if he rode. He was, altogether, a bit of an enigma—a van driver who looked like he should be anything but. Not only that, but from the looks of his van, his transport business probably wasn't a very successful one.

Dani stifled a small sigh. That was probably why he'd perked up like that at the sound of her name. Another fortune hunter, she thought, squaring her shoulders unconsciously. It was nothing new. Over the years she'd certainly met her share. So why, this time, did she find the realization so depressing?

They'd gone about a quarter of a mile when Rick looked over and caught her eye as though something had just occurred to him. "How do you feel about riding bareback?" he asked.

"A lot better than I do about walking," Dani replied. The leather paddock boots she wore beneath her jeans were made for riding, not strolling. Already her feet were beginning to feel the pinch. "Why?"

"I was just thinking that with three horses right here, it's crazy for us to be on the ground. There's no way Trigger's going to let anyone ride him with only a lead shank for control. And Scout feels just about the same way. But Silver..." Rick nodded toward the pretty gray mare. "Now she just might be persuaded."

"Are you offering me a lift?"

"Well..." Rick smiled sheepishly. "Half of one, at any rate. I figured we might both climb on. One of us can steer and the other can pony the other two along behind."

"You want to ride double with me?" Dani decided not to examine why she found the idea unnerving, yet at the same time, far too appealing.

"Sure, why not?"

Why not indeed? "You're on," Dani said, then watched as Rick gathered a handful of silver mane and vaulted up onto the mare's back.

"You're sure Trigger isn't going to object?" she asked as the bay sidestepped nervously. Riding shotgun, it would be her job to hang on to the other two horses. If one of them decided to balk, she would be the one who would end up getting dragged off.

"Don't worry about him." Rick extended down his hand, which Dani took as she hopped up behind him. "He'll settle down once we get going."

Once in place, it took Dani only a moment or two to realize that while Trigger might be a problem, he was not the only one. She gathered both lead ropes into her left hand, then found she was at a loss as to what to do with her right.

Sitting this close, she could not help but be aware of the broad set of Rick's shoulders and the sinewed strength of his back. Both were clearly defined by the molded fit of the dark T-shirt, and both were only inches from her nose. Though her legs wrapped themselves around Silver's flanks automatically, she still needed more of a hold. Yet somehow the idea of slipping her free hand around Rick's hips and snuggling up against his back seemed all wrong.

Up in front, Rick willed himself not to laugh with effort. Imagine that, the princess agreeing to a bareback ride, and double no less! When he'd proposed the idea, he'd never thought she'd accept. Now he could just imagine what was going through her mind.

Lucky for him that she couldn't read his, or else she'd know what a dirty trick he'd pulled. Oh, he'd told the truth about Trigger all right. But while the bay was apt to be a bit ornery, the other gelding, Scout, was actually as docile as a lamb. There was no need for them to have climbed on Silver together. In fact, if the truth were known, he probably could have handled all three himself right from the beginning. Right this minute she could be cool and comfortable riding in that fancy Porsche of hers. Then Rick did grin. There was no reason she ever had to know that, was there?

Rick settled back, feeling pretty smug. "Feel free to grab hold of anything that catches your fancy," he invited.

Though she couldn't see his face, Dani knew he was grinning. "You wish!" she retorted, settling for draping her arm loosely around his waist.

Abruptly Rick straightened in his seat. He'd known she'd have to hold on to him—it was hard enough to maintain your balance riding bareback without the added distraction of ponying two extra horses as well. Yet somehow the gentle, almost tentative way she gripped his waist came as a surprise, as did the tremor that rippled across his skin at the spot where their bodies touched. With more vigor than he'd intended, Rick nudged his heels into Silver's flanks. Immediately the mare shot forward, breaking into her easy, rolling canter.

Behind him, Dani leaned forward and adjusted her weight to the pace. She ventured a look out from behind Rick's back, then ducked her head quickly to one side to avoid a low-hanging branch. "Doesn't this animal have any gaits between stop and full speed ahead?" she gasped breathlessly.

"What's the matter?" Rick tossed out. "Can't you take the pace?"

"Don't worry about me," Dani shot right back. "I'm doing fine. It's Trigger and Scout who are having their feet run off."

"If there's one thing I can't stand," Rick muttered under his breath just loud enough for her to hear, "it's a back seat driver."

"And if there's one thing I can't stand, it's a speed demon. I'll bet when you were a kid you had one of those souped-up jalopies with huge tires and jacked-up wheels."

"Not me," said Rick. He paused, then added, "Actually I couldn't afford a car at all. I had to save all my money for college."

"Oh," Dani murmured. She thought about her first car—a vintage MG convertible that her father had had gift-wrapped and waiting in the driveway on the morning of her sixteenth birthday. She wouldn't have mentioned it for gold.

Then the white barns of the hunt club became visible in the distance, and Rick reined the mare in to a more sedate pace. Relaxing back on her seat, Dani unwound her arm and settled it across her thigh.

"Don't leave on my account," Rick said, and she could hear the amusement in his tone. "I was just getting used to not being able to breathe."

"Don't be silly. I wasn't holding on to you that tightly."

She was right, Rick conceded to himself; she hadn't been holding him tightly at all. Her touch had been thoroughly impersonal—firm enough to do the job, and no more. So why did he find himself missing it now that it was gone?

Despite their necessary physical proximity on the back of the horse, Dani had managed to maintain an unstated but careful distance between them. All at once Rick felt compelled to bridge the gap.

"If you've left any bruises," he continued outrageously, "I'm a big believer in a kiss making things better."

Dani stared at him in consternation. "That makes one of us," she snapped. "I haven't believed in that sort of healing since I was six years old."

Rick shook his head reprovingly. "Don't you know that there are some things that just have to be taken on faith?"

She knew he was only kidding around, but still the teasing words stung. Her upbringing—parents divorced before she'd reached the age of five; a mother who thought that children were, at best, an inconvenience to be tolerated; and a succession of surrogate "fathers" who alternately coddled or ignored her, depending on their moods—was simply not the sort to promote taking anything on faith.

So she was a cynic about life—what of it? If there was one thing she had learned at an early age, it was that the only person she could truly depend on was herself. Despite their pretty words and good intentions, other people came and went. Eventually Dani had realized that it was simply a matter of survival not to let a little piece of herself go with each one.

Love was an indulgence, she'd decided, not a necessity. It was one she had learned to do without.

Lost in thought, Dani inhaled deeply of the rich pine-filled air, then let out her breath in a long, wistful sigh.

"Don't tell me I'm boring you," Rick said with a chuckle.

"Hardly." Whoever Rick Malone was, Dani thought, he certainly was sure of his appeal. In fact, it was just for that very reason that she couldn't resist taking him down a notch. "I was just thinking of all the things I have to do this afternoon," she said casually.

"Such as?"

Behind Rick's back, Dani made a face. He would have to ask, wouldn't he? Until half an hour ago, her only concern for the day had been to put Spencer Hamilton III out of her mind. Then with a start, she realized just how easily Rick had accomplished that very thing. As distractions went, the man was obviously top-notch. Unconsciously she lowered her eyes, tracing once more the smooth, hard planes of his back, the breadth of his shoulders and the sinewy strength in the arms that held the spirited mare so casually in check.

"Well?"

With a gulp, Dani snatched her gaze upward as she tried to remember the question. Oh, yes, her plans for the afternoon.

"The first thing I'd planned on was a long ride through the woods," she said. "And then I have a dressage lesson at two—"

"Dressage?" asked Rick, sounding surprised. "I'd have figured you for something a little more robust."

"To tell the truth, I'm really more of a polo player," Dani admitted. "At the moment, the dressage lessons are an experiment. I'm teaching my ponies some of the more basic haute école movements to see whether or not it will benefit their game."

"Do you really think that knowing those stylized movements will help in a hard, fast match?"

Dani smiled, pleased by his interest. "I don't know yet. But I don't see how it can hurt. After all, when you think about it, dressage promotes strength and flexibility, as well as increasing a horse's sensitivity to his rider's aids."

"Not a bad idea," Rick said slowly. "All right, go on. What comes after that?"

"Then," Dani continued, blithely ticking off the chores on her fingers, "I need to make sure that the splint on Fanfare's leg is healing properly. After that, Trumpet will need some stick work. And, of course, there's always the training sessions with the two young colts I've got at home—"

"Okay, okay." Rick laughed. "I think I get the picture."

Dani smiled to herself. Unless she'd misread his interest earlier, that was his cue. Now was his chance to make a move, to say something terribly original like, "But surely someone as lovely as you can't spend all her time in a stable," and then launch into whatever come-on he was using at the moment. Which one would it be? Dani wondered. By this time it seemed as though she'd heard them all.

But when Rick turned slightly, looking back at her over his shoulder, Dani found she was in for a surprise. "It sounds as though you spend a lot of time on your game," he said thoughtfully. "It must be very important to you."

"It is," Dani replied, telling herself firmly that she was not disappointed in the least. After all, she hadn't been planning to fall for his line; she'd simply wanted to hear it. "I'm determined to build both my game and my credibility and I'm finally now reaching the point where the men at Silverbrook are beginning to take me seriously as a player."

"Have you been playing long?"

"Not as long as I'd like," Dani admitted. "Really just since college. I learned to ride when I was very young, and even then I knew what I wanted. I had my first polo pony by the time I was thirteen, but back in those days polo was considered to be a sport for men only. At the time I was both too young and too inexperienced to buck the system."

Rick nodded, understanding what she'd been up against.

Encouraged by his interest, Dani continued. "By the time I got to Yale, I was determined to go after it. I'll always be grateful that the coach there turned out to be very liberal about such things. He taught me a tremendous amount in those four years, and I soaked up everything I could."

Dani paused, grinning wryly. "Having had the good fortune to study under him, I've been telling myself ever since that it must be my penance now to have to return to Silverbrook and try to launch these cavemen into the twentieth century."

Rick's brow lifted. "You mean, nobody here approves of what you're doing?"

"I wouldn't go that far," Dani said slowly. "Some of the other players don't really seem to mind at all. But I can't say that it's been easy, either. It's not just enough for me to be as good as the men, I've had to be better, sometimes much better. I've got a two-goal handicap now, and if nothing else, they have to respect that. The best player we've got is a three-goal man, then there are two other twos at the club beside me, so this year, for the first time, I've finally managed to solidify my position on the four-man team.''

"Good for you," said Rick, sounding genuinely pleased by her success.

Abruptly Dani realized that she'd been talking virtually nonstop for the past ten minutes. Though his questions had seemed sensible, she wondered if he really had any idea what she was talking about. Maybe it was time she started asking some questions of her own.

"I've been monopolizing the conversation," she said as Rick guided the mare off the road and up onto the edge of the Silverbrook polo field. The meticulously kept expanse was off-limits to riders, and Dani and Rick slipped off and sorted themselves out to walk the last hundred yards. "You haven't said a thing about yourself."

No, he hadn't, thought Rick. Why would he, when he was much more interested in learning about the intriguing blonde the fates had seen fit to send his way? Of course, there wasn't any reason not to answer her questions. After all, she'd find out who he was soon enough anyway.

Rick glanced over, caught her gaze and smiled. "What do you want to know?"

Dani deliberated for only a moment. "For starters," she said, "whose horses are these, and why are you delivering them to Silverbrook?"

"Why, they're mine." Rick made no attempt to hide his surprise. It had never occurred to him she might think otherwise. "As of last week, I'm the club's newest member. I've spent the past three days vanning them up from Arizona, and believe me, that's one trip I'm happy to have behind me.''

"Arizona," Dani repeated thoughtfully before looking up. "You wouldn't happen to mean the Sunnyridge Polo Center, would you?"

Rick nodded.

"You mean, you've come here to play on the Silverbrook team?"

Dani's mind worked furiously as she sorted out the possibilities. No wonder his name had sounded familiar. The Sunnyridge Center was renowned throughout the entire polo world for the caliber of its players. "What's your handicap?" she demanded eagerly.

Rick looked almost sheepish. "I've been playing a good deal longer than you have," he said. "I've got a five-goal rating."

Dani's first reaction was one of pleased surprise, followed by a surge of pure elation. A five-goal handicap! That placed Rick among the upper ranks of all the players in the country. It would be a tremendous boon to the Silverbrook team to acquire a player of his caliber. Dani chortled gleefully. She couldn't wait until Black Rock, their arch rival, found out!

Without stopping to think, she turned and threw her arms around Rick's shoulders, gathering him close for a welcoming hug. "That's terrific!" she cried.

Terrific wasn't the half of it, Rick decided with a smile. He liked a lady with enthusiasm; and to be perfectly honest, he enjoyed it even more when that enthusiasm was pointed in his direction. Dani Hawthorne had managed to make his day on both counts.

Rick started to slide his arms around Dani's waist, then felt the lead ropes begin to tangle and thought better of it. When she unclasped her arms, he stepped back reluctantly. Still, he reflected, there were worse ways to be welcomed to the neighborhood than with a warm hug from a beautiful lady polo player. Business had brought him to Connecticut; now he was beginning to suspect that the move might turn out to be a pleasure.

It wasn't until they'd sorted out the horses and gotten them heading toward the barn once more that Dani finally stopped to consider the full import of Rick's arrival. For a moment she'd been so dazzled by the idea of having him in residence that she'd quite overlooked the problems his coming was going to cause. Now reality came crashing back with a vengeance.

As they walked around the field to the club, Dani snuck a glance at Rick out of the corner of her eye, forcing herself to remember her earlier misgivings. Suddenly she had a feeling she was going to need all the self-defense against this man that she could get.

The club's newest member, Rick Malone—a five-alarm charmer and possible fortune hunter—was also the man who was going to knock her off the Silverbrook polo team without so much as lifting a finger.

Chapter Two

Dani awoke early the next morning. Bright ribbons of sunlight fell across the bed, streaming in through the open French doors that led outside to a small balcony. She hopped up eagerly and crossed the room to walk outside, clad only in an old, oversized T-shirt that covered her to midthigh.

The morning air was crisp and cool, and Dani breathed in deeply. Leaning stiff-armed against the white wrought-iron railing, she gazed out over the twenty acres of rolling lawn, woods and pastures that made up the family estate, Greenfields. The house that formed the centerpiece of this magnificent acreage was a red brick Georgian mansion, complete with tall white columns and leaded windows. Every inch the impressive showplace, its interior had been designed by her mother, whose tastes ran to Bokhara rugs, Louis XIV furniture and pre-Columbian art.

The resulting decor had always seemed much too stiff and formal to Dani, but then nobody had ever chosen to consult her anyway. That her tastes were much more casual was evident only in the appointments of her own suite—a bedroom, bathroom, sitting room combination on the second floor of the west wing. From her balcony there, the view was unbeatable.

To the left lay the tennis court; to the right, the stable. A brick terrace ran the length of the house in the back. Just behind it was the pool, a free-form design bound by rough-hewn rock rather than concrete, an exacting feat of human engineering that succeeded in looking just like a natural mountain pond. Beyond that, hidden in a small clump of trees, stood the only incongruous touch on the perfectly landscaped grounds—a tall and rather unwieldy looking windmill—the legacy of her mother's third husband, a frustrated would-be conservationist who'd been sure that his creation would generate enough electricity to heat the swimming pool.

Looking out over the windmill now, Dani grinned. There were times when she found the perfectly sculpted perfection of her surroundings tedious, even depressing—a little like being caught in a fairy-tale wonderland from which there was no escape. But somehow the sight of that silly, lopsided and utterly frivolous windmill always had a way of restoring her perspective and her sense of humor. Even the rich, it seemed to be telling her, don't always get everything they want.

For all its lavish display, however, Greenfields was her home, the only constant she had known during the unsettled and often baffling years of her childhood. No matter that it was just a building, to Dani it represented a small measure of the security she had yearned for as a child, but never found. Although she had considered moving out and finding a place of her own, in the end she had never been able to make the break.

After all, Dani told herself, why should she? Everything she needed was already there—a place to eat and sleep, a small stable where she housed several of her young horses in training. Why should she give up all that for the dubious pleasure of living alone? Already she had known too much loneliness to ever think of solitude as an advantage.

Besides, Dani mused, it certainly wasn't as though she lacked privacy. Indeed, this summer was a prime example of how things were apt to go. Her mother had been gone for several weeks and wasn't due back again until Labor Day. By then, who knew where Dani herself might be? With any luck, they probably wouldn't run into each other for months, as had often been the case during her boarding school years when sometimes their only contact had been at her mother's periodic, and lavishly staged, weddings.

Back inside her room, the alarm on the clock beside the bed buzzed loudly. Roused from her reverie, Dani sighed. She walked back inside, mentally counting off the fifteen seconds it would ring before setting off the automatic switch on her stereo.

By the time the first strains of the Pointer Sisters' vibrant music filled the room, she was down on the floor, ready to begin. Ten minutes of stretching served as a warm-up before Dani picked up her free weights and began her strengthening exercises in earnest. After so many years, the routine had become almost second nature, and now she completed the sequence automatically. She might have been blessed with an athlete's natural grace and ability, but Dani had no intention of taking her body for granted.

Besides, she thought as she finished her exercises and moved on to the shower, after what had happened yesterday she could only assume that a battle she'd thought was finally won was now about to begin all over again. Standing under the soothing jets of steaming water, Dani pondered the potential upheaval that would be brought into her life by the sudden and unexpected arrival of one Mr. Rick Malone.

What a shame that he had to come along now, of all times! Just when she'd been so sure that the number three position on the team would be hers for the whole season. It would have been her chance to prove herself. Now, just as simply as that, it was gone.

Frowning, she considered the team's new line-up. Of course Rick, and Jim Lynch, the club's three-goal handicap player, would both be guaranteed a spot. That left the three two-goal players—herself, Harley Greer and Trip Malloy—to fight it out for the remaining two. That, thought Dani, had every indication of turning into a free-for-all.

Trip Malloy was no problem. She got along well with him, and their styles of play complemented each other nicely. Harley, however, was another matter entirely. Not only was he a strong, aggressive player, he also tended to be rather bullheaded as well.

Riding the number two position to her number three, Harley's play tended to be either decidedly brilliant or decidedly dangerous. He had no fear whatsoever and played every match to the hilt. Many of the club members agreed that it was nothing short of miraculous that so far he'd managed to contain his injuries to minor cuts and bruises.

She might be brave, thought Dani, but she wasn't stupid. The prospect of having to go head-to-head with Harley to maintain her position was definitely not an appealing one.

"All because of you, Malone," she muttered with feeling as she stepped from the shower stall and reached for a towel. As usual, her instincts had been right. She'd known from the first minute she'd laid eyes on him that that was one man who was going to be trouble!

Slipping into a pair of jeans and a cotton madras shirt, Dani pulled her long hair back into a careless ponytail. Quickly she packed a leather duffel bag with the clothes she would need for the scrimmage that afternoon—a pair of white twill breeches, brown knee-high boots and the green-and-yellow jersey bearing her number. The rest of her equipment—a polo helmet, thick leather knee guards and her collection of mallets—was in her locker at the club, ready and waiting for when she could grab a moment to slip into the dressing room and change.

Several moments later she was barreling headlong down the curved staircase when the shrill ring of the telephone brought her up short. Pausing on the bottom step, Dani watched as Preston, the portly British butler, glided noiselessly out of the dining room and lifted the receiver on the telephone stand hidden beneath the stairway.

"Just one moment please, I'll see if Miss Hawthorne is in." Turning, Preston eyed her outfit balefully before covering the receiver with one large hand and announcing, "Mr. Spencer Hamilton would like to speak with you, Danielle."

Scowling, Dani shook her head. "Tell him I'm not here." A careless toss sidearmed the duffel bag onto a delicate Duncan Phyfe settee in the front hall before she continued on into the dining room.

"Just some toast, please," she told the housekeeper, who nodded and left the room. Dani walked over and helped herself to a cup of hot, fragrant coffee from the pot on the sideboard.

"You will have to speak to Mr. Hamilton some time, you know," Preston said, his tone clearly conveying his disapproval as he entered the room.

"When hell freezes over," Dani retorted with feeling. She settled into the chair that Preston held out for her, pointedly ignoring the way he rolled his eyes heavenward at her language.

"Will you be dining in tonight?"

Dani shrugged, sipping her coffee slowly as her eyes skimmed over the headlines on the newspaper beside her plate. "I guess so."

Her whole wheat toast arrived from the kitchen, and Preston served it to her with aplomb, then stepped back and stood at attention behind her chair. "Shall I have the cook prepare some lamb chops?"

"Fine," Dani replied absently. "Anything would be fine. You know perfectly well that I'd be just as happy with a rare hamburger on a paper plate. Look at this." Her finger flicked disdainfully at the heavy silverware sitting beside her plate. "What a lot of bother to go to for one person, and at breakfast no less! Don't you ever get tired of polishing this stuff?"

"Not me, miss," Preston replied stiffly. "It's not my job."

Surprised by his tone, Dani looked up, realizing for the first time that he was still standing in his best British butler's pose behind her chair.

"Oh, for Pete's sake," she said, frowning. "What on earth are you doing hovering back there, Preston? Sit down and have a cup of coffee with me."

"If you wish," Preston replied, his next words chiding her gently. "Although for what little we've seen of you in the past few weeks, I thought this was what you wanted—to use this house as a way station where you could receive quiet, deferential service—"

"Preston." Dani grinned at him engagingly. "Are you sulking?"

"Certainly not." Preston walked over to the sideboard and poured himself a cup of coffee, then joined her at the table.

"You know perfectly well how much time I've been devoting to the Pegasus Program, not to mention all that has to be done to get ready for the start of the polo season. And on top of everything else, you should hear what's happened now . . ." Propping her elbows on the table, a breech of etiquette that Preston politely ignored, Dani cupped her chin in her hands and proceeded to tell him all about Rick Malone's arrival and the problems it was bound to cause.

It had always been like that between them, ever since the time when Dani was six years old and the butler had found her in the closet beneath the stairs, crying because her mother was not going to be able to make it home in time for Christmas. Over the years, Preston had been friend, helpmate, mentor, and confessor, and in the often confusing world in which she had grown up, the closest thing to a parent that Dani had ever known.

"So you can see why I've got a lot on my mind right now, can't you?" she finished several minutes later. "Just when I thought I was all set, along comes this guy Malone, who knocks the pins right out from under me."

"In more ways than one, I'd wager," Preston observed, watching her closely.

"Oh?" Dani's brow lifted.

"Danielle, you needn't prevaricate. It's been quite some time since I've seen your eyes sparkle with such enthusiasm. Indeed, if I remember correctly the last occasion that prompted such a response was the day you succeeded in outbidding both Robert Sangster and the sheikh from Dubai at the Keeneland Yearling Sales." Preston paused before adding solemnly, "It seems to me that your association with this Mr. Malone might prove to be very interesting indeed."

"I don't know what you're talking about," Dani scoffed. Dammit, her eyes weren't really sparkling, were they? No of course not, she decided. It was nothing more than an old man's fancy. On more than one occasion, Preston had been known to declare that what she really needed was a good man to settle her down—a sentiment with which Dani heartily disagreed.

"Perhaps I should tell the cook to plan on two for dinner?" he suggested artlessly.

"Oh, no, you don't!" Dani cried, shaking her finger at him as she rose from the table. "You stay out of this, Preston."

Instead of replying, the butler merely shrugged, drawing his features closed in a look that Dani had always referred to as his pinched frog face.

Damn, she thought, there he went sulking again. It was definitely time to change the subject. Leaning down, she cocked her head from one side to the other, studying him critically. "You look very good, Preston. You've lost some weight, haven't you?"

Preston permitted himself a small smile. "Six pounds," he announced proudly. "It's those exercises you showed me. I've been doing them three times a week."

"Good for you!" Dani grinned. "We'll have you down to fighting weight in no time."

"Heaven help us," Preston replied with dignity. He stood up as she strode from the room.

Looking back over her shoulder at his imposingly correct stance, Dani laughed. "You'll see, I'll get you into a leotard yet!" she threatened teasingly, then swept up her bag and hurried out the front door before he had a chance to retaliate.

Her car was waiting by the door, and Dani made short work of the drive to the hunt club. Once there, her first stop was at the clubhouse, a white colonial-style building with a row of graceful columns and a wide veranda overlooking the polo field. She stowed her gear in the locker room there, then hurried upstairs to the main lobby where the teams for that afternoon's scrimmage were posted.

As it was only a practice session, both teams would be made up of Silverbrook players, which meant that everyone would have ample opportunity to play. Eagerly Dani skimmed down the list, noting with pleasure that she and Rick were slated to play the number two and three positions on the green team, while Harley, Trip, and Jim Lynch would all be playing for yellow.

Three one-goal players made up the rest of the positions, leaving the green team with a combined handicap of nine and the yellow with eight. The score at the start of the match, therefore, would be one to zero in favor of yellow.

Anxious now to get her work out of the way, Dani hurried out to the stables. She spent the first half of the morning schooling the two ponies she wasn't planning to use in the scrimmage and the second half prepping those that she was. It was almost noon by the time she finished.

Kneeling on the floor in the aisle, she wrapped the last pony's legs in their colorful protective bandages, then released him from the cross-tie and sent him back into his stall. Time for lunch, she thought, heading purposefully toward the stable door.

Once there, she paused, considering. There was still plenty of time before the scrimmage. More than enough, she decided, to satisfy her curiosity.

A casual inquiry to Harry, the groom in charge of her aisle, elicited the information that the new arrivals from Arizona had all settled in nicely. Talking around the thick wad of tobacco clenched perennially in the corner of his mouth, he directed her around the corner to three stalls overlooking the courtyard.

Though Dani had, of course, seen Rick's horses the day before, at the time she'd been too preoccupied to pay them more than scant attention. Now, however, she took the opportunity for a leisurely, and thorough, inspection. Pausing beside the first stall, Dani stuck her head inside.

Nice, she thought to herself several moments later. Very nice. Rick Malone was obviously a man with an eye for a good horse. Then again, considering the heights he'd attained in the game, that was hardly surprising.

Moving slowly from one stall to the next, Dani assessed each animal in turn. Trigger, the firebrand, was a muscular bay with a powerful hindquarter that looked as though it had been built for speed. The other two horses were equally impressive. Silver was a delicate gray mare with a dished face and intelligent eyes; while Scout, the chestnut, was a cobby half Arab.

Still, Dani mused, she'd have thought that a player of Rick's caliber would have more than three ponies in his string. Given the demanding nature of the game—six seven-and-a-half-minute chukkers, each one played at a relentless and sometimes bruising pace—and the attendant necessity of changing mounts often, it didn't take a mathematician to see that he had only enough ponies to make it through the game with each one playing twice. And if, as often happened, one was injured during the course of the play, he'd be out of luck.

Then again, Dani decided wryly, with Malone's self-confidence, not to mention that irrepressible optimism, good luck was probably one of those things he simply took for granted.

"Looking for something?"

Dani spun around and found herself looking up into Rick Malone's inquiring eyes. "Nope," she said, flashing him a cocky grin. "Just checking out the merchandise."

"And?"

Dani's grin widened. "They'll do."

They'd a lot better than do, thought Rick, and he suspected that Dani knew that every bit as well as he did. Briefly his eyes skimmed over her, noting the worn jeans, faded plaid shirt and plain hairdo. Though she was dressed as simply as any of the grooms, he knew she would never be mistaken for one of them. There was something in the way she carried herself—the regal bearing of her shoulders, the confident tilt to her chin—that would always set her apart. Still a princess, yes, but once again, a surprise as well.

"Looking for something?" Her voice was cool and challenging as she mimicked his words.

Slowly Rick raised his eyes to her face. "Maybe," he drawled. "When I find it, I'll let you know."

He wanted her to blush, Dani realized. With equal determination, she decided not to. As usual, generations of Hawthorne reserve stood her in good stead.

He wouldn't be the first man who had met his match in her. Nor, she decided, her eyes flickering over him disdainfully, the last. Malone was an attractive man. She'd grant that. But that didn't mean she was about to let him have things all his own way.

In fact, Dani mused, he wouldn't have to push her very far before he found himself being shoved right back. A small quiver deep in her stomach confirmed the suspicion that she might enjoy the tussle.

"I just stopped by the barn to make sure everything was in order." Rick's gaze flickered up and down the row of stalls. "Since it seems to be, that just about leaves time to grab some lunch at the Grill. Have you eaten yet?"

"No." Dani shook her head. "And I'm starving."

"Good." Rick's dark eyes gleamed. "I hate to eat alone."

"Don't flatter me too much," Dani grumbled as they started down the aisle. "I might get spoiled."

"My thoughts exactly," Rick agreed.

Dani started to sputter a reply, then thought better of it and shut her mouth. Why snap at Malone, when she'd much rather simply kick back and enjoy his company? Preston, damn his perception, had been right. It had been quite a while since anyone made her light up the way Rick Malone did.

And if, as she suspected, it turned out that he was more than a little interested in her money, then that was just too bad. That had happened before, and it was bound to happen again. He'd find out soon enough that there was little percentage in his plans. But for now, the important thing was that he *was* interested. So who was to say that she shouldn't enjoy herself in the meantime? After all, men like this one didn't come along every day.

Ten minutes later Dani and Rick were seated in the Grill, a small, informal dining room on the ground floor of the clubhouse. After giving their order to the waiter, Rick leaned back in his chair and looked appreciatively around the room with its dark wood paneling, framed hunting prints and glass-fronted trophy case.

"This is nice," he commented. "Very plush. It's exactly how I imagined such a room should look."

"But surely you've—" Dani began, then stopped in confusion. His ulterior motives notwithstanding, she'd assumed he was a man of *some* means. Yet to her surprise, he seemed fascinated by their surroundings, as though he'd never seen anything like them before.

"Surely I've what?" asked Rick. "Grown up in a place such as this?" Looking at her across the small table, he shook his head. "Hardly. When I was little, the idea of belonging to a country club was something my family could only dream about. Just because I happen to be very good at a rich man's sport doesn't mean that I was raised with all the advantages."

"But you are here now," Dani pointed out, curious to learn more about his background. "And running a string of three ponies as well—"

"And working damn hard to do it."

"What do you do for a living?" Dani asked, wondering idly what sort of job let their employees off work for Wednesday afternoon scrimmages.

"Management consulting. After Stanford, I went with Arthur Anderson. I spent five years there, the last two on a big project in Arizona. I'd never been to the northeast, but I always had the impression that, as far as business was concerned, this was where things were really happening. When I finally decided I'd had enough of being at somebody else's beck and call, I knew I had to give it a try. This month I'll be opening my own office in Stamford.''

"How do you think you'll do?"

Rick shrugged. "It's never easy getting started, even with solid credentials like mine. I've been doing some groundwork for the past six months or so, and it's just about time for something to break. At least it better be.'' He paused, frowning. "It's not easy supporting a family of four, you know. Do you have any idea how much oats those horses eat in one day?''

Smiling, Dani shook her head. "Not to the quart, no.''

"Try to the dollar,'' Rick advised.

"You must be in finance. You sound like a man with his eye planted firmly on the bottom line.''

"Self-defense, pure and simple,'' Rick groused good-naturedly, as the waiter appeared to deliver their food—two thick hamburgers on hard rolls, with matching orders of french fries. For a moment they both fell silent as they concentrated on the meal.

"Now that you've heard all about my less than thrilling origins,'' said Rick, pausing between bites, "I want to hear about you.''

"There isn't really much to tell,'' said Dani. She picked up a french fry and swirled it through the ketchup on the side of her plate, wondering how to condense the story of her life down to twenty-five words or less. Gloss over the surface, she supposed. That was usually the best method.

If there was one thing she'd learned, it was that people never really wanted to hear the truth. No, all they were looking for was to have their own fantasies verified. Never mind that the reality of her childhood had been nothing like everyone imagined it should be, the story they wanted to hear involved lavish parties, fast cars and weekend trips to the Riviera, and they weren't satisfied until they heard it.

"You know how it goes." Dani waved her hand through the air, bored already by the recital. "Danielle Hawthorne, daughter of James and Amelie Hawthorne. Presented to Queen Elizabeth at the age of three. Boarding school in the winters, Europe in the summers. Top-ranking rider on the horse show circuit as a teenager, then Debutante of the Year. After that came Yale, and I've been concentrating on polo ever since."

Setting down his hamburger, Rick frowned at her across the table. "Very good," he said. "You've just written your own obituary. I'm sure it will read very well in the society papers someday. Now suppose you cut out the crap and answer my question."

Dani stared at him in consternation. "I don't know what you mean," she stammered finally.

"Don't you?" Rick demanded. "I can see now why you recognized me as a finance man right off. After all, it takes one to know one. I asked what makes you tick, and you gave me everything but the number of your Swiss bank account."

"I did no such thing!" Dani denied immediately on principle. Could she help it if he was right?

For a moment Rick merely stared at her speculatively, then his features softened, and he smiled—a real smile that lit up his eyes with warmth. "All right, I'll let you get away with that for the time being. Now, how about if we start over?"

His eyes were such a dark shade of brown that they were almost black, Dani realized suddenly as she let her gaze linger appreciatively. They were surrounded by a fringe of thick, dark lashes and a network of tiny lines that radiated from the outer corners. The eyes of a dreamer and a scoundrel. For the first time in a long time, maybe ever, Dani wondered what on earth she had gotten herself into.

"Hey, princess," Rick said softly. "I can't hold up this conversation all by myself, you know."

"Princess?" Dani's brow furrowed.

"If the shoe fits . . ."

Dani felt her temper begin to rise. "Oh, really?" she snapped. "Well, if that's what you think, you know nothing about my life. Nothing at all!"

"I'm listening," said Rick.

He'd wanted to goad her out of her complacency, and he'd succeeded. Now, however, her anger had led to silence, which gained him nothing at all. Ask most of the women he knew about themselves, thought Rick, and they could chatter on for hours. He was used to having his interest reciprocated, rewarded, not shunted aside as though it didn't matter.

Now Dani's obvious reticence only made him all the more curious. Rick held back a grin. Curious, hell! He was intrigued. It was time, he decided, to start prodding again. "Tell me, Danielle Winslow Hawthorne, are you an only child?"

Dani nodded. She'd come to a decision. So he wanted the truth, did he? Then she'd damn well give it to him!

"In fact, if my mother had had her way, she probably wouldn't have had any children at all." Rick's raised brow prompted her to continue. "She married my father for his money," Dani explained, shrugging lightly. "But before you start making any judgments about her morals, you have to understand that my father married her for exactly the same reason. They produced a child because it was expected of them, but that was as far as their involvement went. They neither wanted me, nor needed me, and they made that perfectly clear."

As she spoke, Rick remained silent. His dark eyes watched her closely, and Dani wondered what was going through his mind. She knew she'd probably said too much already, but having come this far it suddenly seemed important that she lay all his illusions to rest at once. Perhaps then he'd understand that she was not the easy mark she'd first appeared to be.

Her voice was flat, a monotone void of emotion as she continued. ''They got divorced when I was very young. My father went back to his offices in Chicago. I've seen him maybe a dozen times since. He's a very busy man, or so I read in the papers. He always remembers my birthday, though. I imagine his secretary must have it marked with a red star on his calendar. He sends something big and splashy and wildly extravagant, and I suppose he thinks it makes up for the other three hundred and sixty-four days in the year when he doesn't even know I'm alive.''

''And your mother?'' Rick asked quietly.

Dani shrugged. ''She married a count last year, her fifth husband, but probably not her last. In her own way she's very busy, too. . . .'' Her voice trailed away as the waiter approached the table once more.

Damn! Rick frowned, frustrated by the interruption. He scowled up at the waiter, whose timing was nothing short of atrocious. After spending the first half of the meal parrying his questions, Dani had finally begun to open up. He'd been genuinely interested in what she'd been about to say—especially since he'd found the facts she'd already revealed nothing short of shocking.

Before he had a chance to say anything, however, the waiter slid the check down onto the table between them. His thoughts still churning, Rick reached for it absently. To his amazement, Dani beat him to it, deftly nabbing the chit from beneath his fingers, then signing her own name at the bottom. Then, as if to forestall whatever he might want to say, she rose quickly from her seat.

"We'd better be going," Dani said, her voice tense with a sense of urgency, when in fact they still had plenty of time. The truth was that all at once she felt self-conscious about their conversation and how much of herself she'd revealed. Now she couldn't wait to get away.

Frowning once more, Rick stood beside her. He'd been outmaneuvered by a pro, and they both knew it. He'd let her get away with it for now, Rick decided, at least until he'd had time to gather his thoughts.

They separated at the door to the locker rooms, then met up again outside the clubhouse after both had changed. Together they walked back out to the barn—Dani striding quickly, forcefully, away, Rick brooding in silence beside her.

In the courtyard, Harry had both their ponies waiting. Hurriedly Dani donned the equipment she was carrying, pulling on leather knee pads, cotton gloves and the protective polo helmet. Beside her, Rick did the same.

She had taken her gelding's reins from Harry and was preparing to mount when Rick finally spoke. "That's quite a story," he said slowly. The time that had passed since they'd left the Grill had done nothing to blunt his initial reaction. He'd been disturbed then; he was still disturbed now. Still, he was determined not to let the incident pass without comment. "I'm afraid I don't know quite what to say."

"Then don't say anything!" Dani snapped, feeling vaguely cornered. Why on earth had she told him all those things anyway? She didn't give a damn about anyone's opinion of her. She'd never had to before, and she wasn't about to start now. So why had she ever thought it was important to try and explain? He wouldn't understand what it had been like. No one ever did.

But Rick refused to be put off. "I guess it must have been pretty rough on you."

Dani knew, for some reason that she was better off not analyzing, that Rick's gentleness was all she needed to set her off. She had flipped the reins up over Ringo's neck and was about to swing up into the saddle, but now she stopped and whirled where she stood. "Is that what you think I want, your pity? Because if so, you're dead wrong!"

Deliberately she turned her back, hauling up the saddle flap so that she could tighten the girth. Then Dani pulled the stirrup down its leather with a sharp snap and vaulted up into place.

"Come on, Malone, mount up," she snapped. "The last thing I need is for you to stand around here feeling sorry for me!" Snatching the stiff cane mallet that Harry held out to her, she looped the thong around the back of her hand, securing her grip.

"Suit yourself, princess," Rick growled, swinging up into the saddle beside her.

"Oh, I do, Malone," Dani purred, her spurs nudging Ringo forward into a brisk trot. "Believe me, I always do."

Chapter Three

God, he was good, thought Dani. She shook her head in admiration. Rick Malone was really good.

Riding parallel to the goal, she'd backhanded a lateral pass to him across the field, and he'd stroked it deftly between the posts as though the two defending players riding hard on his tail, with every intention of preventing just such a move, had been nothing more than a minor distraction.

Holding her stick upright in the rest position, Dani cantered her pony back to the center line for the toss-in that would begin the play again. A bead of sweat trickled down the side of her cheek, and she shook her head impatiently, flinging it away. The green jersey, which only an hour earlier had seemed so crisp and cool, was now molded to her body like a coat of paint. The moisture it had absorbed during the hard-fought match caused it to cling uncomfortably.

It was near the end of the third chukker, and so far the scrimmage had been fairly routine. Vigorous play by both teams had resulted in a number of goals being scored. Although the green team was now marginally ahead, the lead had seesawed back and forth regularly.

Rick was playing the number two position, which meant that he was the team's chief offensive player. Dani's post, number three, was both offensive and defensive. Like Rick, she had a responsibility to cover the entire field. Hers was the pivot position on which the game often hinged and, as always, Dani was exhilarated by the pressure. She reveled in the demanding pace, delighting in the speed and skill it required.

Riding backup to Rick's forward post, she was in a perfect position to watch him play, and everything she saw was impressive. Though the teams had been handicapped as evenly as possible, Dani knew that with Rick's superior ability and experience, he could easily have piloted the green team to a commanding lead. Instead he was content to use the scrimmage as the practice session it was intended to be, passing the ball frequently to other players and setting up shots for Dani and the other forward rather than always taking them himself.

The short, sharp blast of a horn signaled the end of the chukker. Dani reined in her mount, then made her way over to the sidelines where a hotwalker was waiting to take the horse from her as soon as she slid down out of the saddle.

"Not bad, Malone," she called out as he trotted past, her admiring grin adding volumes to the casual comment. Smiling, Rick raised his stick in acknowledgment before riding on by.

Most of the players were using the midgame break to change their shirts, a luxury unavailable to Dani without a trip back inside to the locker room. Deciding it was simply too much trouble, she wandered over instead to the ice chest that had been set out beside the veranda and helped herself to a drink.

Although the teams were only practicing, they had, as usual, drawn a crowd of spectators. Those who had been watching now took their turn on the field, walking around to push the divots back down into place.

Feeling about as fresh as a used washcloth, Dani pressed the cold soda can against her hot cheeks, then closed her eyes and leaned back against the porch railing for a moment's rest. It didn't last long.

"Dani, darling!"

Dani's eyes slid open slowly to the sight of Sabrina Dare picking her way carefully across the well-trampled polo field. Her long glossy black hair hung in loose waves about her shoulders, the day's sultry heat enhancing its style rather than detracting from it. Her violet eyes were large and luminous, set in a face of cool patrician beauty. Dressed in a pair of linen pants, a mauve silk blouse and a pair of flimsy sandals, which were eminently unsuited to the terrain, she was the picture of sophisticated elegance.

How on earth did she manage it? Dani wondered. Nobody should be able to look so cool and collected on a day as hot as this one. Yet that never stopped Sabrina. From the tips of her impossibly long nails to the top of her carefully coiffed head, she always looked perfect. It just wasn't human!

Dani straightened as Sabrina drew near. She stepped away from the veranda, a smile forming on her lips. Then the two women were embracing delightedly, throwing their arms around each other as they pressed their cheeks together in greeting, first on one side, then the other.

They pulled apart, and Sabrina grasped Dani's shoulders lightly, holding her at arm's length to look her over thoroughly from head to toe. "Darling, it's been simply ages!" she gushed. "Let me have a look at you. Those tiny little breeches are marvelous on you! Don't tell me you've been dieting?"

Dani only grinned. She'd known Sabrina for years. They'd met in prep school, roommates first, and then bosom buddies, and she'd long since grown used to her friend's effusive manner of speaking, knowing that it stemmed from a nature as warm as it was genuine.

"Stuff the compliments, Brie," she retorted fondly. "You're among friends, remember?"

Sabrina's lower lip trembled. "I meant every word I said," she insisted. "I would never tell a lie. You know that."

"But you have been known to embellish the truth a little, haven't you?" Dani asked mischievously. "Like the time I heard you tell Mrs. Dickerson that her little Harold with the tin ear had all the makings of a concert pianist?"

Sabrina's shrug was a study in grace. "All right, so maybe I didn't bother to mention that classical music isn't my forte. Can I help it if I was born to boogie?"

"You're impossible. You know that, don't you?"

Totally unruffled, Sabrina nodded.

"But I love you anyway," Dani sighed as she led the way up the steps onto the shaded porch.

"Well, of course, darling," Sabrina replied. "Who wouldn't?"

They had just sat down on the long wrought-iron bench that flanked one side of the veranda when Rick appeared around the side of the building, accompanied by two of the other players. The three men were intent on their conversation, and Dani and Sabrina went unnoticed as they dug cold sodas out of the ice chest on the bench below, then continued on their way back out to the field.

Sipping her cold drink, Dani watched with amusement as Sabrina's gaze shifted over the three men idly, slipped away, then snapped back in a quick double take. As soon as they were out of earshot, she turned to Dani curiously. "I can see it *has* been too long since I came down to watch polo. Who *was* that gorgeous man?"

"Down, girl," Dani said quietly. Though she smiled, her tone held just the barest hint of steel. "I saw him first."

Raising her eyebrows, Sabrina lifted a hand to buff her already immaculate nails on the front of her shirt. "So? You were the one who always said that a little competition was good for the soul."

"Not this time," Dani snapped, surprising herself with her own vehemence.

"All right," said Sabrina, "if that's really the way you want it, I'll keep my hands to myself." She turned her head, letting her gaze linger once more on the calm self-assurance of Rick's easy stride as he walked along the sidelines. "Although if you ask me, from the looks of that one, he could probably handle both of us."

He probably could at that, Dani realized with a vague ripple of uneasiness. After all, when it came down to the bottom line, Sabrina's net worth was no trifling matter either. Perhaps Malone would simply take one look at the sultry dark-haired beauty and that would be that. As far as he was concerned, she'd be washed up, finished, yesterday's news.

Never one to back away from a challenge, Dani immediately rose from her seat. No time like the present to find out. "Come on, Brie," she invited, tossing her empty soda can into the garbage. "It's almost time for the next chukker. If you want to walk back out to the field with me, I'll introduce you."

"What a wonderful idea," Sabrina cooed. She reached up and ran her fingers through her hair, somehow achieving an artfully tousled look that would have taken Dani half an hour and a can of hair spray to duplicate. "I've always been curious to see just what sort of man it would take to really get your motor running."

"My motor's been running fine, thanks. It's just that some people idle at a little lower speed than others, that's all."

"Perhaps." Sabrina smiled wickedly. "And then again, darling, some of us are never idle at all."

Rick glanced up as they approached the sidelines. His gaze slid from Dani to her companion, then back again, before he quickly excused himself and strode over to meet them.

"Dani!" he said, "I've been wanting to compliment you on your play. You handled the ball out there like a real pro."

"Yes, she is very good, isn't she?" Sabrina paused, waiting for Dani to make the introductions.

"Sabrina, this is Rick Malone," Dani interjected. "Rick, Sabrina Dare."

Without even realizing what she was doing, Dani hung back slightly as her friends shook hands. She waited subconsciously for fireworks to shoot off, cannons to explode, the two of them to launch themselves into each other's arms, but nothing of the sort happened. Instead, Rick merely stepped back as well, including her in the circle once more.

"She's an amazingly good player," he agreed, nodding in answer to Sabrina's question. "I'd be happy to have her riding behind me any time at all."

Though his tone was bland, a smile played at the corners of Rick's mouth, and Dani couldn't help but remember the way she'd ridden behind him the day before, her arm circling his lean waist. Then Rick glanced her way with a broad wink, and she realized that the phrasing of his compliment had been no accident.

"You make a pretty good front man yourself, Malone," she retorted.

"Yes, you do," Sabrina agreed, politely ignoring the undercurrents that swirled around her. Laying her crimson-tipped fingers on Rick's arm, she deftly included herself back in the conversation.

"Thank God you've arrived just in time to rescue us from the recurring ignomy we suffer every summer. I'm sure you realize that the Fairfield Challenge Cup is coming up in July, but what you may not know is that Silverbrook is the only area team that's never won it.'' Drawing a deep breath, Sabrina sighed prettily, bemoaning their past record. ''At least this year, with you on our team, we might have a chance.''

''I'll certainly do my best,'' Rick promised.

The warning bell sounded up in the stands and, on cue, Harry appeared beside them, leading the two ponies they were going to ride in the next chukker.

Flipping down the chin strap on her helmet, Dani pulled on her cotton gloves, then reached for the pinto pony's reins. Charm was the first polo pony she had ever owned. A nondescript gelding with more spunk than breeding, he had taught her almost everything she knew. Over twenty years old now, his neck didn't arch quite as proudly as it had in his youth, his muzzle had gone gray, and there was a definite dip in his back just behind the withers where the saddle rested. Still, he played his heart out for her every time. Now, anticipating a good ride, Dani reached up to run her hand fondly down his long, sleek neck.

''My word, Dani,'' Sabrina laughed. ''Don't tell me you're still riding that old thing!'' Covering her mouth with her hand, she added in a teasing aside to Rick, ''She's had that pony twelve years if it's a day. Talk about getting your money's worth!''

Rick looked Charm over slowly, assessing him from head to tail. ''You know,'' he said, turning to Dani, ''Sabrina does have a point.'' He reached up and caught one of the pony's large furry ears in his hand, cupping it down toward his mouth as he said in a loud stage whisper, ''Have you ever thought to inquire about your pension plan, old man?''

''Not you, too.'' Dani groaned. ''I've tried to retire him. Believe me, I've tried. But he seemed so dejected being left out in the field when everyone else went off to work. Every day when I'd take the other ponies out to be schooled, he'd run along the length of the fence, trying to come with us.

"Finally it dawned on me that he loves this game every bit as much as I do." Dani paused, shrugging helplessly. "I know he's not as young and as fast as he used to be—but he doesn't. And when it came right down to it, I just didn't have the heart to stop him from playing."

"Good for you," Rick said softly. He didn't know many people who would place their own needs second to those of a loyal friend. Now he found himself absurdly pleased that Dani could be counted among them. Then, abruptly, the second bell chimed, drawing them apart. Quickly Dani and Rick vaulted up into their saddles, grabbed their mallets from Harry and trotted out onto the field.

If the first half of the scrimmage had been routine, the second turned out to be anything but. Perhaps because his team was now behind by several goals, Harley Greer was now expending an all-out effort, as though the outcome of the match depended solely on his ability to control the play.

Since Harley was riding the number two position for the opposing team, it was Dani's job to cover him. By the end of the fifth chukker, his hell-bent-for-leather style was beginning to cause her problems. Several times he had fouled her intentionally, his tactics ranging from crossing her line when she had the ball to bumping into her roughly and knocking her pony aside when she went for a shot.

Dani knew those maneuvers were part of his game. Harley was simply one of those men who felt that a woman's place was not on the polo field, and he was not above using physical intimidation as a means of proving his point. That the two of them would ultimately be in contention for the same spot on the club team only added an extra spark of vigor to his assault.

Unfortunately for Dani, since it was only a scrimmage, the referees were inclined to be more lenient than usual. Though they caught some fouls and awarded penalty shots, they let just as many slip by in the interest of keeping the game moving.

"You and I are switching positions," Rick informed her tersely during the brief break before the last chukker. His frustration had grown during the past hour as he'd watched Harley Greer use Dani as his own personal punching bag. Now he was determined to put a stop to the situation before somebody got hurt. "For the rest of the match you're up at number two, and I'll be riding number three."

"We'll do no such thing!" Dani fired back, knowing full well what he was trying to do. "I can handle Harley Greer. So far he's only managed to score one goal."

"That's right," Rick agreed with a frown. "And I'll tell you the reason why. The man has spent more time trying to figure out how to trip you up than he has making shots for his team. From now on I'll be covering him!"

Without waiting for her reply, Rick whirled his pony about on his hindquarter and galloped back onto the field, leaving Dani with no choice but to follow along behind.

Of all the pompous, self-important jackasses! she fumed silently as she jockeyed her pony into position for the toss-in. Who did he think he was, ordering her around like that? Harley Greer might be a pain to deal with, but at least he patronized her openly rather than subtly undermining her credibility under the guise of being helpful.

Didn't Malone realize that if she let him take her knocks for her, she'd lose all the trust and respect she'd managed to build up over the past three years? Then she'd be right back where she started, and anything was better than that. No, Dani decided, she'd much rather suffer the odd bump here or there than go back to the prejudice she'd fought in the beginning when the men had played around her carefully as though she were made of glass—not exactly hindering her game, but certainly not helping it either.

She was still fuming when the referee rolled in the hard wooden ball, and the play began. Then adrenaline shot through her veins, and she urged Melody on, forgetting everything save the small white sphere and the necessity of propelling it through the goal posts at the end of the field.

Her stick whistled through the air, and there was a sharp crack as it connected cleanly with the ball, sending it flying upfield to where her number one teammate was waiting. He overrode the ball, and his shot was weak and wide. It was easily picked off by the opposing back, who dribbled the ball out toward the sideboards.

For the next several minutes, play was centered in the middle of the field, each team striving for the advantage and briefly finding it, but neither penetrating the other's territory deep enough to launch an attack on the goal. The heat and the effects of the arduous game were beginning to tell. The ponies were straining and covered with lather, and the riders were tense, tired and drenched with sweat.

Caught up in the throng of players who battled for control of the ball, Dani's nostrils were filled with the smell of horses and hard exertion. Her ears rang with the clash of sticks and stirrups. Her throat was parched and dry, her body yearning for the relief of a cool breeze. But her pulse raced with excitement and her eyes blazed with zeal as she shoved, scrambled and fought.

Then suddenly through the confusion of players, Dani saw the opening she was looking for. Guiding Melody with her legs, she urged the mare forward. The first stroke of her stick sent the ball flying free. Immediately six players scrambled across the field after it.

She had raised her mallet a second time, preparing to pass the ball to Rick, when abruptly her stick simply stopped and hung in midair, hooked by one of the opposing players. A quick glance to the side confirmed her guess—Harley, of course.

Swearing vehemently under her breath, Dani tried to disengage. Rather than swinging free after successfully blocking her shot, however, Harley gave yet another mighty tug. The saddle was wet and slippery between her legs. Off balance as she leaned out to reach the ball, Dani knew she was in danger of being dragged off. Quickly she twisted her fingers free of the thong. Letting go of the grip, she watched helplessly as her stick sailed away in a wide arc.

Aiming a murderous glare at Harley back over her shoulder, Dani raced for the sidelines and grabbed another stick from the stack set out for just such an emergency. But the seconds she had lost made all the difference, and by the time she rejoined the play the yellow team had pressed its advantage and was driving toward the goal. This time it was Rick who thwarted the opposing team's efforts. He rode in and intercepted a pass, then cleared the ball back out to the sideboards once more.

Determined now to prove her mettle, Dani summoned every bit of energy she had left. She was aware that the clock was ticking. There was just enough time left for one last play, and she meant for it to be hers.

When a poor pass gave her a line on the ball, Dani had her chance. Leaning low over Melody's neck, she raced after the ball, mallet poised and ready. This time she defied Harley, defied anyone, to try to stop her!

The sound of thundering hooves just behind her left shoulder gave her pause, but only for a moment. Then to her amazement she heard Rick's voice. "Leave it!" he ordered, calling the shot for himself.

Dani's head snapped up in indignation. All at once she saw the reason for his interference. Harley Greer was galloping directly at her from upfield. Judging from the collision course he had set, it was obvious that he intended to keep her from making the shot at any cost.

Squaring her shoulders angrily, Dani never hesitated. Her heels spurred Melody forward, but before she was able to reach the ball, Rick caught her. Pulling up alongside, he used his hands and legs to swerve Trigger suddenly to the right.

The two horses bumped, then straightened, then bumped again. Melody grunted from the impact, and Dani felt a brief flash of pain as her knee ground against Trigger's shoulder. Then the mare was forced to give way and veer off to one side. Untouched, the ball passed by beneath their hooves. As Dani watched in helpless fury, it was Harley who got to it, taking one last shot before the horn sounded and the match was over.

What on earth could he have been thinking? Dani wondered incredulously. She glared at Rick's departing back as he galloped off toward the sidelines. Good Lord, she mused, it just wasn't possible! She'd actually been ridden off a shot by a member of her own team!

Pulling her tired pony down to a walk, Dani left the field slowly, taking a few minutes to compose herself and her thoughts. It didn't help. By the time she'd delivered Melody into the waiting hands of the hotwalker, pulled off her helmet, pads and gloves and run to catch up to Rick as he walked up the slope in the direction of the barn, she was still blazingly angry.

"Stop right there, Malone!" she ordered harshly. As she came up behind him, Rick paused, then turned slowly. His face was calm, the set of his shoulders relaxed.

"Do you want something, Dani?"

"Damn right I do!" Dani stopped before him, her eyes glinting with a fire that Sabrina could have warned him had the power to wilt corporate presidents and desert sheikhs alike. "I want to know just what the hell you thought you were doing out there. You rode me off that last shot. Don't try to deny it!"

"Why should I deny it? From my point of view, you were the one in the wrong. I'd called that shot, remember? The fact that we both missed it was your doing, not mine."

"Don't be ridiculous! I had the line on that ball, and you know it."

"Yes, you did," Rick growled. He felt his temper rise to match hers. "It's a pity Harley Greer didn't plan on recognizing that fact."

"Then you admit it! You *were* trying to protect me!"

"Somebody had to. Hasn't anybody ever told you that you're supposed to keep one eye on the ball and the other on where you're going?"

"I knew perfectly well where I was going. It was Harley who was headed the wrong way, not me."

Rick glared down at her. "A fine lot of good that would have done both of you as you sat in the emergency room having your broken bones set."

"Oooh!" Clenching her teeth tightly together, Dani all but screamed her frustration. "Listen, Malone," she snapped, "No matter what the reason, I don't ever want you to do such a thing to me again. I can take care of myself. Do you hear me?"

Unexpectedly Rick grinned. "Yes, I hear you, loud and clear. In fact, I wouldn't be surprised if half the town was able to hear you."

"Good," Dani said stiffly, not backing down an inch. "Then there won't be any more misunderstandings like this in the future."

Rick shook his head in reluctant admiration. So this was what happened when the princess went on the rampage. In earlier times, no doubt she'd have summoned a courier and shouted, "Off with his head!" Come to think of it, she didn't look as if she were above such a tactic right now. Good thing for him she'd laid down her stick before coming after him, or he might really have had some trouble on his hands.

He looked around, fielding several curious glances. Dani was probably used to being the center of attention, but it made him more than a little uncomfortable. Of course he could just walk away. But why should he when he was having such a good time drawing her fire? Obviously she was accustomed to riding roughshod over these pretty East Coast society boys, but she'd soon find out that he responded to this kind of treatment a little differently. This was one princess who was just begging to be dragged from her ivory tower. He'd be damned if he wasn't the man for the job.

Still grinning, Rick stepped forward to close the space between them. "You're one tough cookie, aren't you, Dani?"

Damn him, thought Dani. Why did he have to keep looking at her like that? His smile made it perfectly clear that he was throwing her challenge right back in her face. Not only that, but he was standing too close, just as he'd no doubt intended.

She was near enough to feel the heat his body generated, near enough to realize that, warm from the exertion of the game, he exuded a smell that was faintly pungent and devastatingly male. Despite her intentions, it played havoc with her senses.

Where was that famous Hawthorne reserve when she needed it most? Dani wondered desperately. Inexorably control of the situation seemed to be slipping through her fingers, and that realization unnerved her as nothing else could have. Without thinking, she lashed out in response.

"Bravo, Malone!" she cried. "It's about time you started getting the message."

If anything, Rick's grin widened. "Oh, I get the message all right. I just hope you realize what it is you're sending."

Dani's glare was steely. "Drop," she said, slowly and clearly, "dead."

Rick's gaze skimmed quickly over her, missing nothing from the angry gleam in her blue eyes to the belligerence of her stance. She had to be the most infuriating, intimidating, intriguing woman he'd ever met. And although he'd be more than happy to go a dozen rounds with her, now was neither the time nor the place.

"Not a chance," Rick said. He draped an arm companionably around Dani's shoulders.

Before she even knew quite how it had happened, Dani found herself walking beside him back toward the barn. "Cut it out!" she cried, shrugging his arm away. "How do you expect me to fight with you if you don't fight back?"

"I don't," said Rick. He settled for taking her hand in his. "That's exactly the point."

Maybe it was at that, thought Dani, her resistance draining away. But that didn't mean she was about to let him have the last word. "Try a stunt like that again, Malone, and you'll find yourself wearing my mallet as a hood ornament!"

Rick shrugged. "The way I see it, I was only protecting my own interests."

Dani looked up at him blankly.

"You and I are going to be good together, Dani."

Oh, no, not again, thought Dani, groaning inwardly. Twice in two days? This was really too much! Why was it that every man she looked cross-eyed at suddenly got the notion that he was on the fast track to fame and fortune? Why, this one had barely even waited one day before trying to stake his claim.

"Look, Malone," Dani said quietly, "it'll be simpler if we understand each other right from the start. Don't get the wrong idea, because I have no intention of marrying anyone, and that includes you."

For a moment Rick looked truly taken aback. Then a smile spread slowly across his face. "You might try waiting until you're asked."

Damn the man, thought Dani. He was laughing at her again, while she didn't see anything funny about the situation at all!

"Don't hand me that," she scoffed. "I've been this route before, and I know just how it goes. A few dates, a few flowers, and then bang, it's how soon can we get to the altar? Believe me, I should know. Virtually every man I've ever gone out with has asked me to marry him."

Rick's eyes lit with interest. "Princess, you must be one hot date."

"Don't be obtuse!" Dani snapped. "It has nothing to do with me. It's the money."

"The money?" To Dani's amazement, Rick threw back his head and roared with laughter. "In that case, you must be beating them off with a stick!"

Dani tried valiantly to maintain her anger. In the face of Rick's growing amusement, however, she found the task next to impossible. Finally she simply gave up, acknowledging the absurdity of the situation with a reluctant smile.

"Sometimes I do," she retorted.

Grinning, Rick refused to take the warning personally. "If you ever need any help in that department, just let me know," he offered. "I've been told I swing a pretty fair mallet myself."

"I'll remember that."

"Oh, and if you want to start making plans, I think an autumn wedding might be nice—"

"Don't start with me, Malone."

Rick's expression was bland with innocence. "I didn't," he pointed out. "If you remember correctly, the whole thing was *your* idea."

Dani glanced up. "You know, Malone," she said pleasantly, "you're really beginning to get on my nerves."

Rick grinned wryly. He'd rather she'd have felt compelling attraction. Failing that, a friendly interest might have worked, too. Then again, any reaction was probably better than none. All this meant was that he was going to have to work a little harder to make her realize what a truly irresistible fellow he was.

"It wasn't exactly what I had in mind," he said softly. "But I guess it will do for a start."

Chapter Four

"Rick, old man, you've come down in the world if you call *this* an office."

It was Wednesday evening. Rick had gone straight from the scrimmage to his office, where he was sitting on the floor, engaged in unpacking yet another box. After a week devoted to the task of turning the rooms in the Landmark Square Building into a habitable space, he was finally beginning to feel as though he might actually succeed.

Now, at the sound of the voice, Rick looked up and saw what looked like a large rubber plant attached to a pair of human legs, standing in the doorway. Though the face behind the plant wasn't visible, he'd have recognized that Texas drawl anywhere. It belonged to his good friend and old college drinking buddy, Billy Matlock.

"We all have to start somewhere, Billyboy." Rick stood up and dusted off his hands. Billy lived and worked in New York City, and he'd had a standing invitation to drop by ever since Rick had come east. Now, as far as Rick was concerned, his old friend's timing was perfect: he was delighted by the opportunity to take a break. "Is your head sprouting foliage, or did you actually bring me something?"

"It's what you might call an office-warming present." Billy strode into the empty room that constituted Rick's outer office, the heels of his weathered cowboy boots rapping sharply on the bare wood floors. He set the rubber plant down in the corner, then straightened and took a look around. "I can see it's a good thing I bothered. This office looks as though it can use all the warmth it can get. Don't you even have a desk?"

Rick jerked his thumb over his shoulder. "It's in there. This part's the reception area. The next room's where I actually intend to work."

Billy walked across the room to the second doorway. "Well, now," he said heartily, "this is much better." At least there was a desk. It was made of oak and buffed to a high shine. Bookshelves had been partially assembled along one wall. A computer, still boxed, sat atop the credenza. The only other furniture in the room was a worn corduroy-covered couch. "I think."

Rick grinned, undaunted. "It could be worse."

"Keep telling yourself that," Billy advised. "It'll make you feel better every time you open your eyes and look around."

"Come on," said Rick. "Don't tell me you wouldn't be just a little bit tempted to trade your fancy office in that high-powered brokerage firm for this and all the freedom that comes with it?"

"More than a little," Billy agreed. "In fact, lately I've been thinking about it more and more." He looked at Rick and grinned. "The way I've got it figured, you can take the first shot. That way, when the time comes for me to strike out on my own, you can tell me the pitfalls to avoid."

"Thanks," said Rick. He perched on the edge of the desk and waved Billy to a seat on the couch. "It's nice to be appreciated."

"Don't mention it." The couch creaked as Billy settled his bulk down onto the cushions. "So," he said, looking around, "obviously you're not spending your time on interior decorating. Does that mean business is booming?"

It was a long moment before Rick answered. "There aren't many people I'd admit this to," he said finally, "but frankly, Billy, business stinks."

The Texan nodded sympathetically. "That bad, huh?"

"I've had proposals in the works for months, but so far not even a nibble."

Billy leaned back, resting his outstretched arm along the length of the cushion. "These things take time. The word is out that you've gone out on your own. Now it's just a matter of waiting for people to figure out what to do about it. Once the ball starts rollin', you'll look back at these days and laugh."

"I know." Rick frowned. "But that doesn't make things any easier now."

"Looks like I came at the right time," Billy said. "It seems to me you could use some cheerin' up." He reached inside his jacket and pulled out a tall bottle wrapped in a brown paper bag. When he stripped off the wrapper, a bottle of fine, aged bourbon was revealed. "Kentucky's finest," he said proudly. "I figured two old friends might want to share a drink in honor of your new company. Got any cups around here?"

"Maybe." Rick rifled quickly through the drawers in the desk, coming up finally with a pair of Dixie Cups.

"Perfect." Billy sniffed the mash appreciatively as he poured it into the cups. He set the bottle aside, then held his cup aloft. "To new ventures!"

Billy downed the finger of bourbon in a swallow. Rick raised one brow slightly, then shrugged and followed suit. Immediately Billy refilled the cups.

"To old friends!" said Rick. The two cups were emptied, then quickly refilled once more.

"To beautiful women!" cried Billy.

"You would think of that." Rick's throat burned slightly as he tossed the bourbon down. The next toast was his. "To life's little frustrations!"

"Interesting juxtaposition," Billy commented as he poured. "Don't tell me you've found yourself a filly up here already?"

"Filly, no," Rick corrected. "Woman, yes." He stared thoughtfully into the depths of his bourbon. "Maybe more woman than I can handle."

Billy chuckled softly. "Can't say as I ever recall hearing you say that before."

"I've never met anyone like Dani Hawthorne before." Rick tilted back his head and emptied his drink. Then his fist closed over the cup, crushing it into a ball before flipping it into the wastebasket on the other side of the room. "Maybe that's precisely the problem."

"How so?"

Rick shook his head. It was a sharp, frustrated motion. "She's the kind of woman that'll knock you right off your feet, then pick you up again and make you glad she did. The kind who can look so cool and ladylike one minute, then ride like a banshee the next. She's full of surprises, some good, some bad, but all of them interesting as hell."

"I don't know." Billy shook his head slowly. "Sounds to me like the kind of trouble you don't need at this stage of your life."

Rick eyed his friend suspiciously. "What stage?"

"You know." Billy gestured at the spartan office. "It looks to me like you're running enough risks already without taking on more."

"Maybe," Rick said slowly. He pictured the way Dani had looked on the polo field Sunday—the wind rippling through her hair, her cheeks flushed with pleasure, and most important of all, the spirit, the zeal with which she'd thrown herself into the game. Like him, she was a fighter—the kind of woman who could not only go the distance but who would enjoy every minute of the challenge. In his whole life, Rick hadn't known many women like that; he had every intention of getting to know this one better.

Leaning down, Rick reached into the drawer and pulled out another cup. "Fill 'er up, Billy," he said, extending his arm.

"Sure." Billy poured a generous ration with pleasure. "What are we drinking to this time?"

Rick grinned as he held his cup in the air. "To risks!"

"To risks!" Billy echoed. The bourbon disappeared in a single fiery swallow.

THURSDAY AFTERNOONS were one of Dani's favorite times of the week. That was when the Pegasus Program, an organization that offered riding instruction to handicapped children, held lessons at the Silverbrook Hunt Club.

Dani had first gotten involved with Pegasus when she'd brought her horses back to Silverbrook after college. Nan Blakely, the woman who ran the program, was always on the lookout for extra mounts, and she'd immediately tapped Dani as a possible source. Though several of her ponies were quiet enough for an inexperienced child to handle, Dani had been reluctant to allow their use until she had seen for herself exactly what was involved.

Nan had invited her to one of the weekly sessions, and from the very beginning, Dani had been hooked. She'd seen children, some withdrawn, others belligerent, embrace the experience with wide-eyed enjoyment as they explored their potential on horseback in a way they'd never been able to before. For many, unable to get around without mechanical or human assistance, it was their first taste of what freedom really meant.

Immediately Dani had known that she wanted to be a part of the program. She'd volunteered not only the use of her horses, but also her own time as well. Beginning the following week, she'd thrown herself into the endeavor with complete dedication, progressing quickly from an assistant to a full-fledged instructor. She loved the work, and was gratified by the knowledge that, for the first time in her life, something she was doing was really making a difference.

In January, when Nan had moved to another state and the program had languished due to lack of care, she had found herself assuming many of the administrative duties as well. Now Dani not only taught classes but was also involved in fund-raising, public relations and organizing the program's annual horse show. Pegasus required a lot of time and effort, but each Thursday when the children arrived, their eyes shining with wonder, hope and excitement, Dani knew that it was worth it.

By the time the riders began to arrive at three o'clock, an assortment of twelve horses and ponies were ready and waiting. Dani helped the first arrivals onto their mounts, making sure that each was wearing a regulation hard hat, with its plastic safety strap fastened securely in place. She had just finished settling a towheaded boy on a palomino pony and was leading him into the ring when an excited shriek rent the air.

"Dani, come and look what I've got!"

Dani turned, a smile forming on her face as she saw ten-year-old Missy Johnson waving to her from the side window of her mother's station wagon. Though Dani tried very hard not to play favorites, she and Missy had formed a special attachment during the two years the little girl had been involved with the program.

At just under four feet tall, Missy was small for her age. She had curly black hair, big blue eyes and an engaging grin that was often in evidence. She also had cerebral palsy.

Some of the handicapped children Dani worked with felt sorry for themselves. Missy, on the other hand, considered herself lucky that her speaking, hearing and eyesight were all unimpaired. Her arm movements were slow and often jerky, and her slender legs were encased in heavy braces as she struggled to learn to walk, but Missy faced the world undaunted. Her spirit and good humor were unflagging, and Dani couldn't help but feel that if anyone could beat the odds, Missy was the child who could do it.

"What have you got now?" asked Dani. She walked over as Celia Johnson parked the car in a slot beside the ring. The previous week Missy had shown off a chocolate ice-cream cone. The week before that, a box of crayons. "Is your mother spoiling you again?"

"Nope." Missy giggled. She shook her head, her black curls bouncing. "Dr. Bregman is."

Missy's mother climbed out of the car, and Dani glanced at her inquiringly.

"Don't look at me," Celia said. "This was all Dr. Bregman's idea."

"Well?" Dani opened the door on the passenger side where Missy was waiting. "What is it?"

"Look!" Missy cried gleefully. She held up a much-worn Cabbage Patch doll. "Now Matilda Grace has braces, just like I do!"

Dani took the doll from Missy's hands and inspected it carefully. Wound around its chubby cloth legs were a pair of shiny metal braces. She caught her breath as a lump gathered in her throat.

"Isn't that the neatest thing?" Missy chattered on. "Dr. Bregman did it for me 'specially. It was a surprise. Now Matilda Grace and I are both going to learn to walk at the same time."

Summoning a smile, Dani nodded. "That's neat all right," she said quietly.

"Matilda Grace didn't used to be very good at walking," Missy continued gravely. "But now with these new braces,

I'm sure she's going to be much better. She didn't like them at first because they were hot in the summer and they made her itch. But I told her that was okay because it wasn't forever, and if she wears them now, someday she'll be able to walk, just like I will. Right, Mommy?''

"Right, Missy." Celia tousled her daughter's curls as she helped the child from the car.

Watching them together, seeing Celia's calm assurance and determination, Dani knew where Missy drew her strength. Mother and daughter had a wonderful relationship. That realization brought thoughts of Amelie, and with them, a quiet sigh. Shaking her head, Dani hurried over to the gate to take the reins of the last mount—Charm, her polo pony, who was Missy's favorite.

"Up you go," she said, boosting the little girl into the saddle. Adjusting Missy's feet in the stirrups, she looked up into her smiling face. "Ready?"

"Roger wilco." Missy giggled. "Ten four." She guided the horse into the ring.

Dani latched the gate behind her, then walked to the center of the ring to begin the lesson. All went well, and the hour passed quickly. In what seemed like no time at all, the parents were back to collect their tired but elated children.

As the procession of cars wound down the driveway, Dani took stock of what needed to be done. The other volunteers had taken care of all the mounts but one—Rocky, a roan gelding from her own string. Aiming one last wave at the departing cars, she turned away to lead the horse back into the main barn.

Years of practice had honed the routine to a science. In less than ten minutes she had the roan untacked and washed down and was letting him graze at the end of a lead rope while his coat dried. As the gelding munched on the lush grass in the stable's courtyard, Dani leaned back against the post and rail fence that enclosed its end. Her eyes slipped closed as she let her thoughts drift.

Standing quietly on the other side of the yard, Rick watched Dani for several minutes before a finely tuned awareness of her surroundings alerted her that he was there. He knew the moment it happened. One minute he'd been admiring the long, luxurious line of her body as it reclined gracefully against the fence, the next she had stiffened, then braced her arms and stood, her posture every bit as regal as the imperious tilt to her head.

"You're riding late today," Rick commented, walking forward.

Dani glanced down at the slim Ebel watch on her wrist. "And you're here early. You must be working bankers' hours."

Rick shrugged. "I have an in with the boss. When there's nothing much going on, he lets me cut out early."

"I should be so lucky," Dani muttered, thinking of the mountain of Pegasus paperwork that awaited her. She reached down and ran a hand under the belly of the roan. He was just about dry.

"You work?"

Rick didn't mean the comment the way it sounded. Well, maybe he did. It was just that he couldn't for one minute imagine the princess doing anything that might be construed by the world at large as actual labor. But that still didn't mean that he'd intended to blurt out his thoughts so bluntly. He knew he'd made a mistake the moment he saw the frown that darkened her face.

"You sound surprised." Dani's tone was haughty. It matched the chill in her gaze.

"I am." Too late to back down now, Rick plunged in with both feet instead. "You don't look the type."

Dani's eyes narrowed. "What type is that?"

"Most people consider work to be an unpleasant but necessary fact of life. From what you said the other day, I got the distinct impression that you don't do anything you don't want to do."

Dani shrugged. "Usually, you're right. However, this is something important and, as it happens, I am the only person willing to do the job."

"I see," said Rick. Briefly he wondered what it was that someone like the princess would find worthwhile to disrupt her routine for. Come to think of it, he mused, there was quite a lot about her that was making him wonder.

Rick hated questions without answers, almost as much as he disliked school yard bullies, and puzzles that nagged at his subconscious until he found himself losing sleep at night. Since meeting Dani two days ago, it seemed as though his life had been plagued by all three. It was time to do something about it.

"Does this job of yours take long?" he asked.

"No more than an hour or two."

"Then you'll be finished by Saturday?"

"I should hope so." Dani glanced up suspiciously. "Why?"

"I was thinking you might like to join me for dinner that night."

Unaccountably an image of Preston and his extra lamb chops swam before Dani's eyes. She willed it away and asked again, "Why?"

"Does there have to be a reason?"

"There usually is." Dani folded her arms across her chest and waited.

"How about physical attraction?"

Dani considered for a moment, then shook her head. "Too easy."

At least she hadn't denied it, thought Rick. It wasn't much, but it was something. "Common interests?"

Slowly Dani ran a caressing hand down the roan's smooth neck. "My dentist and I share an interest in my teeth and I don't date him."

Rick grinned. He'd known she wouldn't make things easy. "I'll bet your dentist is fifty and bald."

Dani returned the grin. "Sixty, and very debonair. Have I ever told you I have a thing for older men?"

"No, and with that you've just answered your own question."

Dani stared at him blankly.

Rick gazed back at her, then smiled. It wasn't often he'd seen Dani at a loss for words. He almost wanted to savor the moment. Even more, however, he wanted to assure himself of her acquiescence. "I think we're a lot alike, Dani," he said softly. "And I think we could be very good for each other. I want . . . no, I need to get to know you better."

The words, quietly spoken, caught Dani off guard. The warmth behind them reached out, tugging at her own needs, willing her to comply. She looked up at the man who stood before her, his virile body silhouetted by the rays of the waning sun. His dark hair ruffled slightly in the breeze as he awaited her response. All at once she wanted very badly to go out with him, and yet . . .

After so many years her defenses were so much a part of her makeup that Dani didn't even realize that they'd risen into place. She tossed back her head, the movement part defiance, part frustration. How could she deal with his needs when she wasn't even sure of her own?

"What if you don't like what you find?" she asked.

"I'm willing to take my chances, Dani." Rick's eyes, dark and intent, found hers and held them. "Are you?"

There it was, thought Dani, the sixty-four-thousand-dollar question. She'd never backed away from a challenge before. Her gaze floated over him once more. She sure didn't see any reason to start now.

"Dinner it is," she conceded. "Pick me up at eight."

JUST LIKE THAT, thought Rick, as though he'd been given an imperial summons to appear. It was Saturday night, seven-thirty, and he was in the process of getting dressed.

Fresh from the shower, he strode naked across the bedroom of his rented condo. The open door of the walk-in closet revealed a row of suits in muted blues and grays. Rick snorted softly under his breath. If one wanted to make it in business, one had to look the part. But on Saturday nights, he answered to no one but himself, and that included one Miss Danielle Winslow Hawthorne.

Rick pulled open the top drawer of his dresser and fished out a pair of cobalt-blue jockey shorts. As he stepped into them, he tried to imagine Dani with any of the single men he'd met at the club. It wouldn't wash.

Of course their breeding was impeccable. And, of course, they had financial statements to match. But for some reason Rick couldn't bring himself to take most of them seriously. Perhaps it was their bright, vacant smiles, or the soft hands that clasped his in an equally soft handshake. Or maybe, he thought, grinning, it was their penchant for loud sportswear.

What were those colors again? Oh, yes, poison pink and Greenwich green. Worst of all were the patchwork pants that combined the two. He could just imagine what Dani would say if he showed up in a pair of those!

Rick swept a pale yellow shirt off its hanger and settled it across his broad shoulders. No, the princess didn't believe in pulling her punches. Mentally, if not physically, she was every bit as strong as he was, and she was determined to let him know it.

No doubt about it, thought Rick as he pulled on a pair of taupe linen slacks. As far as Dani was concerned, he was in for a struggle. Then that thought brought a smile. He had every intention of making the most of it.

Twenty-five minutes later Rick guided the nose of his Jeep Cherokee through the high wrought-iron gates that guarded the entrance to the Greenfields estate. He whistled softly as he drove down the quarter-mile gravel driveway that led to the house. Old money, he thought. Tactful, understated and reeking of good taste. He hadn't expected anything less.

Dani was upstairs putting the finishing touches on her outfit when she heard the front doorbell chime. She swept up her purse, then paused by the bedroom door, purposely giving Preston a moment or two alone with Rick. Her gaze darted to the mirror over the dresser and she studied her reflection less with a critical eye than with curiosity concerning the image she had concocted.

Her hair was soft, shiny and clean. Worn loose around her shoulders, it gleamed like gold in the muted light. Her jumpsuit was silk, the fabric so supple that it draped her curves lovingly, concealing her body while at the same time flattering it outrageously. Its vivid blue color matched the shade of her eyes, drawing attention back to the fine-boned features of her face.

She'd do, Dani thought, then frowned. She'd better. She'd spent almost an hour getting ready, and when was the last time she'd done something like that? "If Preston says so much as one word..." she muttered with feeling.

The knock on her door was brief, discreet. "Danielle?"

"Coming, Preston." Dani threw open the door and grinned. "Did I give you enough time to check him out?"

Preston drew his shoulders back stiffly, his chest puffing out like a ruffled hen. "I don't know what you mean."

"Sure you do," Dani said easily. "You always vet my dates for me. You've been doing it since I was fourteen years old."

"Fifteen," Preston corrected. "You weren't allowed to date until then."

"Doesn't mean I didn't, though." Dani started down the hall, her stride long and jaunty.

"Ah, yes." Behind her, Preston sighed. "Biff Applebaum."

Dani stopped dead in her tracks. "You knew about him?"

"Of course." Preston sniffed disapprovingly.

"But I . . . but we . . ."

"Used poor Curtis Renfrew as a decoy. Yes, I know."

Dani giggled, remembering. "He was into geometry and chemistry and wore glasses half an inch thick. We figured you'd love him."

"Not," Preston said gravely, "when you were seeing Biff on the sly."

"I was only fourteen, remember? It was all on the sly."

"So it was," Preston agreed, his displeasure obviously undimmed by the intervening years. "Biff Applebaum, of all boys. I nearly purchased a shotgun on his account."

"Preston!" Dani was shocked. "You wouldn't really have run him off, would you?"

"More than once I was tempted. He was much too old for you, Danielle."

"Sixteen," Dani said with a sigh. "Ah, young love. I thought he was something else."

"Until Joey Blackman came along."

Dani's eyes widened. "You didn't miss much in those days, did you?"

Reaching the end of the hall, they descended the staircase together. "I still don't," Preston said meaningfully.

"Don't what?" asked Rick, who was waiting at the bottom of the stairs.

"Don't ask," Dani advised him. "Believe me, you don't want to know."

She looked terrific, thought Rick. Not that he'd ever doubted she would. But still, after the rumpled jeans and sweat-stained riding clothes he'd seen her in before, the silk jump suit made a pleasant change. Another facet to the princess, he mused. One he'd anticipated, to be sure, but no less enjoyable for it.

"Good night, Preston," Dani said firmly. She took Rick's arm and led him toward the door. On another night, with another man, she might have invited him into the library for a drink. Now, however, the gleam in the butler's eye was entirely too smug. "Don't wait up."

"Certainly not," Preston replied, holding the door. He inclined his head toward Rick. "Good night, sir. Have a pleasant evening."

"Thank you." Rick grinned broadly. "I intend to."

Was it her imagination, Dani wondered, or did they actually exchange a wink? It just wasn't possible, she decided as Rick opened the door to the Jeep and she hopped up onto the front seat. Preston wouldn't be caught dead winking at somebody.

On the other hand, she realized, the butler had failed to give his standard lecture about careful driving and not staying out too late. Maybe Preston was actually mellowing in his old age. Or maybe, she thought, casting a sideways glance at Rick, Malone had had something to do with it.

"So," she said as he started the Jeep and they headed down the driveway. "Did you and Preston find something to talk about while I was getting ready?"

"Sure did." Rick nodded, his eyes on the road.

"Well?"

"Well what?" It must be a flaw in his character, Rick decided, that allowed him to enjoy baiting her so much.

Dani counted slowly to ten before continuing. "Preston has been known to subject anyone who comes to the house to take me out to a very thorough inspection."

"Really?" Rick's brow lifted. "I didn't notice."

Like hell, thought Dani, deciding to humor him. "What *did* you and he talk about then?"

"Sports," said Rick, his voice low and amused.

"Sports?" Dani turned to stare. "You must be kidding! Preston wouldn't be caught dead discussing anything as pedestrian as that. He thinks the whole idea of organizing games for the masses is vulgar."

"Oh, yeah? Try telling that to the bookie who took his bet on the World Cup."

Dani choked on a laugh. "Preston has a bet on the World Cup?"

"Uh-huh." Rick nodded. "He won a bundle on the Stanley Cup and decided to let it ride."

"Now I know you're crazy. Preston would no more watch ice hockey than—"

"Than what?"

"Than moon the queen!"

At that, Rick laughed out loud, and after a moment, Dani joined in.

"If it'll make you feel any better," Rick said several minutes later, "Preston did tell me to be sure and have you home at a reasonable hour."

Dani smiled fondly. "To tell the truth," she admitted, "it does. Preston's routines are so deeply engrained that when he breaks with tradition I begin to get worried."

"He cares about you, too," Rick said quietly. Indeed, in the course of his conversation with Preston, he'd been surprised to discover the depth of the butler's concern.

They'd approached each other as adversaries—each cautious and more than a little wary. Yet in the space of several minutes time, they'd wound up allies instead. It pleased Rick to know that Dani had someone like Preston looking after her, whether she seemed to think she needed it or not.

Dani gazed at Rick as he drove, trying to decipher the odd look on his face. "I'm sure you put his fears to rest," she said, probing.

"Of course." Rick's expression lightened as he turned to face her. "I told him I'd have you back by Monday morning at the very latest."

"Monday morning?"

"Well, I do have to work, you know."

"You know, Malone," Dani muttered, "sometimes your overconfidence is truly staggering."

"Thank you," Rick said modestly. "I consider it one of my best features."

There was simply no way for Dani to answer that, so she decided not to even try. Instead she sat back in her seat and spent the remaining minutes of the drive humming softly along with the Vivaldi concerto that emanated from the stereo speakers on either side of the Jeep's interior. When they arrived at their destination, she was pleased to discover that Rick had chosen one of her favorite restaurants—a small clapboard-covered café right on the beach overlooking Long Island Sound.

"I hope you like seafood," said Rick.

"I love it," Dani replied. Without waiting for him to come around, she hopped down out of the Jeep and slammed the door behind her. "And this place is one of the best."

"So I've been told," said Rick. After entering the restaurant he gave his name to the maître d', who led the way to a quiet table in an alcove near the back of the room.

A waitress appeared to take their drink order, then recited the list of the evening's specialties. Both Dani and Rick left their menus untouched, choosing instead to order from the day's catch. That done, they sat back to enjoy the view through the sparkling bay window.

A candle, encased in a small glass globe, flickered on the table between them. In its light, Dani realized, the planes of Rick's face gentled. His eyes, already dark, took on an air of mystery. The line of his mouth softened in repose, his lower lip was sensuously full. He looked less like the determined, hard-riding polo player she'd met on the field and more like the sort of man a woman would want to have as a friend . . . or a lover.

The waitress delivered their drinks, and Dani picked up her dry martini and sipped at it thoughtfully as she pondered the reason they had come. He'd said he wanted to get to know her better. All at once Dani realized she wanted to get to know him better, too.

"Have I lost you?"

"Hmmm?" Dani looked up to find Rick's dark eyes trained on her.

"You looked so deep in thought. I just wondered if anything was wrong."

"Wrong? Not at all." Dani smiled. "At least not unless you have something against satisfying my curiosity."

"Go ahead," said Rick. He picked up his Scotch and swirled it in its glass. "Shoot."

"If I'm out of line, you can tell me, but I'm curious as to how a self-confessed poor boy ever got started playing polo."

"That's easy." Rick grinned, pleased by her interest. "It was necessity, plain and simple."

"Necessity? Don't be ridiculous." Dani cocked her head to one side. "Nobody plays polo because they have to."

"Maybe not," Rick allowed, enjoying the way the gesture of skepticism exposed the long line of her throat. His gaze followed it downward, tracing the smooth skin of her shoulders, the spill of golden hair. "But people do take jobs because they have to, and sometimes that means taking whatever they can find. At fourteen and trying to hold down a full load of freshman courses, the best offer I had was a chance to muck out stalls before and after school at a private stable down the road.''

Dani's brow lifted. Once again she couldn't help but be struck by the differences between their upbringings.

It was ironic that she, who had supposedly been raised with all the advantages, was the one who had been left with bitter memories of her youth. Rick, for his part, didn't seem concerned in the slightest that he'd been forced to earn a living at a time when most boys his age had had nothing more on their minds than trying out for the football team or testing their prowess with girls.

"Go on," she prompted, resting her elbows on the table and leaning closer to listen.

"In the beginning, the only reason I took the job was because we needed the money. But, working in the stables every day, it wasn't long before I fell in love with the horses. Ben Kingston, their owner, had some of the finest Arabians this side of Poland. I thought they were the most gorgeous animals I'd ever seen.''

Rick's voice was low, almost reverent, and Dani smiled at his enthusiasm. She understood just how he felt.

"Anyway, aside from breeding Arabs, Ben's other passion was polo. He noticed the way I took to the horses, and pretty soon he had me riding. Ben thought that real riders were born, not made, and at least in my case it seemed to be true.

"The first time I climbed onto the back of one of his horses, I felt as though I'd come home. The next thing I knew, Ben had stuck a mallet in my hand and I was riding his string and working out with the team. From there the whole thing just kind of snowballed.''

"You and Ben must be very close," Dani commented. She felt a small pang as Rick's features clouded over.

"We were," he said slowly. "Ben died two years ago.''

"I'm sorry," Dani murmured.

Rick nodded. "He was a wonderful man, and a wonderful friend. I met Ben at a very bad point in my life. I had just lost my own father, and there were times when I wondered how my mother and I would ever manage to go on. Then I got the job with Ben and started playing polo, and gradually, things began to come together again. Ben meant a great deal to me. Like my father, I still miss him. I guess I always will."

Leaning back in her chair, Dani watched the play of emotions across Rick's expressive face. He seemed so comfortable with his feelings, in a way she herself had never been. He wasn't afraid to admit that he had cared, or that that caring had caused him pain. He had both strength and softness. It was, Dani decided, a compelling combination.

"Now it's your turn to answer a question for me," said Rick.

Dani nodded. "I guess that's only fair. What do you want to know?"

"I don't understand why you got so upset after the scrimmage the other day. I know it wasn't because I called your shot. You're much too good a player to resent something like that. So what was really going on?"

Dani sighed softly. On Wednesday she'd been far too angry to explain. Besides that, she wasn't used to being in the position of even *wanting* to explain. But now, seeing how sincerely confused Rick appeared to be, Dani knew she had to try to make him understand.

"Every time you interfere on the field," she said slowly, "you only make things worse."

Rick's eyes never left hers. Some women were meant to be savored by candlelight, he decided. Some were merely meant to be savored. He reached across the table, his hand beckoning. Surprised, Dani hesitated a moment, then slipped her fingers into his. He squeezed gently, his grip both strong and reassuring. "Tell me how."

"When I first started playing polo at Silverbrook, the other players drove me crazy. They were too polite, too careful. Either that or they played around me as if I wasn't even there. I have their respect now, and believe me, I've earned it. The only reason I have any credibility now is because they've learned that I don't let anyone push me around. And that has to include you, or everything I've accomplished so far will have been for nothing."

"I see," Rick said slowly. And for the first time he really did. Dani's refusal to accept his help hadn't been a pigheaded denial of her need, but rather a calm acceptance of the fact that polo was an inherently dangerous game—no more so in her case, yet no less, either. He still didn't regret the impulse that had sent him flying to her aid, but at least now he understood what had triggered the outburst that had followed.

"Then you won't get in my way again?"

"Probably not."

"Probably?"

Rick looked up and grinned, enjoying the cobalt fire that burned suddenly in her eyes. When the princess was calm, she was beautiful. Angry, she was nothing short of glorious.

"All right," he said, "I promise I won't interfere again." He paused, then added. "Unless I have to."

Dani's outraged glare could have melted ice.

Rick's grin grew broader still.

Damn him, thought Dani. And damn that silly, sexy, irresistible grin. She was angry, wasn't she? So why did she feel like doing nothing more than laughing with him? A moment passed, then another. Finally she just couldn't help herself. A smile twitched at the corners of her mouth, then blossomed full force.

Shaking her head, Dani picked up her martini and tossed off the ice-cold gin that remained. If she wasn't careful, Preston was liable to wind up having the last laugh yet.

Chapter Five

They were eating dessert when Rick brought up the subject of marriage. "Is it time yet?" he asked.

Dani looked up from a Linzer torte on which she was happily lavishing a good bit of attention. "For what?"

"The proposal."

Dread rose within her, an unwanted specter like the ghost of Christmas Past. Reluctantly she pushed the torte aside. Then she noticed that Rick was grinning again—a sure sign of trouble. "What proposal?"

"You know the one. You told me about it yourself. A few dates, and then bang! That proposal."

"Oh." Dani nodded, considering the matter. At least he didn't sound entirely serious. "Has it occurred to you that you're several dates short?"

"You know what they say," Rick said cheerfully. "Never put off till tomorrow what you can do today."

"Not in this case," Dani muttered. "Trust me, this is one topic that is better off postponed." She reached once more for the torte, cut off a large wedge with her fork and stuffed it into her mouth. The dessert she'd been enjoying so much only a moment earlier now tasted cloyingly sweet.

"I take it I haven't hit upon your favorite subject." Rick's eyes were bright with curiosity. Funny that a woman who exerted such a commanding presence in so many situations could be unnerved by a simple topic of conversation.

"You take it right."

"You're not planning to get married, then?"

Dani looked up. "Not if I can help it."

"Why?"

"Maybe I'm too liberated to consider giving up my freedom." It was a stock answer, delivered without thinking, and they both knew it.

"Maybe," Rick said slowly. And maybe not. "Has it ever occurred to you that in a good marriage, people gain a good deal more than they could ever give up?"

No, thought Dani, it hadn't. To tell the truth, she'd never given the matter much thought. Since she had no intention of ever falling in love, she'd always assumed that that omission automatically precluded marriage. And since she didn't plan to marry, she'd never seen the point in spending a lot of time thinking about it.

All of which was a good deal more than she had any intention of explaining. No, all things considered, it was much easier to toss the conversational ball back to Rick and let him run with it.

She propped both arms on the table and leaned closer across the space that separated them. "Why don't you tell me what your idea of a good marriage is?" she invited.

Rick felt a stab of reluctant admiration. She certainly was good at ducking things she didn't want to talk about. No, make that *very* good. Once more, he was forced to revise his opinion. Dani Hawthorne was only nine-tenths princess—and one-tenth artful dodger.

"A good marriage is the best kind of partnership," he said firmly. "Two people working together to achieve common goals—respect, good communication, lots of laughter, and above all, plenty of love."

"It sounds like an awful lot to ask," Dani said with a frown. "Do you really expect to find all that?"

"I certainly intend to try. My parents had that much. I don't see why I should have to settle for anything less."

Dani muttered something—part sigh, part epithet, under her breath.

"What was that?"

"I said, good luck."

Rick glanced up when he heard the tone in her voice. She didn't seem at all convinced that he would succeed, and that didn't surprise him in the least. What did surprise him was that rather than being smug, she'd sounded almost wistful, as if she wanted to believe that such things existed but couldn't quite bring herself to do so.

It was obvious that someone, somewhere, had really done a number on her. And remembering what little she had told him about her past, Rick could think of several likely culprits. If her own parents were the only example she'd had, it was no wonder she was turned off the idea of forming a lasting relationship with a man.

She was definitely in need of enlightenment, Rick decided. From what he'd seen so far, however, the princess was just about the most stubborn person he'd ever met—excluding himself, of course. That meant that a sincere attempt at persuasion would probably get him nowhere; he'd have to make his point another way. He'd start by loosening her up a bit.

"Oh, don't worry about me," Rick said, flashing her a cheeky grin. "I don't need luck. When it comes to picking a wife, I have a foolproof plan."

"I'll just bet you do," Dani said, smirking. As far as she could tell, Malone was prepared for just about anything that came his way. "I know I'll probably live to regret this, but why don't you tell me about it?"

Rick sat back in his chair, assuming center stage with aplomb. "The secret to a good marriage is picking the right partner—in my case, a wife."

"I should hope so." Dani's eyebrows waggled up and down teasingly.

"Shh, don't interrupt."

"Sorry, just trying to interject a little levity."

Rick offered himself a silent congratulations. The princess he liked best was back—tart, sassy and just itching to give him hell. Wait until she heard what he was going to say next.

"In order to insure that I don't make any mistakes, I've compiled a list of qualifications."

Dani nodded thoughtfully. "A comprehensive guide to wife shopping. That's very interesting. You could probably market this and make a fortune."

"Don't tell me we're going to have to discuss money, again."

"Sorry." Dani giggled, sounding anything but. "Just trying to interject a little prosperity."

Rick smiled sweetly. "Shut up, and drink your coffee, would you?"

Dani matched the smile with one of her own. "I think I can guess the first qualification already. Obviously your perfect woman needs a 'Me Tarzan, you Jane' type of personality."

"Better than 'Me Tarzan, you Cheetah.' "

"Not necessarily."

Rick glared. "Would you like to hear the list, or not?"

"Of course," Dani conceded graciously. "By all means, describe your perfect woman. I can't wait to hear all about her."

"Laugh all you want, but this wife shopping is serious business. A man shouldn't have to settle for anything less than the best."

"I should say that depends on his own qualifications," Dani said archly. "Wouldn't you?"

"Agreed. But of course, in my case—" Rick preened for his appreciative audience "—the material is above reproach."

"Self-reproach anyway."

Ignoring her, Rick continued. "The woman for me would have to be beautiful—"

"You realize, don't you, that that's a rather sexist request?"

"Not at all. Every woman is beautiful in her husband's eyes. Now intelligence, that's a less subjective matter."

"Are you aiming high or low?"

Rick affected a wounded air. "That's a low blow."

"Just checking."

"And of course, to be honest, if she were rich, it wouldn't hurt."

"It never does," Dani said dryly.

"She'd need a terrific sense of humor—"

"Obviously."

"Oh, and by the way, she'd better be able to cook."

"Just out of curiosity," said Dani, "where do you expect to find this paragon?"

"Oh, I don't know." Rick's shrug was elaborately casual. "How are *you* doing so far?"

He was sneaky, all right, Dani decided, lulling her into a false sense of security with his gentle teasing and his ridiculous list. It had taken him a while to work his way around to it, but now all of a sudden, there they were, right back where they had started.

The only problem was that he had actually succeeded in lulling her into a mellow frame of mind. She'd relaxed with him, and enjoyed his company, and now she simply couldn't see the point in ruining all that by getting mad. Rather than fighting, always fighting, all at once it simply seemed much easier just to go with the flow, to play along, and see where the game took them.

Sitting back in her seat, she pretended to consider the list. "Well," she said finally, "I can't cook."

"No problem." Rick waved his hand magnanimously. "If there's one thing every budding tycoon learns, it's to be flexible. In your case, I think I'd be willing to make a few exceptions."

There he went again, thought Dani. It was time to put a stop to this, once and for all. "Listen, Malone—"

"Let's dance, shall we?" Abruptly, Rick stood and held out his hand.

"But—"

"Enough talking. It's time for a little action."

He wasn't going to let her voice her objections, Dani realized. Trying to tell Rick Malone something he didn't want to hear was roughly comparable to placing oneself in the path of a runaway train. He simply wasn't going to be deterred for a moment.

With a shrug, she rose and let Rick escort her to the other side of the room. It was probably for the best, she decided. Talking always seemed to get them into trouble. Maybe they'd fare better on their feet.

The dance floor was small, dark and very crowded. They found an opening and moved out into the swirling dancers. Leaning into Rick's body, Dani placed her arm behind his nape and began to move slowly in time to the music. A couple jostled them, and Rick gathered her closer. Her cheek rested, then nestled, against his shoulder. The music washed over them, melding them together as they swayed to its beat.

He'd been waiting all evening for this moment, Rick thought, then realized he was wrong. He'd been waiting all week. Almost from the first moment they'd met, he'd wondered what she'd feel like in his arms. The reality, he discovered now, was even better than he'd imagined.

The song ended, and another one began. The tempo of the music changed, growing slow and languorous. Dani shifted slightly, pressing closer, relying on Rick's strength to guide them as they spun around the room. She floated dreamily in the safe harbor of his embrace. Despite her size, Rick held her easily. She'd never met a man who'd made her seem petite before, yet now, sheltered in Rick's arms, she felt small, almost fragile. It was an unaccustomed sensation.

Unconsciously Dani stiffened. Not only was it a feeling she wasn't used to, it was also one she was distinctly uncomfortable with. Damn it, she wasn't fragile. She was five feet ten inches of solid muscle. Her riding and her weight training had seen to that. So why, surrounded by Rick's strength, did she suddenly feel as delicate as a summer blossom?

Dani felt a chill that rippled the length of her spine. The problem with summer blossoms was that they were easily crushed. They were picked, admired, then discarded. Whatever she was, it would never be that. All at once she was angry at Rick for making her forget her own strength, for exposing a weakness where she'd been sure there was none.

Rick felt the difference immediately. One minute Dani had been swaying, soft and pliant, in his arms, the next her back had straightened and her head lifted as she tried to wrest control. In an instant harmony vanished. Rick drew back, meeting Dani's glare with one of his own.

"Stop trying to lead, dammit!"

Dani's eyes widened. "I'm doing no such thing!"

"A moment ago you weren't. Now I keep tripping over your feet."

Dani smiled sweetly. "Try chalking it up to bad technique."

"Bad technique?" Rick muttered something unintelligible under his breath, then added louder, "Did I mention that those feet are heading in the wrong direction?"

"That," Dani said firmly, "is all a matter of your point of view. From down here they seem to be doing just fine."

"Well, from here, they seem to be waltzing me all over the floor. I know you told me you were strong, but this is ridiculous."

At that, Dani allowed herself to enjoy a small, private smile. "Did I ever mention that in college I earned a brown belt in karate?"

Rick shook his head wearily. "I don't think I want to hear about it."

"Okay, if that's the way you feel." Dani's blue eyes sparkled. "I just thought you should know what you were up against."

"Believe me," Rick said with feeling, "I'm beginning to get the idea."

Relaxing once more, Dani let herself be drawn back into Rick's arms. She felt much better now, stronger, more herself. She was no longer teetering on the edge he'd brought her to earlier. No, she was in control once more—both of herself and the situation. It was the way things should be.

Dani sighed softly. That something—that elusive feeling of shared sensuality that had spun around them as they'd swayed to the music—had been lost in the process was inevitable. Only a fool would think she could have everything, she told herself firmly. Only a fool would allow herself to care.

At midnight the trio of musicians packed up their instruments for the evening. As Rick and Dani left the restaurant, night breezes, heavy with cool, moist air, blew up off the sound. The moon was a shimmering silver crescent, hanging low in the velvet sky. Beyond the café, several small boats were moored at the pier. The sound of water slapping against wooden hulls echoed through the quiet night as the boats bobbed gently in their slips. Rick and Dani stopped by the edge of the parking lot to admire the scene.

"Are you tired?" Rick asked suddenly.

Dani raised her face to his. "Not at all. Why?"

"Let's go for a walk on the beach."

"Now?"

"Of course now. Can you think of a better time?"

Laughing, Dani shook her head. As Rick stepped out of his loafers, she reached down to slip off her sandals and roll up the pants on her jump suit. They tossed their shoes into the back of the Jeep, then joined hands and sprinted down to the beach. Stumbling in the deep sand, they clutched each other for support, giggling delightedly when they reached the water and the foamy shallows washed up over their feet.

"Ahh!" cried Rick, jumping back hastily. "That stuff's cold!"

"Of course." Dani laughed. "What did you expect?"

"Cool maybe, but not frigid." A small wave broke over Rick's ankles, and he hopped up and down in place.

"That's Connecticut for you. Up here in the northeast we like our temperatures brisk."

"Brisk is one thing. This water's like liquid ice."

"That's the trouble with you Arizona boys. You're too soft."

"I'll show you soft," said Rick. He held out his hand, fingers beckoning. "Come here, warm me up."

"Uh-uh." Grinning, Dani shook her head. The breeze caught her hair, swirling it around her shoulders like a golden cloud. Part of her ached to float into his arms. Another, more prudent part, demanded caution. She settled for teasing him instead. "You think I'd make things that easy for you?"

"No." Rick shook his head, knowing it was the truth. "Never."

"You're learning, Malone."

Then Dani looked up into Rick's face, and her smile slowly died. He looked gorgeous in the moonlight, she realized. His hair was windblown, the normally controlled locks in glorious disarray from the run. His deep-set eyes were trained on her, their color dark against the golden hue of his tan. His smile revealed a row of white, even teeth, and the confidence of a man who's seen what he wants and intends to go after it.

It was just that thought that made Dani stoop down into the surf. Dipping her fingers into the water, she splashed a fine spray into Rick's face. Before it had even hit its mark, she spun around and raced down the flat hard-packed sand.

"Why you—!" He blinked away the salty mist and took off.

Dani was fast, but even so she was no match for Rick. He caught her before she'd gone ten yards, scooping her up off her feet midstride and swinging her into his arms. Automatically Dani reached up to wrap her arms around his neck. Her eyes widened as the wave beneath their feet receded and Rick followed it out.

"Malone?"

His answer was part grunt, part triumphant growl.

"Are you going to do what I think you are?"

"Quite possibly." Rick reached up to finger the silk jump suit. "This thing's wash and wear, right?"

Dani sighed. She'd learned long ago that it was useless to fight the inevitable. "Right."

"Although if you ask me very nicely, I suppose I might be persuaded to put you down."

"Sorry, that's not my style." Dani nestled her head in the curve of Rick's shoulder. For as long as the ride lasted, she intended to enjoy it. "Of course," she continued, "you're going to have to weigh any satisfaction you might feel now against the fact that Preston will probably kill you when we get home."

"Idle threats." Rick waved the objection away. "I heard him say he wasn't going to wait up."

"Preston always waits up." Dani grinned into Rick's shirt front. Then, because the idea amused her, she nipped at his collar, catching it between her teeth.

Rick felt the even cadence of her breath, warm and sweet upon his throat. Desire rocketed through him like a blow to the solar plexus. Did she have any idea at all what she was doing to him? Could she possibly understand how he'd felt watching her roll up her pants and frolic in the surf like a child?

In the moonlight, her skin was like alabaster, her hair a shimmering veil of light. She'd slipped from his grasp like quicksilver—ethereal, ephemeral—dancing away like a half-forgotten goddess from his dreams. When she'd run from him, he'd known he had to follow. Had there ever been any choice?

Rick swallowed uncomfortably. Though he held her in his arms, he sensed that she was running still. Her body might be quiet, but her emotions were in full flight. Worse still, when she left, she'd never look back. For the first time in his life, Rick knew the feeling of wanting something that was beyond his control. He didn't like it one bit.

"Well?" Dani demanded. The suspense was killing her. The spot Rick had waded out to wasn't even deep enough to wet his pants. Still, it was ample for a dunking. What she couldn't understand was why he'd stopped, without saying a word.

Abruptly Rick turned and headed back to shore. "You're no good to me wet," he said gruffly. "You'd only mess up the Jeep."

"Of course," said Dani, as though his statement made perfect sense. "I should have thought of that myself."

She gazed upward quizzically, trying to gauge his mood. They'd certainly run the gamut tonight. A moment ago, he'd been playful as a puppy. She'd honestly believed he'd take his revenge. Nor would she have blamed him. Then suddenly his arms had tightened around her—arms that were already holding her closer than was strictly necessary, and he'd backed down. And she had no idea why.

That was the problem with Malone. He didn't make anything simple. Not only that, but nothing in her experience had prepared her for what she felt when she was with him. She'd enjoyed the calm, well-ordered balance of her life, the symmetry of knowing what would happen and when. It was certainly easier than this tumultuous sensation of rushing headlong into the unknown.

Then again, Dani mused, a little excitement wasn't all bad either, especially not when it came wrapped in a package like this one. Obviously Malone was around to stay. It was time to press him a little. With any luck, she might find out just how very complicated her life was about to become.

Abruptly Dani felt herself being set upright as they reached dry sand and Rick released his arm from beneath her thighs and swung her down to her feet.

"Can you walk?" he asked.

"Been doing it for years."

Her flip answer brought only a grunt in reply as Rick started up the beach toward the parking lot. Frowning, Dani hurried after him. "Hey!" she said, grasping his shoulder. "What's the rush?"

"Preston's waiting, remember?"

"Big deal." Dani stepped around in front of Rick, placing herself squarely in his path. "Let him find his own date."

"Dani, come on." Rick's voice was tight, impatient. "Enough playing around. It's time to go."

"I don't want to go home yet." The words were simple, the yearning was not. Was he going to make her do everything?

Rick stood, totally still, until it was simply too late to move. Drawing a hoarse breath, he reached upward, his fingers grazing the smooth skin of her cheek. With a soft oath, he took a step back. He needed distance. Even more, he needed to touch her again.

Dani's voice floated to him on a sigh. "Kiss me."

Had he been waiting all his life to hear her say the words, Rick wondered, or did it simply seem that way?

It made no difference which one of them moved first, because suddenly they were together. Rick's lips were warm and firm, his taste sweet and heady like the wine they'd drunk with dinner. His tongue skimmed the surface of her lips; they parted for him with a small moan.

She'd wanted to know, thought Dani. And now she did. Rick Malone was going to be very big trouble indeed. She hadn't known she could feel this good, so good that she wanted the kiss to go on and on and never stop.

It didn't make sense at all, Dani mused. She knew how to control desire; she'd certainly done it often enough in the past. But now suddenly there was a vortex burning within her, a whirling inferno that raced through her veins, igniting her senses, twisting and turning reason until she could no longer remember why she'd wanted control in the first place.

With an urgency born of need, Dani strained closer. Rick's palm pressed against the small of her back, drawing her into the cradle of his hips. Their bodies rubbed, and the friction they caused was a delicious accompaniment to the heated movement of their mouths.

Slowly Dani felt reason slipping away. Something inside her was sweeping her along, molding her to its rhythm like a primitive tide. It felt heady, dangerous and vaguely alarming. It felt so very right.

What was she doing to him? Rick tried to pull back and found that he couldn't. He was trapped in the spell Dani had woven around them. He tried to think, and found it impossible. His senses knew nothing save the taste of her. He had known she was not a woman to do things by halves. Now he wanted everything, the best she had to offer. And what then? Rick wondered. Would he ever be satisfied with anything less again?

With that thought came the knowledge that things were moving much too fast. He drew back slowly, his breathing every bit as ragged as his thoughts. So much for the ice princess, he mused dimly, revising again to add one part tigress to the mix. Would he ever know all the facets Dani had to offer? If not, he was beginning to suspect he might spend the rest of his life wondering.

"Well," Dani muttered under her breath, "I guess that answers that question." Obviously there were complications, and there were *complications*.

"What question?"

Dani looked up quickly. "Nothing. I was just talking to myself, that's all."

"I guess we'd better be getting back then." He needed space and he needed time, thought Rick. And the sooner he got them, the better.

"Yes, of course."

On the trip out, Dani had assessed Rick as a cautious, law-abiding driver. On the trip back to Greenfields, he could have set records. Feeling more than a little miffed, Dani watched the speedometer climb. Obviously he couldn't wait to get rid of her.

Perhaps Malone was the type of man who had to be the aggressor in a relationship, she mused, because they'd been doing fine until she'd kissed him. Then the same kiss that had left her feverish with longing had somehow ended with him cool and remote. Dani frowned slightly. Or then again, maybe the problem was even more basic.

She knew she wasn't a particularly sexy woman; she'd known it for a long time. As far back as junior high, Dani had seen what it was that boys found appealing—girls who were small, soft and helpless, girls who were everything she was not. The body that had been too tall and gangly in her youth was too strong and streamlined now. If Malone had found her a disappointment, she supposed he wouldn't be the first. And if that was what was going on, Dani decided, they may as well get it out of the way right now.

"Well?" she demanded as the Jeep pulled up in front of her door.

"Well what?" asked Rick. He was stalling, and he knew it. He wanted time to think, to try and sort out the feelings that had overwhelmed him on the beach. But from the look on Dani's face it was obvious that she didn't intend to give it to him.

"Was it my fault?"

Rick's confusion turned to genuine bewilderment. "Was what your fault?"

Dani glared at him. He wasn't helping at all. "Look," she said, "I know I'm not the sexiest woman..."

Rick frowned as comprehension began to dawn. She was worried about the way he'd withdrawn from her so abruptly. At the time he'd been so wrapped up in his own thoughts that he hadn't even stopped to consider how his actions might appear to her.

"You do, do you?" Rick reached across the seat that separated them. His fingers cupped her chin, tilting her face up to his. "Who told you that?"

His dark eyes were filled with such tenderness, such caring, that for a moment Dani almost allowed herself to give in to the warmth she saw there. Then she remembered what had happened the last time. Instead, her shoulders stiffened. "Surely you don't want references?" she said tartly.

"Dani." Rick sighed quietly, shaking his head at the futility of trying to explain what he didn't understand himself. "Nothing that happened was your fault. Nothing at all. You were wonderful."

Dani's gaze was still troubled. "So wonderful that you couldn't wait to get me home, right?"

Rick's fingers caressed the soft skin of her cheek. "So wonderful," he said slowly, "that if we hadn't left when we did, we might have found ourselves getting in over our heads."

Rick watched as Dani digested that for a moment in silence. "Have you ever been on a runaway horse?" he asked finally.

Dani nodded, smiling faintly. "Once, when I was little."

"I feel like that sometimes when I'm with you," Rick admitted. "I'm not sure I like it."

Dani's chin lifted. "I wouldn't."

"Then you see my problem."

There was a wry tilt to Dani's mouth. "Yes," she said slowly. "I guess I do."

Obviously she'd been hoping for something more, Rick realized as he gunned the Jeep down the driveway after seeing Dani to her door. He'd managed to allay her insecurities, but not necessarily her confusion. How could he, he wondered, when he couldn't even seem to deal with his own?

Chapter Six

Under normal circumstances there was almost nothing that could induce Rick to go to his office early on a beautiful Sunday morning. Then again, one of the first things he'd learned upon opening his own business was that when you worked for yourself there was no such thing as a normal circumstance. From answering the phones to taking the red-eye to the coast to meet with a prospective client, if something needed to be done, you did it, period.

Now there were less than twenty-four hours before he'd be submitting a proposal to the CEO at Telecomm. The job, if he secured it, would be large enough to get Malone Inc. up and running. Thanks to his research into the company, he'd slanted the proposal to stress his familiarity with what he suspected they needed most—the restructuring of long-term debt. This morning he wanted to have one last look to make absolutely certain that everything was as it should be.

Rick entered his office with an impatient stride. The sooner he was through there, the sooner he could get out to Silverbrook and begin his preparations for the afternoon's polo match. Oblivious to the dramatic view of the Stamford skyline visible through the window, he sat down behind his desk and switched on the computer. Moments later the file was on the screen. Quickly he began to scan through the figures.

Ten minutes later Rick sat back in his chair, rubbing a hand over his half-closed eyes. Though the numbers on the screen told him he was on page five, he couldn't remember a thing he had read. His thoughts kept wandering, focusing instead on another, more beguiling image.

Finally Rick gave in to the impulse, allowing himself to remember the way Dani had looked the evening before on the beach. He saw again her deep blue eyes, alive with laughter at first, and then, after he had taken her in his arms, smoldering with a passionate response whose intensity had nearly pushed him to the limits of self-control. But that wasn't all. No, her eyes had betrayed a third emotion the night before—bewilderment. Abruptly Rick felt again the pang of conscience that had tugged at him then.

He knew he'd behaved badly; he could offer no excuse. None except perhaps bewilderment of his own. From the very beginning the effect Dani had had on him had been undeniable. She'd blown into his life like a summer storm, and in less than a week's time, succeeded in turning it, and him, inside out.

Billy had been right when he'd said that Dani was the last sort of complication Rick needed. And yet, he knew, he wouldn't change a thing that had happened between them even if he could. Nothing, he mused grimly, except perhaps the timing. A year, even six months from now, he'd have been ready for her. Rick's gaze swept around the sparsely furnished room. A whole lot readier than he was now.

Standing, Rick leaned on his arms, his hands gathered into balled fists on the empty blotter of his desk. For the first time he wondered about the wisdom of the venture he had embarked upon. Whereas only days earlier he'd looked around his office and seen limitless potential, now he saw little more than empty space and unbilled time. He'd known from the beginning that starting a new business was never easy, that it took time and skill to get an enterprise like his off the ground. Last week he'd accepted that; now he couldn't. And all because of Dani.

The night before he'd realized things wouldn't be easy no matter what developed between them. There were simply too many differences between them, and too many variables to take into account. He had no intention of letting money be one of them.

"You always did have too much pride for a poor boy." Abruptly Rick grinned as Ben's words floated through his thoughts. Ben had been right. And though he wasn't a poor boy any longer, Rick still had a lot of pride. He had no desire for Dani to see his place of business and compare it, consciously or subconsciously, to others she had known. When they did come together, he wanted them to meet as equals.

Of course, he thought wryly, part of the problem was that he didn't seem to have too much say in the way things were going. Ten days ago, had he been told what was about to happen, he'd never have believed it possible. He'd laid his plans carefully; the concept of Malone Inc. was well thought out. He wouldn't have imagined that a chance meeting with a fiery blonde could possibly be capable of throwing everything into such a state of turmoil.

The night before, he'd pulled away from Dani because he'd sensed that things were moving much too fast. But now, twelve hours later, his emotions were still humming with the same vibrant tone. The mere thought of her sent adrenaline coursing through his body at the same breakneck pace.

Timing be damned! Rick thought. He was enough of a realist to know when he had no choice. Too restless to stand still, he moved out from behind his desk and strode across the room. If this wasn't love, he was in big trouble. If it was, the trouble was bigger still.

Rick stood in front of his window, staring at the view and seeing none of it. No wonder he'd been confused. Love was the last thing he'd counted on finding in Connecticut. One thing was sure: this overwhelming, invigorating, head-over-heels emotion had taken him by surprise—as had the lady who had provoked it.

Rick shook his head slowly. He'd never taken the easy route in life before; obviously this time would be no exception. He'd picked himself a wildcat all right. Nor did Rick doubt for a moment that it was a large part of Dani's appeal. He'd known his share of interesting women—pretty ones, too. But a woman who could challenge him on his own turf, match him toe-to-toe, eye-to-eye, and never falter once? She was one in a million.

All of which, Rick reflected quietly, was the very last thing that Dani would want to hear. She was wary of both love and commitment, and justifiably suspicious of anyone who offered a claim to either. Obviously he was going to have to handle himself very carefully. And that, he realized, was the second good reason for taking things slow.

The thought of time passing made Rick glance down at his watch. He swore softly under his breath. So much for the work he'd intended to do that morning. The proposal was simply going to have to wait. He had a polo match to play.

BY TRADITION, each summer the Silverbrook and Black Rock Hunt Clubs played their first polo match of the season against each other. Over the years the rivalry between the two clubs had intensified to the point where sportsmanship had become a forgotten virtue. Winning and losing were all that mattered. It was for that reason that it was especially important Dani play her best. Small mistakes and minor gaffes might be overlooked by the board in other games, but in a match with Black Rock, never.

On Sunday afternoon she checked the bulletin board outside the locker room as soon as she arrived at the club. As she'd expected, both Rick and Jim Lynch had been named to the starting team. She, Trip Malloy and Harley Greer were to play four chukkers each, switching in and out in the other two positions.

It could have been worse, Dani realized as she made her way out to the barn. At least the way things were structured she'd only have to deal with Harley for no more than a third of the game. After what he'd put her through during scrimmages, that was going to seem like a breeze!

"All set here, Miss Hawthorne."

"Thanks, Harry." Dani took Trumpet's reins from the groom. Declining his offer of a leg-up, she swung up into the saddle, then trotted the bay pony down the hill toward the polo field. Several players were already out on the field warming up, and she scanned the group anxiously, relaxing when she saw that Rick was not among them.

It was just as well that they weren't going to have a chance to talk, she decided. After the way things had turned out the night before, she wouldn't have known what to say to him anyway.

No sooner had the match started than Rick realized that the Black Rock players had been warned about his addition to the Silverbrook team. Riding the number two position, his task was a demanding one, and it quickly became obvious that the opposing team had no intention of letting him do his job. Two players rode him continually, providing a constant buffer between him and the ball.

Unprepared for the strategy, the Silverbrook offense fell into disarray. By the end of the first chukker, Black Rock was leading by a goal, and Rick was glowering. As the horn sounded and they rode off the field, he gathered the Silverbrook players on the sidelines for an impromptu meeting.

"Can't you see what they're doing?" he asked. He looked around the circle at each of his teammates in turn. "By putting two men on me, they're leaving their defense wide open. We can capitalize on that." His gaze swung back to Harley Greer. "We should have already."

"That missed shot wasn't my fault," Harley whined. He nodded in Dani's direction. "If her pass hadn't gone wild, I'd have made it easy."

"It doesn't matter who's to blame," Jim cut in. "The fact of the matter is, Rick's right. Their strategy isn't sound in the long run, and it's up to us to prove it to them."

The warning bell chimed, and the team scattered to find their mounts. Harry had Charm ready and waiting, and Dani smiled as she saw that the pinto's fuzzy ears were pricked in anticipation. She pulled down the chin strap on her helmet and was just about to mount when Harley strode angrily across the field to block her path.

"You're not seriously thinking of riding that old nag, are you?" he demanded.

Dani sighed quietly. "It looks that way, doesn't it, Harley?"

"This is a polo match, not a trail ride. He'll never be able to keep up."

"He's always kept up before," Dani snapped. "He may be old, but what he lacks in speed, he makes up in know-how. This pony's been playing the game longer than all of your horses combined."

Harley's sneer was an ugly approximation of a smile. "Well, isn't that reassuring? I guess it's good to know that someone on your side has some idea of what he's doing!"

The bell sounded for the second time. Fuming, Dani swung up into the saddle. If Harley was trying to rattle her, he was doing a good job of it. Nor did it help matters when she heard him say in a loud voice as she trotted away, "Wouldn't you think she could find something else to replace that old nag? Lord knows, she has enough money to throw around!''

Then suddenly from out of nowhere, Rick was at her side. "Don't pay any attention," he said, swinging Silver in next to Charm. "Harley's just jealous, that's all."

"Jealous?" Dani stared at him in disbelief. "Of what?"

Rick flashed her a brief grin as the horses jockeyed for position for the toss-in. "Watch yourself play sometime, princess. You'll see."

Dani's face warmed to his words, but there was no time to think about them or anything else as the referee tossed in the wooden ball and the match resumed. This time the Silverbrook team managed to work together as a cohesive unit, controlling both the ball and the play. Within minutes, Jim had scored their first goal, followed only moments later by a similar effort from Rick. When the chukker ended, this time it was the Black Rock team that trotted glumly from the field. The four Silverbrook players were smiling and jubilant.

Dani sat out the next two chukkers as Trip Malloy went in to take her place. As always, she found it much harder to watch than to play. Filled with nervous energy, she paced up and down the sidelines, applauding good shoots, bemoaning bad ones and muttering vigorously under her breath about the ebb and flow of the game. When the time came for her to mount up again, she couldn't wait to get back into the fray.

By the time the match ended half an hour later, Dani was flushed with elation. A near perfect pass from Rick in the final minutes of play had set her up for her first score of the season. Since Silverbrook was already ahead at the time, the goal had only served to enhance the margin of their win. Still, Dani was thrilled. Nor did it hurt that Harley, who was now complaining loudly about the officiating, had ended the game scoreless.

"Nice job," called out one of the Black Rock players who was riding by as she dismounted.

"Thanks." Dani looked up with a smile. "My first of the year."

The player saluted her with his upraised mallet. "To many more," he said, then added with a grin, "Just not against Black Rock."

She laughed. "Believe me, I'm not choosy. I'll take them anywhere I can get them."

Dani handed Ringo's reins to one of the hotwalkers, then paused by the sidelines to pull off her helmet and gloves. Reaching up, she unwound the elastic, then ruffled her fingers through her flattened hair.

"Hey, Rick, over here!"

Dani glanced up as Malone rode past her and pulled up beside the grandstand where two of the spectators, obviously his friends, were waiting. As she bent to remove her knee guards, she couldn't help but overhear the conversation. From the sound of it, Rick was undergoing quite a razzing.

"You call that playing?" one of the men drawled in a thick Southern accent. "Why that little lady over there rode rings around you!"

"Scored your last goal, too!" chortled the other.

Dani turned away to stifle a giggle. Even though the jibes were unwarranted, she couldn't help but enjoy seeing Rick be on the receiving end for once.

"Dani!" She spun back to find him waving in her direction. "Come on over. There are some people here who'd like to meet you."

Dani left her gear on the ground and walked over to where Rick was waiting. He greeted her with a broad grin, then introduced her to his friends. "These two gentlemen, and I use the term loosely, are Billy and Joe Matlock. We were in the same fraternity in college. Unfortunately, as you can see, they never amounted to much.''

Billy was frowning as he gazed at Dani speculatively. It was Joe who stepped forward to take her hand. ''Pleased to meet you, pretty lady,'' he said, enveloping Dani's hand in his beefy paw. ''What'd you say your name was again?''

Dani started to answer, but before she had a chance, Rick stepped between them. His arm settled around her shoulders, asserting proprietorship.

''Didn't I tell you?'' he said. ''You've met my trusty horse, Scout. This, of course, is my faithful companion, Tonto.''

Dani sighed. Just like men everywhere, she thought. Put them back with their old college friends and they immediately regress to a college age level of maturity.

''Tonto, huh?'' Joe repeated thoughtfully, looking at her blond hair. ''Funny, you don't look like you got Indian blood.''

''Sure I do,'' Dani replied, falling into the spirit of the game. She glanced down at her polished leather boots. ''Blackfeet.''

Beside her, Billy roared with laughter. ''She got you there, little brother!''

Rick grinned, appreciating her quick wit. ''We're on our way up to the clubhouse for a beer. Would you care to join us?''

Dani considered for only a moment before shaking her head. Last night Rick had been the one to put distance between them. Now she found herself doing the same.

She didn't think of it as a power play. In fact, she'd have been horrified if anyone had suggested such a thing. It was just that the idea of swigging beer and swapping tall tales with a pair of back-slapping college buddies really wasn't her style. Besides, she still hadn't caught up on all the Peg-

asus paperwork that needed to be done, and the remainder
of her afternoon was fully booked.

"Thanks, anyway," Dani said, smiling up at him, "but
I'm afraid I can't."

Though he hadn't really expected her to accept, Rick
found that his disappointment was keen. Take it slow, he
reminded himself silently. For now he simply had to be
content to let her set the pace.

"Too bad," Joe drawled meaningfully. "You want a rain
check on that invitation, little lady, you just let me know."

For the second time Rick found himself moving to step
between them. With effort, he curbed a swift stab of irritation. He should have remembered the way Joe Matlock had
of moving in on a woman, any woman, in two seconds flat.
Maybe he hadn't because it had never mattered to him before. Suddenly, however, it seemed to matter a lot.

"Don't pay any attention to Joe," said Rick. He aimed a
smile, edged with desperation, in Dani's direction. "He was
dropped on his head as a baby." He began to walk, herding
Billy and Joe ahead of him. "I'm sorry you can't join us."

"Me, too," Dani replied.

Rick glanced back, taking one last look over his shoulder. Their eyes met, then held. The contact was brief, but
still it was long enough to warm Dani clear down to her toes.

Rick saw her expression soften, and he smiled. It wasn't
much, but it was all he had. For now it would have to be
enough.

DANI SPENT THE REST of the afternoon and most of the next
morning working on the fund-raising that the Pegasus Program depended on so heavily. By Monday afternoon she had
a cramp in her hand, a crick in her back and was beginning
to wonder whether the phone had become a permanent fix-
ture attached to her ear. When Sabrina called and an-

nounced that she was coming over for a swim, Dani jumped at the chance for some time off.

She changed into a sleek midnight-blue maillot, did a quick mile's worth of laps and was floating on a raft in the middle of the pool when Brie arrived.

"Miss Dare is here," Preston announced. He held open the French door that led to the terrace.

"Thanks, Preston," Sabrina said, breezing past him. "I can take it from here."

The butler's nose rose a notch. "As you wish. Danielle, do you require anything?"

Dani opened one eye and squinted up to where he stood. Something was wrong; she knew it in a minute. Though he was apt to keep up appearances in front of guests, Preston had known Sabrina for years. The only other reason for him to have gone all stiff and formal like that was if something serious was bothering him.

"No thanks, Preston, we're all set." Dani rolled gracefully off the raft and sluiced through the water to the side of the pool. Before she could say anything else, however, the butler had nodded his head and disappeared inside. Leaning her arms on the lip of the pool, she frowned after him.

"What do you make of that?" she asked.

"Of what?" Sabrina hoisted her canvas bag onto a lounge chair and began to unpack a supply of tanning lotions that would have done a pharmacy proud.

"Preston. Didn't he seem odd to you?"

"No more than usual, darling. As far as I can tell, he's always the same—heavily starched."

In spite of herself, Dani laughed. Then Sabrina stood up and drew her flower-sprigged sundress off over her head, and her giggle ended in a gasp. "What is *that*?"

"A bathing suit, of course." Sabrina held out her arms and twirled for effect. "The latest thing from Rio. Don't you just love it?"

"I'm reserving judgment till I see the rest of it," Dani said with a grin. She eyed the wearer of the skimpy trikini with unabashed admiration. "If you don't mind my asking, what's holding those pieces on?"

"Sheer willpower," Brie confided, giggling. "With more than a little luck thrown in."

"That's about what I thought." Dani flipped over onto her back and stroked lazily away from the side. "Coming in?"

Sabrina did, swimming just long enough to cool off before they both pulled themselves up out of the pool and stretched out on two chaise longues to lie in the sun. "I was at the match yesterday," Sabrina commented. She bent her knees, then leaned over to oil her long legs with care. "From the looks of things, your Rick Malone may win the Challenge Cup for us yet."

"Could be," Dani agreed languidly. "He's certainly got the game to do it." She turned her head to one side, eyeing her friend. "But he's not *my* Rick Malone."

"Oh, no? Try telling that to him."

"What do you mean?"

"Come on, Dani. I saw the way he called you over after the match to meet his friends."

"Old college buddies," Dani said dryly, "are hardly the same as being taken home to Mom."

"Go ahead and play it cool." Brie's tone left no doubt at all as to what she thought of such behavior. "I heard you turn down his invitation, too."

"I had my reasons." Dani frowned in exasperation. "Did you listen to every word?"

"As many as I could hear," Sabrina admitted shamelessly. "What are friends for? Take my word for it, this one's a find."

Dani didn't need Sabrina's opinion to figure that out—not that she was about to admit it. Given any encouragement, Brie would be all over her with good advice. Stubbornly she turned her face up to the sun and said nothing.

"It wouldn't hurt for you to make a little effort, you know," Sabrina continued doggedly.

Too late to escape, thought Dani. Ready or not, here it came.

"Trust me, I know all about these things."

"I don't doubt it for a minute."

"Well, well, well." Sabrina sat up and cocked her head in Dani's direction. "If you're feeling inclined to be nasty, I suppose I must be on the right track."

"I'm sorry," said Dani, her smile contrite. Brie was right. There'd been no reason to snap. The two of them had been friends long before she'd ever even heard of Rick Malone, and undoubtedly they still would be long after he'd ridden off into the sunset. "It's just that Malone and I went out the other night, and nothing seemed to turn out the way it was supposed to."

"Did you have a fight?"

"Not exactly. That's the problem. I don't know what went wrong." Dani paused, then added mischievously, "Although he did yell at me for trying to lead when we were dancing."

Sabrina shook her head. "You never learn, do you?"

"Hmph," Dani sniffed. "I know everything I need to know."

"Except how to find yourself a man."

"Who says I'm looking?"

Sabrina met that question with a silence long enough to make Dani open her eyes and look over to see what was wrong. When she did, Brie was simply sitting there patiently, waiting for her to come to her senses.

"All right," Dani admitted, "so maybe I am interested in Malone."

"Now we're getting somewhere," Brie said with relish, and Dani groaned inwardly. "If you want my advice, the best way to keep a man interested in you is to make him feel strong and in charge."

"Rick is strong," Dani said with a laugh. "And believe me, nothing short of a bulldozer in high gear could make him believe that he wasn't in charge."

Sabrina smiled. "I'll grant you the man does seem to have a mind of his own. But as your best friend, let me be the first to assure you that he isn't the only one. It wouldn't surprise me if the two of you were going head-to-head constantly."

"Me, neither," Dani muttered.

"Take my word for it," Sabrina said wisely, "it wouldn't hurt for you to tone down your act a bit. Try being a little softer, a little more feminine."

Abruptly Dani frowned as the well-meaning advice hit too close to home. Her defenses rose, and with them, her temper. "I have no intention of changing for any man," she declared. "Either Rick Malone accepts me the way I am or he doesn't. The choice is up to him."

"All right, if that's the way you want to play it. But don't come crying to me when the man gets an offer from some frilly young thing, and walks."

"I won't." Dani looked at Sabrina coolly. "Really, after all this time, I should think you'd know me better than that. I never cry, not ever."

"No, you don't," Brie acknowledged, realizing it was true. "Let's just hope Malone isn't the man who gives you a reason to start."

"Don't worry," Dani said firmly. "He won't be."

It was after five o'clock by the time Sabrina left. Dani gathered up her things, then went inside for a shower and change of clothing. That done, she set off in search of Preston. With unerring instinct, she found him in the very first place she looked—down in the kitchen, sampling a batch of eclairs the cook had just made.

"Shame on you," said Dani. She waggled her finger under his nose. "What about those six pounds you lost?"

"I decided I deserved a reward for good behavior," Preston declared, biting into the pastry with relish. He pushed the plate across the table. "Here, try one. They're delicious."

"Not on your life." Instead, Dani chose a bunch of grapes from the fruit bowl in the center of the butcher block table. Making herself comfortable in the chair opposite him, she waited while Preston worked his way through a second eclair, and then a third. No doubt about it, she decided, something was very definitely wrong.

"All right," she said, pulling the plate out of range as he reached for a fourth. "That's enough. I'm not going to sit here and watch you eat yourself into oblivion."

"Fine." Preston sniffed and glanced toward the door. The unspoken message was obvious.

"And I'm not leaving either."

"If you're not going to give me my eclairs, and you're not going to leave, then what are you going to do?"

"Talk," Dani said firmly. "With you."

"Saints preserve us," Preston muttered.

"There's something bothering you, and I want to know what it is."

"Nothing," Preston said stiffly. "Nothing at all."

Like hell, thought Dani, facing him with a frown. She knew that Preston was a very private person. He didn't like to talk about himself, and he refused, on principle, to gossip about others. It was one of the reasons she had trusted him with so many of her secrets when she was younger. He'd always been there for her then, Dani mused quietly. She refused to do less for him now.

"All right then," she said stubbornly. "If you won't tell me what's wrong, then I'll just have to guess. We'll start at the top and work down. You've just been to see the doctor, and now you only have three days to live?"

Preston frowned irritably.

Dani decided to take that as a no. "You forgot to pay your back taxes, and now the IRS has put a lien on your house?"

"I live here, Danielle." The corners of Preston's mouth twitched.

Dani shrugged. "Is it my fault I'm flying blind? Okay, how about this? You bet your pension fund on the World Cup, and your team lost."

The butler's gaze was filled with reproach. "I see Mr. Malone talked."

Dani grinned. "I dragged it out of him."

"Just as you're determined to drag this out of me, aren't you?" Preston asked with a sigh.

Dani nodded.

"I warn you, it's a long story."

"We've got hours yet before dinner."

Preston eyed the plateful of eclairs. "I can talk and eat at the same time."

Dani picked out the largest pastry and handed it over.

Preston bit into it, chewed blissfully, then swallowed. Finally he began to speak. "It all began years ago when the Wentworths had a baby."

"Christopher?" Dani pictured the neighbor's son. "Why, he must be fifteen!"

"I told you it was a long story. If you keep interrupting, it will be interminable."

"Yes, Preston," Dani said meekly.

"You probably don't remember, but they hired a nanny from England to take care of him. Her name was Victoria Fellows."

He was right, thought Dani. She didn't remember that part at all. But then why should she? She wasn't in the habit of keeping tabs on the servants that came and went in the neighborhood. Dani looked up when she realized that Preston's silence had lasted a beat too long. To her surprise, she saw that a gentle flush stained his full cheeks.

"Victoria and I had what you might call a—" Preston paused to clear his throat "—close relationship."

"Why Preston, you sly old fox!" Dani said, her eyes twinkling. "I never even guessed!"

"Of course not," the butler said stiffly. "That would have been unconscionable."

"So," Dani prompted, "then what happened?"

"Well, er, nothing. You see Christopher grew up, and by the time he was five the Wentworths decided he didn't need a nanny anymore. So Victoria moved on. Of course she had no problem securing another position. She put in her name with an agency in London and was reassigned immediately. The only problem was that the family that hired her lived in England."

Without thinking, Dani centered the plate between them and reached for an eclair. "How awful for you."

"Well," he replied, "it really wasn't as bad as all that. Victoria writes a wonderful letter, and if I do say so myself, I'm not such a bad correspondent either. So we've kept in touch all these years. It always seemed as though we had plenty of time, you see. And besides, I thought that as soon as you were grown, all our problems would be solved."

"Me?" Dani paused, eclair dangling in midair on the way to her mouth. "How was I going to solve anything?"

"If you don't mind my saying so, you always seemed to be an eminently marriageable young woman. Once that was done, I figured it would be only a matter of time until Victoria's services would be required on this side of the ocean once more."

"So that's why you keep telling me that it's time to settle down."

Preston had the grace to look sheepish. "In part, yes."

Dani grinned at him mischievously. "Does this mean you've given up on me, Preston?"

"Good heavens, no!" The butler was shocked by the very idea. "It's just that time does seem to be passing. When I got Victoria's last letter, I knew I had to act. Apparently her current situation is going to be ending in a matter of weeks. If I don't do something now, she may lock herself into another position, and it will be years before I have another chance."

"Just what exactly is it that you want to do?"

Preston's large frame heaved with a heavy sigh. "Victoria and I had a wonderful relationship once. I think we could again. These past years we've grown even closer through our letters than we were before. If she'd have me, I'd like to spend the rest of my life with her."

"Preston, that's wonderful!" Dani cried. "You must call her immediately."

"Oh, no," Preston said quickly. "I couldn't possibly, not after all these years. I thought perhaps a letter outlining my intentions—"

"Would be just the thing," Dani finished firmly.

"Do you really think so?"

"Of course. I'm sure Victoria will be thrilled."

Preston looked unconvinced. "What if she isn't? What if she turns me down? We have such a wonderful friendship now. I'd hate for anything to ruin it."

"Ruin it? Are you kidding? Preston, where's your self-confidence, your determination? For all you know, Victoria may have been waiting all these years to receive just such a letter!''

"Do you really think that's a possibility?"

Dani was touched by the older man's uncertainty. Reaching out, she laid a reassuring hand on his arm. "All I can say, Preston, is that if I were in Victoria's place, I'd be honored."

The butler relaxed slightly, sending Dani a grateful smile. "And I'd be on the next plane, too!"

"Goodness!" Preston exclaimed. "I don't suppose things will move that fast, do you?"

"Having second thoughts already?" Dani teased him.

"Certainly not. I'm just trying to make plans, that's all."

"Then you'll sit down and write Victoria tonight?"

"I suppose so . . ."

"Preston!"

"All right, I will." The butler's pinched frog face was back in evidence. "There now. Are you satisfied?"

"Uh-huh." Dani glanced down at the plate of eclairs between them. Though she couldn't recall doing more than a little nibbling, only two of the original dozen remained.

Preston followed the line of her gaze and sighed. "Having gone this far, I suppose it's our duty to finish them off, wouldn't you say?"

Dani picked up the last eclair and held it aloft with a flourish. "To you and Victoria," she said. "May your reunion be everything you hope, and more."

"Amen." Preston said heartily.

Dani stuffed the last bite in her mouth, then swallowed slowly. Suddenly she felt ill. "Preston?"

The butler looked up as she rose quickly from the table.

"Please tell cook not to bother with dinner tonight, will you? I think I'm going to be sick!"

"As you wish, Danielle." He watched Dani rush from the room, holding her stomach, then settled back in his chair for a discreet burp.

Chapter Seven

"Give me a break, Malone! You can't work seven days a week!"

Dani stood on the clubhouse porch, glaring down at Rick, who was settled in a wrought-iron chair, his briefcase open across his jean-clad knees. He held a sheaf of papers in one hand, and a ballpoint pen in the other. A faded red polo shirt stretched across the breadth of his shoulders, outlining the muscles of his chest and the lean contour of his waist. He looked tanned, fit and incredibly handsome.

So what else was new? Dani wondered. In the two weeks that had passed since they'd gone out to dinner, the effect he'd had on her had never been short of heart-stopping. And seemingly he'd managed it without the slightest effort at all. Though Malone hadn't asked her out again, they'd still seen each other frequently—scrimmages on Wednesdays, matches on Sundays and chance meetings at Silverbrook in between. Each time he'd been glad to see her, his demeanor friendly but not effusive. In short, he'd acted like her best buddy.

Except, Dani mused, she wasn't in the market for any more buddies. She wanted more from Rick Malone, and if he wasn't about to take the first step, then she would simply have to do it herself!

Rick looked up from the papers he was studying. With effort, he held back a grin. The princess was in rare form today. Maybe he was finally beginning to get to her, and if so, it was about time. These past two weeks had pushed both his patience and his frustration level to the limit. His only hope was that they'd been as hard on Dani as they had been on him.

"In case it has escaped your notice," he said calmly, "the way you keep interrupting me, I'm not working at all."

"Come off it, Malone," Dani scoffed. "Nobody sits on the clubhouse porch and seriously expects to get any work done. There are too many distractions."

This time Rick did grin. "On a beautiful day like this, I couldn't bear to be cooped up in the office. Besides," he pointed out affably, "the only distraction I see around here is you."

"Sometimes one is enough." Dani perched herself on the arm of Malone's chair and draped her arm over his shoulder. "Are you sure I couldn't make you forget about work, just for a little while?"

If only she knew, thought Rick. This was one lady that was apt to make him forget about sanity altogether.

"I don't know," he said, pretending to consider. "What did you have in mind?"

Immediately Dani leaped to her feet. She swept the pile of papers from Rick's hand, stuffed them into his briefcase, then slammed it shut and set it aside. "How about a ride cross-country?"

Rick rose beside her. "I've already had Trigger out, and both Scout and Silver could use a day of rest."

"No problem," Dani assured him blithely. "Harry's saddling Trumpet and Melody for us right now."

"You're very sure of yourself, aren't you?"

Dani shrugged. "If I'm not, who will be?" Then she looked up and found Rick watching her, his dark eyes intent. He wasn't satisfied with her answer, and they both knew it. Suddenly neither was she.

"Besides," she added, "Preston had the cook make up a backpack for me. It's filled with wine, cheese and all kinds of fruit. I was going to go out for a quiet ride by myself, but when I saw you sitting here, well...I decided I'd rather share."

"Thank you," said Rick, sorry now that he had snapped. Whoever it was that had said abstinence was good for the soul had to be crazy. Either that or a eunuch. He reached down and placed the tip of his forefinger under Dani's chin, lifting her face to his. "I'm glad you feel that way."

Before common sense had a chance to step in and stop him, to insist for the millionth time how much wiser it was to take things slowly, he leaned down and closed his mouth over hers.

"Rick...?" Dani's eyes fluttered shut, then quickly opened. The kiss was over almost before it had begun. Still she felt a surge of tingling heat that started at her lips, then spread to every corner of her body.

"Hmm?" Rick mumbled.

Dani started to speak, then stopped as a group of riders rounded the side of the clubhouse and started up the steps onto the porch. Obviously this was neither the time nor the place for what she wanted to say. Then Dani thought of the meal Preston had packed, and the secluded glade where she planned to enjoy it. She grinned devilishly.

Reaching up, she chucked Rick smartly under the chin. "Hold that thought, I suspect we may get back to it."

THE JUNE AFTERNOON was warm and sunny, and the sky a clear cerulean blue. Perfect riding weather. Rick and Dani made their way carefully around the edge of the polo field, then turned off onto a bridle path that veered away into the woods.

Citing her greater knowledge of the surrounding territory, Dani took the lead. As soon as the trail widened, she nudged the mare into a trot, then, several minutes later, a gentle canter. Trees, heavy with leaves, shaded their way. The thick bed of pine needles, which provided the footing, muffled almost all sound.

For the time being Rick was content to follow. This was the first time since his arrival that he'd had a chance to ride anywhere but the club grounds. Now, though he was sure he could find his way, he was willing to defer to Dani's familiarity with the best trails. He just sat back and enjoyed the ride.

Half an hour passed before Dani slowed Melody to a walk. "This way," she said, indicating a narrow overgrown path that veered off to the right.

Rick looked at the trail dubiously. "It looks like nobody's been down there in months."

Dani smiled. "Exactly." She reined Melody through the opening, rising in her stirrups as the mare hopped over several branches that littered the path. "By the way," she called back over her shoulder as she sent Melody into a canter once more, "you do know how to jump, don't you?"

"Fine time to ask," Rick grumbled to himself as the first fence, a solid-looking stone wall, loomed suddenly in front of them.

He watched in admiration as Dani gathered the chestnut and set her fearlessly at the obstacle. As one, horse and rider leaped into the air, clearing the wall with inches to spare. Rick gave Trumpet his head, and a moment later they had landed on the other side as well.

"Well done," Dani called back to him. Then she put her heels to Melody's flanks and was off once more.

If Rick had expected a quiet afternoon's jaunt, he soon found out how wrong he was. With Dani leading the way, it took every bit of skill he possessed simply to keep up. They leaped fallen trees, forded several small streams, and once, skidded to a halt in order to avoid angering a family of skunks that were crossing the path.

"Are we almost there?" Rick asked when the last of the small white-striped babies had waddled away into the underbrush.

"Uh-huh. It's just ahead, and worth every minute of the trip."

She was right about that, Rick decided a moment later. The spot Dani had led him to was a secluded clearing, bounded on one side by a clear, rushing stream. A profusion of wildflowers had grown up along its banks, and a weeping willow swayed gracefully in the slight breeze.

"It's beautiful," said Rick. He slipped out of his saddle, then ran up his stirrups and loosened the girth. "How did you ever find it?"

"I came here for the first time when I was very little," Dani replied. She knotted her reins on Melody's neck, then unfastened the curb chain so the mare could eat. "Six years old to be exact. I knew right away that it was a special place. I've been coming back ever since whenever I wanted to think, or find some peace."

"Six years old?" Rick looked at her oddly. "What were you doing all the way out here at that age?"

"To tell the truth, we're not that far from civilization. The trails that lead here from Silverbrook are fairly roundabout, but we've been on Greenfields land for the past ten minutes or so. If you felt like crashing through the underbrush that way—" Dani gestured off to the left "—it wouldn't be too terribly long before you found yourself staring down a tennis court."

"I see." Rick nodded slowly to himself. "Then you've brought me home."

"In a manner of speaking." Dani turned away and busied herself with unpacking the backpack she'd worn strapped across her shoulders.

Rick gazed around the quiet glade. "Dani?" He waited until she looked up. "How many other people have you brought here?"

It was a moment before Dani answered. "None," she said finally. "You're the first."

"I'm honored."

Dani threw down the half-empty pack and leaped to her feet. "Don't go reading all sorts of messages into this, Malone! I just felt like coming here today, okay?"

"Okay." Rick smiled. He liked the fact that he'd touched a nerve. He liked the fact that he could. "So," he said, looking down at the feast and rubbing his hands, "when do we eat?"

The bounty in the backpack consisted of ripe Camembert, a small tin of water biscuits, grapes, peaches, strawberries and a bottle of still-cool Chablis. Tucked away, deep in the bottom, Rick found two white linen napkins, followed by a pair of plastic cups.

"Two?" His brow lifted as he handed one over to Dani and kept one for himself.

Dani shrugged. "You know Preston. Hope springs eternal, and all that."

"Or maybe he knows you better than you think."

"Could be," Dani agreed. She spread a thick slab of Camembert on a biscuit and popped it into her mouth. "He knew me well enough to realize that I needed this today."

Rick followed her lead with a wedge of cheese. "Why today, especially?"

Dani shrugged. She started to put him off, then stopped and changed her mind. "Mostly it's this whole business with the team, I guess. I thought that this year I'd finally have it made, and now—"

"Now I've ruined all your plans."

"You might say that." Dani had never been one to pull her punches; she wasn't about to start now. "We're three weeks into the season already, halfway to the start of the Challenge Cup, and I still don't know whether I've made the team or not. The uncertainty is killing me. It's hard to play your best when you know that your every move is being scrutinized."

"The same holds true for Trip and Harley," Rick pointed out. He pulled the cork out of the bottle and poured wine into the two plastic cups. "They're under the same pressures you are."

"Harley, maybe," Dani agreed. "But not Trip."

Rick glanced up curiously. "Why not?"

"Trip has a lot more experience than Harley and I do. Last year we were both one-goal players, battling it out in the ranks, while Trip's been a solid member of the team for the past three years. I can't imagine that the board would pick either one of us over him now."

"So it really is a head-to-head competition between you and Harley. No wonder he has it in for you."

Dani leaned back against a large rock, enjoying its sun-warmed support. "I think the worst thing is that he doesn't fight fair. It would be one thing if all I had to do was beat him on the field, but I don't. Harley knows just about everyone at the club, and he talks to anyone who will listen. Apparently he's been telling people that the only reason I got a two-goal rating at all is because I have enough money to buy the best ponies."

Rick's forehead lowered in a frown. "He's wrong, of course. And anyone who watches you play will be able to see it."

"Anyone who knows what to watch *for*," Dani corrected him. Even though she didn't need Malone's endorsement, it felt good to have him leap to her defense. "But there are plenty of people who just assume that Harley knows what he's talking about.''

Dani finished off her Chablis and poured herself another cup. The sunny day, good wine and wonderful company had combined to put her in a very mellow mood. Now she felt more relaxed than she had in a long time.

''That's the thing about having money,'' she continued with a sigh. ''Especially money you've done nothing to earn. People get very jealous, even angry—as though they think the whole thing's your fault.''

''Really?'' Rick asked, frowning.

''Of course.'' Dani's tone was matter-of-fact. Money, and the problems it inspired, had been a fact of her life for too long for her to get upset about it now. Leaning over, she plucked a wildflower and tucked it behind her ear. It's blue shade, Rick noticed, matched the vivid color of her eyes.

''Then there's the other side,'' she said. ''The people I don't even know who call themselves my friends. It's like the money has an aura to it. If they get close enough, maybe some of it will rub off on them. But how many people do you think there are whom I could depend on if I was really in trouble?'' She stopped, then frowned.

''How many, Dani?'' Rick prompted. He found that he was really curious.

Dani considered her answer for a long time. Once, she glanced surreptitiously at Rick as though thinking something through. ''Two,'' she said finally, nodding with satisfaction at her choice. ''Preston, and Sabrina.''

Rick swallowed a sigh. He supposed it was too soon to ask her to believe in him, but that didn't mean he couldn't try.

''Three,'' he corrected quietly.

Dani looked up, her eyes wide. ''You?''

Rick caught his breath at the brief flare of emotion that passed over her face. Then it was gone, so quickly he wondered if he might have imagined it.

"Yes, princess," he said. "Me."

Dani saw by Rick's expression that she'd been caught. Inwardly cursing the brief moment of weakness, she moved immediately to rebuild the walls. "You're getting serious on me again, Malone," she said, her voice hard and flippant. "I don't like it."

Beside her, Rick knew exactly what she was doing. It was less than he wanted, but no more than he'd expected. He'd thought he might have accomplished something today, here in Dani's special place. A flowering of trust perhaps, or maybe just the beginning of hope.

Instead it was becoming increasingly obvious that their relationship was destined to take two steps back for every one forward. Though he understood the source of Dani's reticence, that didn't make it any easier to take. Now, if she wanted to spar with him, Rick found he was only too willing to accommodate her.

"Why don't you like it, Dani?"

The biscuit that Dani was holding snapped in her hand. The sound was dry and brittle. He was coming too close, closer than she wanted him to be, closer than she could allow. She knew she was the one who had opened the door. It had been a mistake. Because now she was cornered in a trap of her own making. She needed space, and she would have it. Now.

"I don't like to be pushed, Malone." Her voice rose, wavering on the edge of fear. "The next thing I know, you'll be hearing wedding bells."

Rick shook his head. "You're the one who's obsessed with that idea, not me. I wonder why."

"I told you before," Dani snapped. "Every man I've ever gone out with has eventually gotten around to proposing. Even some I didn't even know have done it. Why should you be any different?"

Every emotion within him railed at the injustice of the accusation. He didn't know which was worse—the fact that she had lumped him together with a collection of men whose company he certainly didn't want to keep, or the nagging suspicion that perhaps he wasn't so very different from those men after all. Obviously, for one reason or another, they'd all found Dani to be a fascinating woman. Could he honestly say that the same wasn't true for him?

"Well?" Dani demanded.

"Do you really believe that?" Rick looked at her hard, his eyes demanding that she return his gaze. "Do you actually think that I'm some sort of fortune hunter who's only after your money?"

With a sharp pang, Dani remembered the doubts she had harbored when they'd first met, doubts that had long since been replaced by a growing respect and affection for Rick Malone as a man. "I don't know what to think," she blurted out. "I wish I did."

She didn't want to believe the worst of him, yet how else could she explain what was happening between them? She wasn't beautiful, she'd always known that. Nor was she witty or charming; she'd never tried to be either. As for sexy, well...

Dani drew herself up haughtily. She refused to defend herself. The only other option was to attack. "How else do you explain what's happening between us?"

Rick swore vehemently under his breath. "Has it ever occurred to you that sometimes things simply fit together so well that they don't need any explaining?"

"Things like your debits and my credits, perhaps?"

"That," Rick snapped, "is beneath answering."

"Can you honestly say that my money means nothing to you?"

"No," Rick said slowly. "I can't."

Dani's eyes widened. It wasn't at all the response she'd expected, nor the one she'd wanted. If he'd lied, it would have made things easier. She'd have felt nothing but contempt then; certainly not this grudging glimmer of respect that only made it that much harder to maintain the finely honed edge to her anger.

"Your money is a part of you," said Rick. "For better or for worse, its presence in your life has shaped the person you've become. When I look at you, I don't separate the pieces—I see only the whole."

If Rick hadn't been so angry, he'd have stopped right there. But she'd already pushed him beyond the bounds of good sense, and now he was tired of trying to behave like a gentleman when every primitive instinct within him cried for release. Still, he was almost surprised when he heard himself say the words. "I'm falling in love with you, Dani. I think you should know that."

For a brief moment, etched in time, Dani went perfectly still. Her eyes clouded over with an emotion…shock, pain? Then the moment passed, and the look was gone.

"Oh, hell," she said.

Rick glared at her. "At the moment, I'd have to say that those are my sentiments exactly."

"It's nice to know we agree on something."

"Isn't it?" Rick said wearily.

He stood up and began shoving the supplies back in the pack. Half an hour earlier the small glade had seemed like a peaceful haven; now he couldn't wait to get away. He'd finally done it. He'd laid his cards on the table, and she'd wasted no time in throwing them back in his face.

Well, what else had he expected? Rick asked himself savagely. He'd known it wasn't what she wanted. She'd certainly told him that often enough. But what about what *he* wanted? Didn't that count for anything?

Say ~~yes~~ to
romance

AND YOU'LL GET

---

4 FREE BOOKS
1 FREE WATCH
1 FREE PEN
1 FREE SURPRISE

NO RISK • NO OBLIGATION
NO STRINGS • NO KIDDING

Say yes to free gifts worth over $20.00

Say YES to a rendezvous with romance, and you'll get 4 classic love stories—FREE! You'll get an LCD digital quartz watch—FREE! You'll get a stylish ballpoint pen—FREE! And you'll get a delightful surprise—FREE! These gifts carry a total value of over $20.00—but you can have them without spending even a penny!

MONEY-SAVING HOME DELIVERY!

Say YES to Harlequin's Home Reader Service and you'll enjoy the convenience of previewing 4 brand new books every month, delivered right to your home before they appear in stores. Each book is yours for only $2.49—26¢ less than the retail price, and there is no extra charge for postage and handling.

SPECIAL EXTRAS—FREE!

You'll get our newsletter, *heart to heart*, packed with news of your favorite authors and upcoming books—FREE! You'll also get additional free gifts from time to time as a token of our appreciation for being a home subscriber.

Say yes to a Harlequin love affair. Complete, detach and mail your Free Offer Card today!

RUSH! FREE GIFTS DEPT.

BUSINESS REPLY CARD

First Class   Permit No. 717   Buffalo, NY

Postage will be paid by addressee

Harlequin Reader Service ®
901 Fuhrmann Blvd.,
P.O. Box 1394
Buffalo, NY 14240-9963

NO POSTAGE
NECESSARY
IF MAILED
IN THE
UNITED STATES

She came up behind him so quietly that the first indication he had of her presence was when she laid a hand on his shoulder. He turned and found himself looking down into her wide blue eyes—eyes that had the power to mesmerize him and cause him immeasurable pain. His hand groped for the cheese and came up empty. He couldn't tear his gaze away.

"I'm sorry," she said quietly.

"For what?" There was no humor in his harsh laugh. "You were only being honest."

"You're right," Dani agreed. "I was. I don't love you, Malone. I don't love anyone. To tell the truth, I don't even think I know how. For years I've felt as though that side of me was simply closed off. But that doesn't mean there aren't times when I wish it wasn't so."

"If you wanted to change," Rick insisted stubbornly, "you could."

Dani glared up at him, a sudden burst of fury rocketing through her. "Things aren't that simple!"

"They never are, are they, Dani?"

"Damn it, Malone!" she yelled, pounding her fists against the hard expanse of his chest. "You're the one who's complicating things. Why does everything have to be so difficult? We're attracted to each other. We enjoy each other's company. Why can't that be enough?"

For a moment Rick simply withstood the barrage, making no attempt to deflect the blows. The physical pain felt right. It took his mind off the ache deep inside that throbbed as though his guts were being torn in two. Only when he sensed her anger abating did he reach up to grab Dani's fists, trapping her hands in his.

"I don't have a choice, princess," he said quietly. "Maybe I never did."

Her anger spent, Dani sagged against him. His body was warm, and she leaned into the heat, fighting a chill that came from within. Things could have been so good for them. What right did he have to ruin everything by asking for more than she could give?

"We each make our own choices, Malone."

"Yes," Rick agreed. Hadn't he told her that earlier? It was so hard to think, to concentrate. With Dani in his arms he cared for nothing save the sweet scent of her golden hair, the glorious feeling of her lean body molding itself against his. It was sheer madness, and he never wanted it to stop.

"You feel something for me, Dani," he said. "You can't tell me it isn't true."

Dani drew a ragged breath. Honesty warred with the desire within. She reveled in his nearness, felt her body awakening as it shimmered with heat. She knew he deserved an answer—and had no idea what that answer should be.

Drawing back her head, she looked up into Rick's dark eyes. "I..."

All at once he knew he didn't want to hear what she was going to say. He stopped her the only way he knew how.

Rick brought his mouth down to cover hers. The contact was harder than he'd expected, then he realized that she'd risen to meet him. Her lips were smooth and soft. They parted with a small moan, and he felt the warm rush of her breath. She tasted wild and sweet. Rick sampled, and knew he needed more.

Dani's fists uncurled. In seconds, her arms were around him, and his around her. Her head whirled, then spun. She felt giddy, so light-headed that it was a wonder she could stand. Yet there was an edge of desperation to her need. If she let herself go, would she ever find a way to put the pieces back together again?

Then the wondering passed as Dani lost herself in Rick's embrace. Heat surged and swelled within her. His hands were moving, his touch a kiss of fire. She wanted to feel them everywhere. One palm spanned her breast. Her heart pounded like thunder beneath it.

Rick's lips left hers. They grazed the soft skin of her cheek, then her throat. She tilted back her head, and the hand that pressed against her back tangled itself in the shimmering waves of her hair.

She'd never known, Dani thought dimly. She'd never known it was possible to lose herself, and find herself, all at the same time. No one had ever wanted her like this before. Or perhaps it was she who had never wanted so much. Nothing had prepared her to deal with these feelings—this wildness that came from within, that built and throbbed with an ever increasing intensity until she began to wonder how she could ever bear the strain.

Then all at once it was over. The air felt cool against her fevered body as Rick pulled away. His hands slid from her shoulders, then down the length of her arms. As though he couldn't bear to break contact entirely, his fingers caught her hands and held on, hard.

"Tell me," said Rick. His voice was low, rasping, as he gathered his breath, and his wits. "Tell me you don't feel anything for me, and I'll never bother you again."

Bother her? Dani's eyes opened wide. Was that what he thought he'd been doing? Abruptly she remembered the aftermath of their last kiss and was swamped with uncertainty. With it came pride. She looked up and thrust out her chin.

"Maybe I like being bothered, Malone."

It wasn't the answer he wanted, but it was about as close to an admission as he'd come yet. Rick considered his options and decided he'd come out ahead. His grin was wide, and outrageously sexy.

"Hold that thought," he drawled, repeating her own words back to her. "I suspect we may get back to it."

Chapter Eight

Dani spent the early part of the week working to formulate a mailing list of potential sponsors for the upcoming Pegasus horse show. Since most of the files were housed in one of the hunt club's back offices, she set up shop there, working in a small airless room that she shared with Shirley Devane, the club secretary. By Thursday afternoon she was hot, tired and thoroughly disgruntled.

"If I never see another typewriter again, it will be too soon," she grumbled as she hunched over an ancient manual machine and typed yet another name onto the long list.

"What'd you say?" On the other side of the room, Shirley looked up from the papers she was filing.

"I don't know how you do this day after day," Dani said, shaking her head. "It would drive me crazy to be cooped up in here with only a rickety old air conditioner, and a pre-Second World War typewriter!"

"It is warm in here," Shirley allowed. "Do you want me to send down to the Grill for some more iced tea?"

"Heaven forbid. I feel as though I've drunk a barrel of the stuff already."

"Maybe you'd like to try my typewriter?"

Shirley's machine, a vintage electric, was several steps up from the one Dani was using. Nevertheless she declined. "No, you need it more than I do. You've got plenty of work of your own." She looked at Shirley and grinned. "Amazing, isn't it, that a club as modern as Silverbrook claims to be hasn't heard about the computer age?"

"It's not that they haven't heard of it." Shirley chuckled. "Lord knows, I've mentioned it often enough myself. The problem is that the board doesn't have to do any typing."

Dani nodded, her eye scanning down the remainder of the list. At this rate, she'd be here forever! Preoccupied with what she was doing, she didn't notice Shirley, who was watching her speculatively.

"If you don't mind my saying so," the secretary said finally, "you're not exactly chained to that desk. Why don't you get somebody else to do that for you?"

Dani looked up. Sighing, she reached up and brushed back a lock of golden hair that had fallen down across her forehead. "Believe me, I'd love to. I got involved with Pegasus to teach, not do paperwork. But ever since Nan left there just hasn't been anybody else to take up the slack."

"Speaking of teaching..." Shirley glanced down at her watch. "It's almost three o'clock. Hadn't you better get out to the ring?"

"Damn!" Dani pushed back her chair and stood up. "Is it that late already?"

Shirley nodded, watching as Dani tried to quickly sort the jumbled papers into some semblance of order. "How far did you get?" she asked.

"Almost done, thank God. I'm in the *U*'s—Mr. and Mrs. Thornton Underwood. I can't imagine there'll be too many more names after that, can you?"

"Probably not," Shirley agreed. "Look, why don't you just leave that? My work load's pretty light today. I'm sure I could manage to finish up, if you'd like."

"Could you?" Dani shot the secretary a grateful glance. "I'd really appreciate it."

"No problem. You're not the only one who'd like to see those kids get a break. Hurry up now. They're probably out there waiting for you."

"Thanks," Dani said fervently. As she bolted for the door, she made a mental note to send Shirley a bouquet of flowers for her desk, something light and cheerful, to brighten up the small office.

As the secretary had predicted, the class was waiting by the time Dani got around the back of the barns to the ring. Other volunteers had gotten the children mounted and circling at a walk. Now as Dani climbed through the fence and took her position in the middle of the ring, several of them waved and called her name.

"Look, Dani, no hands!"

She turned, a smile ready. Missy had dropped her reins on Charm's neck and was holding her hands high in the air. The pinto pony stood by the rail, waiting patiently for her next command.

"You know better than to show off like that, Missy." Dani did her best to sound firm. "If you don't hold on to your reins, how is Charm going to know what to do?" She crossed the dusty track and helped the little girl pick up her reins and fit them correctly through her fingers.

"Charm always knows what I want him to do," Missy said proudly. "I talk to him, and he listens." As if to prove her point, the pony flicked a furry ear backward. "See?"

"Uh-huh." Dani smiled. "And if you promise not to tell anybody, I'll let you in on a little secret."

Solemnly Missy nodded.

"When I was your age, I had a pony I talked to, too, just like you talk to Charm."

"Really?"

"I sure did. And he listened to me, just like Charm listens to you. But you have to understand that ponies don't just listen with their ears. They listen through the reins, too.''

"They do?''

Dani nodded. ''That's the way it's easiest for them to understand. When you use your reins to talk to Charm, he'll always know just what you mean.''

"Okay.'' Missy lifted her hands until the reins tightened and she made contact with the pony's mouth.

At the sound of Dani's encouraging chirp, Charm ambled slowly away from the rail. Missy bobbled in the saddle, then righted, and Dani caught herself just in time from offering help where it wasn't needed.

"Okay, class,'' she called, clapping her hands loudly. "Let's go to work!''

Forty minutes later, when Rick stuck his head out of the barn to see if the ring was free, class was still in progress. He'd seen notices on the bulletin board about the Pegasus Program, and recognized immediately what was going on. What he hadn't realized was that Dani was one of the instructors.

Crossing his arms over his chest, Rick leaned against the doorjamb to watch. As a teacher, Dani was firm, but gentle. She controlled the class with aplomb—encouraging beginners, praising achievements and making even the most awkward child feel like a champion.

Slowly a smile spread across Rick's face. The compassion Dani tried so hard to hide from the world, she lavished upon the children in her class. She was freer, more spontaneous with them than he'd ever known her to be. He was seeing yet another facet, Rick mused. Another side to the woman he loved. One that was, perhaps, the most valuable of all.

When class ended, he walked to the gate to meet her. "You're very good with them,'' he said as she ushered the last of the children from the ring.

Dani looked up, surprised. "When did you get here?"

"At least twenty minutes ago. When I realized this was a Pegasus class, I couldn't resist staying to watch."

"I know what you mean," Dani agreed, gazing fondly after the children. "They're really something special, aren't they?"

"Yes, they are." Rick's eyes warmed with approval. "And so are you."

Dani swallowed uncomfortably. Since the weekend before when they'd gone out riding together, she'd been stepping around Rick very carefully. She was used to having men declare their love for her; that was nothing new. What she wasn't used to was having them mean it. And somewhere deep down inside she was afraid that Rick did, which left her feeling uneasy, and very unsure of how to act.

She was sure of one thing, however. She didn't want him to harbor any illusions about who she was. None at all.

"Don't put me up on a pedestal, Malone. I don't belong there."

"No, you sure don't," Rick agreed. His grin was infuriatingly smug. "In fact, offhand, I can think of few women who deserve it less—"

Dani grinned back at him, her mood lightening. "A simple insult will do. You don't have to get carried away."

"Haven't you noticed?" asked Rick. "I like getting carried away."

An uncomfortable silence followed that statement, then suddenly they were both laughing.

"I've noticed all right," Dani jibed, pleased that the laughter had washed away the last of the tension that had eddied between them during the past few days.

She looked down and tapped the face on her watch. "I've also noticed that you have a bad habit of skipping out of work early. Surely that can't be good for business. What about all those mouths you have to feed?"

Rick smiled wanly. "Nobody's gone hungry yet."

Dani peered at him closely. "It sounds," she said, "as though there should be a 'but' on the end of that sentence."

"Like I told you before..." Rick's shrug was elaborately casual "...getting started is never easy."

"Financial consulting, right?" Dani frowned thoughtfully. "You know, I could introduce you to some people—"

Rick reached out and placed a hand on her arm, stopping her in midsentence. He had no intention of becoming the latest in a long line of men who had valued Dani for financial reasons. "Thanks," he said, "but no thanks. I'm doing just fine on my own."

"Really, it's no problem—"

"Dani," Rick said warningly, "I didn't come here today to discuss business with you."

"Oh, no?" A teasing smile played around the corners of her mouth. "Why did you come?"

Because he hadn't been able to stay away, thought Rick. He knew perfectly well Dani had spent the past four days avoiding him—the princess throwing up her nose and playing lady of the manor. Today he meant to do something about it.

"You know the answer to that. Or at least you should. You've been treating me like I had the plague ever since last weekend. I'd like to know why."

Dani saw the trap as the door slammed shut behind her. He was pushing her again, damn him. "I don't have to answer to you, Malone," she said coolly, spinning away on her heel.

"You're right, you don't have to." Rick grasped her arm, stopping her where she stood. "But you will. I made you uncomfortable, didn't I?" he pressed. "I told you some things you didn't want to hear."

"So what else is new?" Dani snapped. "You seem to make a habit of that. I swear, Malone, you truly are the most infuriating man I've ever met!"

"Then why do you put up with me?"

Dani stared at him, nonplussed. "I . . . what?"

"You heard what I said." Rick crossed his arms over his chest and leaned back against the fence. "From what I understand, you've sent any number of men packing. But not me. Why?"

Dani snorted. "In case you haven't noticed, I've tried. You just never seem to take the hint."

"No." Rick shook his head slowly. "I don't think that's it. Despite what you say, princess, I think you like having me around. And why not? After all, I'm a hell of a guy."

"Modesty becomes you," Dani flung back, amused in spite of herself.

"I'm glad you like what you see," Rick said with a grin. "Because this brings me to my proposition."

Dani's brow rose slightly. Knowing Malone, this was bound to be good.

"As it happens, my work load is rather light right now. What do you say we both stop all this feinting and bluffing and try spending some time together?"

"Doing what?" Dani asked suspiciously.

Rick shrugged. "Working on becoming friends, for a start. Beyond that, whatever comes to mind. Think of it as free-form enjoyment. All you have to do is relax and take things as they come."

"And while I'm doing that, what will you be doing?"

Rick puffed out his chest. "Why, trying to acquaint you with all the hitherto unexplored sterling aspects of my character, of course."

"A man who believes in the impossible," Dani muttered, just loud enough that he'd be sure to hear. "I should have known there'd be a catch."

"There *is* a catch," said Rick, suddenly becoming solemn. "You've got to stop fighting me, princess, or this is never going to work."

"I only fight when you make me," Dani insisted stubbornly. "Stop pushing, Malone, and you'd be amazed what an agreeable person I can be."

Rick threw back his head and laughed. "You don't really expect me to believe that, do you?"

With effort, Dani managed a hurt look. "Of course."

"All right, then, it's a deal." Rick draped an arm over Dani's shoulder. "I won't push and you won't prickle."

"You make me sound like a porcupine," Dani grumbled.

"If the quill fits—"

Her clenched fist caught him squarely in the solar plexus. A gratifyingly loud "Oomph!" announced its effect.

Rick's gaze was stern as he waved a finger at her warningly. "You're breaking the rules already, you know."

Dani smiled complacently. "Didn't I tell you, Malone? I'm one of those people who believe rules are made to be broken."

FREE-FORM ENJOYMENT, Rick had called it, and to Dani's delight that's exactly what she got. Over the next two weeks she found herself spending every available extra minute in his care. The experiences he dreamed up for them to sample ranged from visiting a shoreline oyster festival to climbing a hill with a bucket of chicken on the Fourth of July to watch the fireworks explode over Long Island Sound.

"I can't believe you've lived in Connecticut all your life and you've never visited Mystic Seaport," he announced one morning before driving her up the coast to remedy the situation. Nor could he understand her lack of familiarity with Westport's public parks and beaches.

"It's just that it's never occurred to me to come down here before," Dani said, watching as he spread out a blanket to mark their territory on crowded Compo Beach. "When I want to go swimming, I hop in the pool."

"What?" Rick teased, gesturing around at the hordes of sunbathers who took up every available inch of space. "And miss out on atmosphere like this?"

Dani opened her mouth to reply, but no words came out. That morning, when Rick had picked her up, he'd been wearing little enough—a pair of corduroy shorts that doubled as a bathing suit, and a baggy Stanford T-shirt on top. Now, oblivious to her scrutiny, he reached up and pulled the shirt fluidly off over his head.

Dani's breath caught in her throat at the sight of his magnificent body, naked save for the trim-fitting shorts. The sun glistened on Rick's wide shoulders, lending a golden cast to his already tanned skin. Dark curls covered his well-toned chest, narrowing over his flat stomach into a line that disappeared inside the waistband of his shorts.

With effort, Dani pulled her eyes away. When she raised them once more to Rick's face, she saw that he had followed the line of her gaze. Too late for coyness, Dani opted for jumping in with both feet instead. "Maybe," she said in her best Mae West tone, "I never knew what I was missing."

Rick grinned. "Stick with me, little girl," he said, W. C. Fields chomping on an imaginary cigar. "I'll make sure you don't miss a thing."

"I'll just bet you will." Dani laughed as they sat down on the blanket to bask in the sun.

True to his word, Rick spent the afternoon making sure that Dani took full advantage of her day at the beach. When they tired of lying in the sun, they ran down to the ocean for a swim, then followed that with a lunch of hot dogs and candied apples from the snack bar. Several hours later, when the crowds began to thin out, Dani was astounded to see Rick pull out a volleyball net, pound the stakes into the soft sand, then recruit two teams by enlisting any likely looking people who passed by.

Dani had always been reserved with strangers, and now she was amazed by Rick's easy sense of familiarity with people he didn't know. His enthusiasm was contagious: within minutes nearly everyone around them had been drawn into the boisterous game. Following his lead, Dani began to relax. Soon she was throwing herself into the competition with gusto. By the time the sun began to set, and the beach to empty, she was truly sorry to see the day end.

Though their days were hectic, evenings were devoted to simple things: seeing friends, or going out to eat. And through it all, Rick behaved exactly as he'd promised he would. He neither pushed nor prodded her in any direction. Instead, he was simply content to create an environment in which their relationship could grow and flourish.

One evening, when Billy Matlock arrived unexpectedly from the city, Rick suggested that Dani call Sabrina, and the four of them go out. It wasn't until the brunette arrived at Rick's condominium in Westport that the two men revealed what they had in mind.

"Bowling?" Sabrina repeated in a shocked tone.

"That's what they said." Dani laughed, shaking her head. She knew Rick and Billy were enjoying their consternation thoroughly.

"You mean they actually want us to put on someone else's smelly old shoes?"

"That's about the size of it, pretty lady," Billy drawled. "That is, unless you've got some bowling shoes of your own you'd like to take along?"

"No." Brie swallowed heavily. "Rented shoes will be fine."

"They're not exactly a match made in heaven, are they?" Rick asked half an hour later at the bowling alley, where he and Dani were watching Billy and Sabrina argue over selection of the best balls.

"Don't worry about them," Dani said with a chuckle. "Brie's a good sport. She'll come around. And if Billy isn't careful, she'll bowl the pants right off him."

Rick laughed along with her. "Somehow I don't think Billy'd mind that a bit."

Dani waited, wondering if Rick would follow up her suggestive comment with one of his own, but instead he merely took her hand and led her over to the racks against the wall so that they could choose some balls of their own. He'd told her he wanted friendship, Dani remembered. Obviously he'd meant what he'd said.

Dani had called Brie a good sport, Rick mused as the evening progressed, but the same could certainly be said of her. He'd known a bowling alley wouldn't be one of her usual hangouts—indeed she'd admitted to never having set foot in one before. But that didn't stop her from joining in the fun with abandon. He watched with pride as Dani held up the ball, measured her approach, then fired off a strike. He'd ceased being surprised by her adaptability, now he simply enjoyed it.

On the other hand, Rick decided, what he wasn't enjoying was the frustration of having Dani all to himself, day after day, and knowing that he could look but not touch. If looks could burn, he thought, she'd be scorched by now.

Tonight, as always, Dani looked beautiful. She wore little makeup, and needed none. Her hair hung loose and free around her shoulders. Her outfit—a camisole top and flowing skirt—showed off her trim body to perfection. Rick's eyes roamed hungrily over her bare shoulders, then to the lacing that traveled enticingly downward between her breasts.

He groaned softly under his breath. He'd promised himself he was going to take things slowly. They both needed time—he to build up his business; Dani to learn to trust in both him and the feelings he had to offer. What he hadn't known was how impossible the waiting was going to prove to be.

They bowled three games, with Rick and Dani finally eking out a narrow margin of victory. Magnanimous in defeat, Billy and Sabrina offered to spring for the drinks. There was a small, dimly lit bar attached to the bowling alley and, after trading in their shoes, the foursome went inside and found a table.

"I hear that new software package you've been waitin' on has finally hit the market," Billy commented to Rick as they sat down. "I bet you snapped one right up."

"Not yet." Rick's smile was thin. He signaled for the waitress. "Shall we order?"

"But you told me yourself six months ago that MoneyPro was going to revolutionize—"

"Billy," Rick interrupted, shooting his friend a glare. "I don't think the ladies care to listen to us discuss business. I'm sure they'd much rather talk about something else."

Billy cleared his throat uncomfortably. "Of course, anything you say." He laid a hand on Sabrina's shoulder as he rose from the table. "Come on, pretty lady. What do you say you and I belly up to the bar and rustle us up some drinks?"

Dani waited until Billy and Sabrina were out of earshot before turning to Rick. "All right, Malone, out with it. Is something wrong with your company?"

"No," Rick said quickly. "Nothing beyond the usual start-up problems. In a couple of weeks everything will be ironed out. I'm sure of it."

Dani gazed at him evenly. "In other words, you don't care to discuss it."

"Trust me," said Rick. "This stuff is dull, through and through. I'm letting you off easy. Next time you might not be so lucky."

"Don't worry about me, Malone," Dani said, her voice dropping to a low, enticing drawl. "I'm willing to take my chances."

Once again she hoped Rick might pick up on her double entendre, but once again he merely smiled. By the time Billy and Sabrina reappeared with the drinks, Dani had sighed, settled back in her seat and resigned herself to discussing polo ponies.

And as the following week progressed, nothing changed. Although Dani gave Rick what she considered to be any number of openings, Rick was still determinedly treating her just like a good pal. If she didn't count the times that he'd reached out and taken her hand, interlacing his fingers with hers, she thought crossly, he'd barely touched her at all. Indeed, he was so adept at maintaining the carefully polite distance between them that by the end of the week Dani was sure she was going quietly crazy.

When Rick proposed that they go to the movies, she acquiesced readily, hoping that the feature would be something hopelessly and utterly romantic to help her set the mood. Instead, she discovered by reading the marquee that the movie Rick had chosen was a children's classic.

"Old Yeller?" she said incredulously, turning to him as he parked the Jeep.

"Sometimes you have to take what you can get. Westport's a small town."

"Not that small."

Rick shrugged disarmingly. "All right, so maybe I have a weakness for sad movies about big sloppy dogs."

Inside the movie house, Rick bought two sodas and a huge tub of popcorn, which Dani eyed skeptically. So much for thoughts of snuggling inside the darkened theater. From the looks of the bucket, it was going to take Malone every minute of the movie just to dispose of the food.

As it turned out, Dani's prediction wasn't far off, but by then she was beyond noticing. Like Rick, her eyes were glued to the screen, as she too became enmeshed in the tragic story. By the time Old Yeller's owner was forced to get a gun and shoot the dog who had saved his life, Dani had forgotten all about Rick's reticence.

Leaning over, she grasped his arm, then leaned her head on his shoulder. She felt him stiffen, then shudder at the sound of the gun's loud report. A moment later she heard a quiet sniffle. Surprised, she raised her head.

"Rick?" she whispered. "Are you all right?"

"Fine." He dabbed at eyes that were suspiciously moist. "I hate this movie."

Dani chewed at her lower lip in consternation, her own involvement forgotten. "But that's exactly what it is—a movie."

"So?"

"So there's no reason to let it get to you."

Rick turned in his seat to look at her. "Maybe I like letting things get to me, Dani. Look around you," he said, waving his hand. "Look at everybody here. They've *all* let this movie get to them. Everybody except you."

"That's not fair!" Dani bristled. "Just because I'm not crying doesn't mean I don't have feelings."

"Oh, you have feelings all right," said Rick. "It's just that you've buried them under so many layers of self-defense that I doubt if even you know how to reach them anymore."

Dani glared at him angrily. "You're pushing again, Malone."

To her surprise, Rick immediately backed down. "You're right," he agreed. "I'm sorry. I told you I wouldn't do that."

Princess, hell, he thought irritably, revising his opinion once more. Where had he ever gotten that idea from anyway? The woman was one part artful dodger, one part tigress and eight parts stubborn as a mule!

LATER THAT EVENING when Rick's Jeep pulled up in front of her door, Dani was out of the vehicle before he'd even had a chance to turn off the engine.

Why should she wait to be walked to her door? she thought irritably. Nothing was going to come of it. For the past two weeks, ever since that incredible kiss in the woods, nothing ever had. Malone had her on tenterhooks. Yet for all the interest he'd displayed, he might as well be her brother. A giant bucket of popcorn indeed!

"Don't bother getting out," Dani said, smiling sweetly. "I know where I live."

Rick hopped out of the Jeep anyway. "A gentleman always sees a lady to her door."

Dani muttered something pungent under her breath as he took her arm. "Who told you I was a lady, anyway?"

"I live in hope," Rick replied calmly. He congratulated himself on his control. Despite her outward show of cool, she was obviously beginning to do a slow burn just below the surface.

Rick climbed the three steps and deposited Dani at the door. When she merely stood, looking at him in disgruntled silence, he added, "First lesson in how to be a lady. This is the point where you smile politely and say, 'Thank you for the lovely evening.'"

Dani stuck out a forefinger and jabbed his chest. "First lesson in being a man. This is the point where you, having speculated for hours on the evening's outcome, try to talk your way in the door."

"What?" Rick asked innocently. "And disturb Preston?"

"No," Dani gritted through clenched teeth. "And disturb me!"

"Oh." Rick considered for a moment, then shook his head. Not quite yet, but they were close.

"Sorry, princess," he said, leaning down to brush a quick kiss across her lips. "But I did promise not to push. I believe I'll wait for an invitation."

Dani's glare burned a hole in his back as Rick turned and left. Damn the man anyway! It wasn't fair of him to use her own words against her like that. "And stop calling me princess!" she called out, shaking her fist in the direction of the Jeep's receding taillights. The vehicle never even wavered.

Scowling, Dani closed the front door behind her, then calmly and deliberately picked up a small Stuben prism from the sideboard. The crash it made when it connected with the wall was satisfyingly loud.

"Danielle, is that you?" Preston hurried into the front hall from the direction of the kitchen. He was wearing burgundy silk pajamas, a navy velour robe and a pair of comfortable leather slippers. In his hand he held a plate piled high with apple pie and vanilla ice cream.

"Yes, it's me," Dani said wearily, her anger spent.

Preston eyed the shattered shards of glass. "Is everything all right?"

"Just fine, Pres," Dani said with a frown. "Can't you tell?"

Preston drew himself up to his full height, managing, even in his robe and slippers, to attain more dignity than most men could in a three-piece suit. "Danielle," he said formally, "you know I do not answer to that form of address."

"So what?" Dani shrugged. "I don't answer to princess, or Tonto either for that matter, but it doesn't seem to make any difference."

Preston raised one eyebrow stiffly. "I assure you, Danielle, never once in our long association has it ever occurred to me to call you Tonto."

Dani had been gazing down at the shattered glass. Now she looked up, feeling faintly exasperated. "Not you, Preston, Malone. He's always calling me names—like princess, or his faithful companion, Tonto."

"Really?" Preston's lips twitched as he turned away and began picking up the larger pieces of glass. "How interesting."

Immediately Dani was down on her knees to help. "Preston, watch out, you're going to cut yourself!"

"If you don't want me to have to pick up shards of glass off the floor," Preston replied, "then you shouldn't go smashing breakable objects against the wall."

"I wouldn't have if I'd known you were still up. I'd planned on throwing my little tantrum, then removing the evidence all by myself. And speaking of which," Dani added, seizing gratefully on a way to change the subject, "why *are* you still up? I know perfectly well this is past your bedtime."

Preston dumped the glass in a wastebasket, then headed into the kitchen for a dustpan. "As you can see, I am indulging in a small midnight snack."

Dani eyed the pie à la mode balefully. "That's plenty for three midnight snacks, not to mention enough indigestion to keep you up all night. What gives? And don't try putting me off, because I know you better than that. You wouldn't be up and eating in the middle of the night unless something was wrong.''

Silently Preston reached into the pocket of his robe. He withdrew a much-creased sheet of lavender-scented paper. "Victoria's reply," he said, then knelt down and busied himself with sweeping up the rest of the glass.

Quickly Dani skimmed through the letter once, then read it through a second time. She couldn't seem to make any sense out of it at all. Though Victoria claimed to appreciate Preston's "offer" and had promised to give it some thought, she had stated unequivocally that she was unsure of the advisability of relocating without a firm situation in mind.

Frowning, Dani looked up. Preston was there, waiting. "I don't understand," she said. "What does this part about wanting a firm situation mean?"

The butler cleared his throat uncomfortably. "She means a job, miss. Victoria would like to know that there is a family here awaiting her services before she comes."

"A family?" Dani sputtered. "But, Preston, I thought you and she . . . well, I understood that you meant to—"

"Propose?" Preston supplied unhappily. "I did. However, things don't seem to have turned out that way."

"They certainly don't," Dani muttered, staring down at the delicate sheet of paper.

"You see, I thought at the time that a bit of subtlety was indicated. After all, any student of romance knows that these things are meant to be done in person, not through the post. I figured it was far better not to spring everything on her at once. After Victoria had arrived, I thought there would be plenty of time for things to sort themselves out."

"But if you didn't ask her to marry you, what reason did you give for asking her to come?"

Preston's cheeks flushed a delicate shade of pink. "I told her that I'd won a bit at the races and had some extra money. I mentioned how nice it was when we were working in the same neighborhood all those years ago and offered to pay her way if she wanted to come to the States again. I thought perhaps that might be sufficient inducement, but as you can see..." Preston's voice trailed away lamely.

"As I can see, Victoria doesn't know a good thing when she hears one," Dani declared stoutly.

"Oh, no," Preston said, leaping to Victoria's defense. "This really isn't her fault at all. Victoria is, after all, a very well-brought-up woman. It seems that she thought that it would simply not do for her to have to depend on a man until she got her bearings."

"There's only one solution," said Dani.

Preston looked up hopefully.

"You've got to write to her again."

"But—"

"No buts, Preston," Dani said firmly. "You've got to tell her how you feel."

"If you insist..."

"I do. Trust me. This is no time to be shy."

Only when she was satisfied that Preston truly intended to write to Victoria did Dani head upstairs to bed. Talk about muddled relationships! she thought. Between the two of them, they hadn't even managed to get to first base. Frowning, Dani thought of her mother's five marriages and shook her head. It was probably something in the water.

Chapter Nine

Sunday's polo match was an away game, scheduled for four o'clock at the Ox Ridge Hunt Club in nearby Darien. To Dani's delight, Harley Greer was away on vacation, which meant that she and Trip were automatically starting players.

It was one more chance to show off her talent, Dani reflected, a chance she sorely needed. More than a month had passed since the beginning of the season—five long weeks of scrimmages and games, and still the board had given no indication which four players would represent Silverbrook in the Challenge Cup at the end of July. The suspense was driving her crazy.

She was riding well, and she knew it. Her ponies were better trained than Harley's, and better conditioned, too. Dani had been careful to leave no stone unturned when it came to trying to sway the board's decision in her favor. She hadn't because she couldn't afford to.

Harley, for all his faults, was still a skilled polo player. He was also a man. And though no one would dare admit such a thing, Dani knew she was still battling the age-old problem of prejudice. The board was made up of men—eight of them, and none under the age of fifty. In their minds, anything a woman could do a man could do better. It was up to her to prove them wrong.

The Ox Ridge team was a hard-riding one, their players strong and capable. Bearing that in mind, Dani had chosen her mounts with care. First Melody, because the mare was her best, then Trumpet, who was her fastest. After that, Ringo, a scrappy black gelding who didn't mind the hard knocks and always gave back as good as he got. And finally, Charm, because when the chips were down, there was simply no substitute for experience.

Dani maneuvered the Porsche through the stone gateposts of the Ox Ridge Hunt Club, then parked the car beside one of the long, low red barns. The Silverbrook vans had already arrived; the ponies were unloaded and waiting. The first person Dani saw when she headed toward them was Rick.

"What do you think?" he asked, falling into step beside her. "I hear this team is pretty tough. Are you ready for a hard match?"

Dani glanced up, a retort ready. Then suddenly, unaccountably, the words caught in her throat. Malone was dressed no differently than she'd seen him a dozen times before, yet now, for some reason, she couldn't help but stare. Hungrily her eyes toured the sinewed expanse of his chest, so neatly delineated by the trim lines of the clinging yellow jersey. His stomach was flat and hard, his waist and hips trim. Beneath the tight fabric of his twill breeches, she could see the bunched muscles of his thighs contract with each step he took.

Desire, strong and sweet, ripped through her so unexpectedly that for a moment she almost lost her balance. She stumbled slightly on the uneven turf, and Rick reached out a hand to steady her. Dani gazed up into his dark eyes, wondering if he could read her thoughts, hoping that perhaps he might.

"I'm ready, Malone," she said, her voice low and husky. "As ready as I'll ever be."

Rick frowned slightly. "Good," he said, then looked at her again. Was it his imagination—?

"Rick, we've got a problem!"

Pulling his gaze reluctantly away, Rick turned in the direction of the voice. Jim Lynch was bearing down upon them, his face marred by an irritable scowl.

"What is it?" Rick went to meet him halfway. Curious, Dani trailed along behind.

"Somehow between the time the van left Silverbrook and arrived here, your bay managed to throw a shoe. The trip over was pretty bumpy. The driver said he was kicking back there something fierce."

Rick nodded. He'd heard the sound of Trigger's hooves ringing out against the side of the van often enough when he was driving himself. The problem couldn't be helped. What they had to do now was find a solution. He gazed across the field toward the club barns. "Is there a blacksmith available?"

"There's one on call. They're trying to reach him now. But on a Sunday..." Jim's shrug was an eloquent symbol of the futility of such a gesture.

"I won't ride him barefoot," Rick stated emphatically. After last night's rain, the lush green grass was damp and slick. He nodded, his decision made. "Silver and Scout will just have to take up the slack."

"Don't be silly," said Dani, speaking up for the first time. "I can lend you something. I only meant to ride Charm for one chukker, but I'm sure he can manage two. That leaves me with an extra horse. You remember Trumpet, don't you?"

"Of course," Rick said gratefully. He knew how much Dani's polo ponies meant to her. Her volunteering to let him ride one of her mounts in the game was a sign of trust, pure and simple. "I'd love to take him, if you're sure you don't mind?"

"Not at all," said Dani, ignoring the odd look Jim Lynch sent her way. So she wasn't in the habit of lending out her string, what of it? She and Rick might have their differences, but she knew that Trumpet would be safe in his care.

The game got underway ten minutes later, with Rick riding the number three position to Dani's number two. As he'd expected, the Ox Ridge team had obviously come prepared to put up a good fight. From the moment the referee tossed in the ball, the action was hard and fast. Three chukkers passed, then four, with the lead changing sides regularly.

By the end of the fifth chukker, Dani was tired. Wind whipped against her overheated cheeks as she galloped downfield. After almost an hour of strenuous play, her muscles cried out, straining from the exertion. Deliberately Dani ignored them. She'd play on guts alone if she had to. When a clean, hard shot from Trip Malloy sent the ball flying toward the opposing goal, she sent Charm after it, determined to get the hit.

On either side two other players raced with her, their intentions the same. Her peripheral vision revealed only green jerseys. That meant Ox Ridge players—the enemy. Dani knew Charm was neither as strong as he'd been in his youth nor as fast. She wasn't surprised when the men started to pull away. She was surprised, however, when abruptly, the space between them narrowed. They meant to box her out, she suddenly realized.

At another time she might have taken the cautious route and given up the shot for lost. But now, with the Challenge Cup only weeks away, she was acutely conscious of the selection committee's eyes upon her. They wouldn't tolerate any excuses, and she had no intention of giving them any.

She felt Charm check his stride, hesitating as the gap closed further. Obviously he was tired, too. At his age the second chukker had been a lot to ask. But now Dani knew she was going to demand even more.

The gelding's ears pricked warily. He saw the danger, just as she did. Experience told him to yield. Dani's legs in his sides told him to press on. He reached down into the depths of his great heart and summoned one last burst of speed.

Had he been younger, or perhaps fresher, they would have made it. As it was they still came close. Dani was leaning low over Charm's neck, her attention focused totally on the ball, when some sixth sense warned her of the impending crash. Eyes wide, she looked up, only to see that it was too late.

In the last few seconds, Dani knew the impact was inevitable. She tensed for it subconsciously but still was not prepared for the shocking force with which the animals collided. Buffeted from both sides, Charm stumbled, then tried valiantly to recover. Dani's heart leaped into her throat as she realized he wouldn't make it.

Then the world flew out from under her as she catapulted out of the saddle. Twisting, Dani managed to absorb most of the shock through her shoulder as she hit the hard turf with a bruising force that knocked the air from her lungs. Her movements purely instinctive, she gathered herself into a ball and rolled out of the way only seconds before the pinto crashed to the ground beside her. With a rush of wind, hoofbeats thundered past her ear. Then all was still.

Dani knew much better than to get up without checking for injuries first. But now, when she saw with horror the way Charm was thrashing helplessly on the emerald turf, her own welfare was forgotten. She scrambled up and lunged for his head, grabbing the bridle as the old pony tried, once more, to heave himself to his feet. His efforts were unsuccessful, and Charm collapsed back down on the ground, breathing heavily through distended nostrils.

"Shhh," Dani crooned, holding him down. "Don't try to stand. You're hurt." Her fingers caressed the pony's soft neck, tangled in his furry ears. "Don't worry," she murmured, soothing him with voice and touch. "Everything's going to be all right . . . all right . . ."

She was repeating the words, over and over, like a mantra when the first of the other players reached her. "Dani!" Rick's voice was harsh. He slipped out of the saddle before Silver had even slid to a halt. "Are you all right?"

Rick's breath caught in his throat as she turned her stricken face up to his. Her eyes were huge, her skin pale. He could hear the ragged sound of her breathing even before he dropped to his knees beside her. One look at the pony's twisted foreleg confirmed what she must have already known.

Then the players parted, turning their ponies away as the officials were upon them. Hurriedly the vet knelt to make his examination, his sure, steady fingers feeling up and down the length of Charm's leg.

"It's the cannon bone," he confirmed quietly.

"No!" The anguished cry broke from Dani's throat like a keening wail. She cradled the pony's head in her lap, the sound of his labored breathing mingling with her own.

She had to ask, even though she already knew the answer. "Is there anything that can be done?"

The vet shook his head. He opened his bag and began to prepare the injection.

"Dani, come on," said Rick. He grasped her shoulder and tried to pull her away. "You don't want to watch."

"Get away from me," Dani snarled, shrugging him off. Her fingers still stroked, still soothed, trying to bring one last measure of comfort to the pony in her arms. "I won't leave him alone."

The vet held the hypodermic needle up to the sun. One clear drop of liquid glistened briefly on its tip. "I'm ready, miss."

Silently Dani nodded. She felt a sob gather in her throat and fought it back. "Goodbye old friend," she whispered softly. "Goodbye..."

She held the pony until his head lay still and heavy across her lap. Dani felt her heart constrict as the light in Charm's eyes dimmed, then vanished. Gently she pushed the lid shut. It was done. This time, when Rick tried to pull her away, she didn't resist. Standing up, she walked away without looking back.

"I'm sorry, Dani," Rick said quietly. He felt helpless and inadequate. The power of her pain touched him deeply, and his frustration was only compounded by the knowledge that nothing he could say or do would be enough.

"Leave me alone, Malone," Dani snapped. She couldn't deal with him right now. Her emotions were too raw, too near the surface. He wanted to comfort her, and she couldn't bear it. One break, one crack in the facade, and she knew she'd shatter into a thousand pieces right there in the middle of the field.

"Dani, I want to help."

Dani glanced around sharply. Her eyes were wild with grief and pain. "You want to help me, Malone? You really want to help? Then get on your damn pony and play. This game isn't over yet!"

Rick's hands curled into fists at his sides as he watched her stride across the field and snatch Melody's reins from the groom. Without waiting for a leg-up, she vaulted into the saddle, then gunned the mare to the far end of the field. There they trotted endless circles until the field was clear and the match ready to resume.

For seven of the riders, play during the last chukker was subdued. The eighth was Dani, who rode with a vengeance, playing as though the only way to exorcise the demons that haunted her was with speed and frantic motion. She scored one goal, then another, glaring murderously at the Ox Ridge defenders who let her slip past.

When the final horn sounded, marking the end of the game, Dani rode her lathered pony over to the side of the field. Calmly and deliberately, she ran up her stirrups, then pulled off her saddle and dumped it on the ground. Her eyes stared blindly, seeing nothing, as she picked up a cooler and tossed it over the mare's back.

That done, she handed over the reins to one of the hot-walkers, then began to pull off her own equipment. Helmet, gloves, knee guards, all were dropped into a careless pile at her feet. Then she turned away and began to walk.

She didn't know where she was going, and she didn't care. All she knew was that she had to get away—away from the curious eyes and the sympathetic murmurs. She struck out across the field and didn't stop until she'd reached the other side. There were trees there, a narrow band that separated the field from the road. There was solitude and quiet. Dani sank to her knees on the soft ground. Within her, there was only emptiness.

A small sound rose in her throat, a whimper that escaped through trembling lips. It was her fault that Charm was gone. There was nobody else to blame. If she hadn't pushed him so hard . . . if she hadn't wanted so badly to prove that she was the best . . .

Dani gulped frantically for air, her chest heaving. She wouldn't cry. She wouldn't. Somehow she would get through this. Somehow she would deal with the ball of pain that burned within her, expanding until it seemed to block off everything else.

"Just hold on," Dani whispered, her breath coming in shallow gasps. "Don't let go."

Thoughts of the old pony, half-forgotten images from her childhood, rose before her eyes. She had named him Charm because that's what he had seemed to be—a magic talisman who would take her where she hadn't been able to go before. Over the years he had done just that. He had been her friend, more loyal, more honest, than most people she had known. And now he was gone.

Shaking her head fiercely, Dani pushed her thoughts away. A single hot tear welled in the corner of her eye, then trembled on her lashes. Angrily she dashed it away. *Don't think,* she told herself. *Don't feel, just hold on.*

She was curled into a tight ball of misery when Rick found her—her knees drawn up to her chest, her arms encircling them and holding them close. For a moment he hesitated. He'd tried to comfort her before. She hadn't wanted his help then; perhaps she still didn't want it now.

Then, as he watched, Dani's body began to shudder, as though racked by unbearable pain. Instinctively his hands reached out to her—to offer whatever measure of solace she would accept. He'd seen the look on her face when the vet had prepared the injection; he'd known how she was suffering. Now, seeing the extent of her grief, he felt her pain as though it were his own. Rick realized he had to go to her, whether she wanted him or not. For his sake, as well as hers, it was the only way.

Dani sensed Rick's presence only moments before he appeared beside her. Quickly she struggled to compose her features. He wouldn't see her like this. She refused to let him. Sniffling loudly, she turned her face away.

"Dani?" Rick crouched down beside her, one hand resting on his bended knee. The other reached out to touch her shoulder. "Please," he said gently. "Let me help."

"I'm okay," Dani mumbled. "Leave me alone."

Rick sighed quietly. He hadn't expected anything else. Still, there was no way he could honor her request. Instead, he crossed his legs and sank down on the ground beside her. "You're crying, aren't you?"

"Of course not," Dani denied, her chin set at a stubborn angle. "I never cry."

"Look at me." Rick's hand cupped her chin, tilting her face upward.

Dani's skin was devoid of color, which only made her eyes stand out all the more. The pupils were dark and dilated, the lashes damp. Her lower lip quivered, even as she sought to stare him down. It was clear that she was trembling on the edge of control. All at the same time, Rick realized, she looked utterly vulnerable, lost and bereft.

"It's all right," he murmured, the soothing words coming instinctively as he gathered her into his arms. "Everything's going to be all right."

Pity would have made her angry; recriminations, forced her to fight back. But it was his tenderness that sent her over the brink. A gasping sob forced its way out as she surrendered herself to his embrace. "It's not all right," she cried, her head coming to rest against his broad chest. "It's never going to be all right again."

Then all at once the tears came as the blinding flow of emotion she'd tried so hard to contain erupted beyond her control. They streamed down her cheeks and tangled in her hair, staining Rick's jersey as he held her close. Her body shuddered within the circle of his arms, racked by feelings so long suppressed.

"I killed him," she sobbed raggedly, her voice so low that Rick had to strain to hear the words. "It was all my fault."

"It wasn't your fault," he said firmly. His hand stroked the length of her back from shoulder to hip, quieting her as one might a frightened child. "Polo is a dangerous game, and sometimes things go wrong. Nobody can be blamed for that."

Dani shook her head. "I knew he was too old. I never should have pushed him so hard."

"He pushed himself," said Rick. His fingers made their way through her hair to massage the back of her neck. "You told me yourself that the only reason you were still playing him was because he wouldn't let you stop."

"But it was my decision, and now he's gone." Dani's voice broke on a sob. "I just wasn't ready to give him up yet."

"I know," Rick crooned quietly. "I know."

His hand cradled the side of her head, holding her close to his chest. Dani rested against him, drawing more comfort from his calm presence and quiet solicitude than she would have thought possible. She felt his heart beneath her cheek, pounding softly in time with her own. Slowly, gradually, her sobs quieted.

Holding her, Rick was silent, lost in his own thoughts. He understood her feelings. He'd experienced the same crushing sense of grief years earlier when his father had died. And then again when Ben had left him.

Yet for him things had been different. He'd had family and friends from whom to draw comfort. Unless he stopped her, he knew that Dani would draw inward, seeking no solace save what she could offer herself.

"It just isn't fair," Dani murmured.

"Life often isn't," Rick said quietly. He thought of his mother, widowed at thirty-three. And himself, lost and directionless at the vulnerable age of fourteen. "But it goes on. Whether you want it to or not, it goes on."

Her tears dry, Dani gathered her breath in one last shuddering sigh. She felt weak and drained, as though the emotions that had coursed through her body had taken every ounce of her strength with them. Then she lifted her head and looked up into Rick's eyes. The caring she saw there touched something within her. A tiny kernel of warmth began to glow inside, fighting the chill that racked her soul.

Then reason began to return. With it came self-consciousness. In the past half hour, Dani had given in to a side of herself that she'd worked very hard to deny. It was bad enough to be forced to the realization that her efforts hadn't been successful. Worse, that it should happen in front of Rick. All at once she felt naked and vulnerable, and she didn't enjoy either.

"I'm sorry," Dani said stiffly, pushing herself away.

"You have nothing to be sorry for." With regret Rick let her go. "There's no shame in giving in to your feelings, Dani. It's all right to let things out every now and then."

"Maybe." Dani sounded unconvinced. "I still didn't mean to hang all over you like that."

Rick swallowed heavily. She still didn't understand. He'd give it one last try. "I wanted to be here for you, Dani. I'm glad I was able to help. Besides, you weren't hanging on to me. It was I who was holding you."

"Semantics." Dani frowned. She rose, lifting a hand to brush back her tangled hair. When she stood, she could see the polo field, empty now save for the scoreboard and brightly painted goalposts. There was nothing for her there. She turned back, her gaze sweeping the ground, though she couldn't say what she was looking for. "I guess I'd better be going."

Rick rose to his feet beside her. "Dani?"

The face she turned to him was ashen. She barely looked strong enough to stand. Without stopping to think, he reached out his arms. She hesitated barely a moment before moving into them.

With a sigh, Rick gathered her to his body and held her close. There was nothing sexual in the embrace. He did not desire her now, or if he did, the feelings were submerged beneath a stronger need—the need to keep her safe, to make her whole again.

Even as she stepped back finally from the embrace, Rick knew he couldn't let her leave, not alone. "I'll come with you," he said as they started across the field.

Talking was too much effort. Dani merely nodded. Rick's arm was draped around her shoulder, and it seemed entirely natural that she should lean into his side, accepting his support. She felt unbearably weary. The field they had to cross looked a thousand miles long.

They reached the cars sooner than she had expected. Dani found she was loath to relinquish the comforting touch of Rick's arm. "Thank you," she said slowly. Gratitude was yet another unfamiliar emotion. Like the others, it didn't come easily.

"For what?"

Dani looked away, her gaze going out to the empty field one last time. This time she knew what she was looking for. She also knew that she wouldn't find it. "Thank you," she repeated softly, "for being there when I needed you."

"You still need me, princess." Rick turned her in his arms. He braced a hand on each of her shoulders; he wasn't quite sure if it was for her sake or his own. He saw her eyes narrow, and knew she wanted to fight. He also knew she didn't have the strength.

"Come on," he said, turning her gently toward the Jeep. "You're coming with me."

"But—"

"You're in no shape to drive." Rick opened the door of the Jeep and settled her inside. "And besides, you shouldn't be alone."

Dani saw both the wisdom in his words, and the futility of arguing. She leaned back in the seat and closed her eyes, leaving everything up to Rick. He could have driven her anywhere. When the motion of the Jeep stopped and she looked out to see that they were parked in the courtyard of a modern condominium complex, she knew that he had brought her home. His home.

"Out you go," said Rick. He opened the door, his hand reaching in to take hers and guide her to her feet. He was treating her, Dani realized, as though she was either very old or very fragile. At the moment she felt both.

Inside, she paid scant attention to her surroundings. Vaguely her mind registered plush cream colored carpeting and gray streamlined furniture. She found the couch, dropped down into it and promptly forgot the rest. She was still sitting there, staring into space, when Rick reentered the room with a cup of hot tea several minutes later.

"Here," he said. "Drink this. You'll feel better."

Dani stared down at the cup as though it were a foreign object she'd never seen before.

"It's tea, with honey."

Dani's hand shook slightly as she guided the cup to her lips. The liquid burned going down. The heat felt good; it let her know she was alive. Then the taste of it registered, and she frowned.

"I added a little brandy," said Rick, intercepting her look. To tell the truth, he'd added a lot. From the look of her, she could use all the help she could get. She'd been through a violent emotional storm. Now, unless he missed his guess, the numbness was beginning to set in.

"I never drink brandy," Dani said. Her words were measured, and very distinct. "It puts me to sleep."

"Just this once." Rick shielded her hand with his, guiding the cup to her mouth once more. "It's good for you."

Already Dani's eyelids were growing heavy. Between the effort she'd expended during the hard match, and the heart-wrenching turbulence that had followed, her system had simply had enough. Now it had gone into overload; the next move, shutdown.

"It's all right," Rick said soothingly. "Sleep if you want to. It's the best thing you could do."

"Will you hold me?" Dani murmured drowsily.

"I'll hold you, princess."

Only moments later, the sound of her breathing, shallow but steady, let him know that she had drifted off. The hand that stroked her smooth hair didn't stop as he gathered her to him. She sighed dreamily and shifted, nestling closer still. Outside, twilight gathered and the crickets began to chirp. Inside, Rick held Dani in his arms, and knew peace.

They sat that way for more than an hour until Rick's arm had begun to stiffen and his thoughts were sufficiently guilt-ridden to goad him to move. He'd brought her to his place to comfort her, to be with her when she needed somebody, and because, tonight of all nights, he couldn't stand the thought of depositing her in that mausoleum she called home. And as far as that went, it seemed to have worked. She'd been able to relax, to fall asleep. There was no better medicine he could have prescribed.

He should have been feeling relaxed, too, pleased by the knowledge that his ministrations had worked so well. Yet instead his body was a churning mass of nerves. Dani lay in his arms, quiet and trusting, and utterly vulnerable. And he could never remember wanting a woman so much.

With a muttered oath, Rick disentangled himself and rose from the couch. Dani never even moved. Obviously she was going to be his guest for the night. Shaking his head, Rick strode into the kitchen and made a quick phone call to Preston.

When he returned, Dani was still blissfully asleep. Rick smiled softly at the picture she made. Her head was turned in toward the cushions. One pale hand was curled into a fist and tucked beneath her chin. In repose, Dani seemed smaller somehow—as though the tensions that held her straight and tall during her waking hours, had eased away with her dreams. She looked soft, fragile and very, very lovely.

Love blossomed within him, the feeling so strong, so sweet, that unexpectedly tears gathered in the corners of his eyes. She was everything he would ever want in a woman, he acknowledged silently. All he could ever need, and more. Then Dani turned over, moaning softly in her sleep, and Rick forced his thoughts into a more practical vein. It was time he made both of them as comfortable as possible.

As he swept her up into his arms, Rick couldn't suppress a wry grin. He'd imagined spending the night with Dani in his bed. Indeed, over the past several weeks it was fair to say that he'd devoted an inordinate amount of thought to the prospect. Yet somehow the reality was turning out to be a far cry from what he'd imagined.

Abruptly he remembered what he'd told her earlier. At its best, life wasn't fair. At its worst, it felt like a kick in the gut. There was no doubt about which one he'd been handed today.

Rick lowered Dani down onto the coverlet of his bed. She moaned softly as he knelt at her feet and eased off her boots. The tight breeches followed, then the panty hose she wore beneath them. He eyed her shirt and decided against it. She wouldn't thank him for any of this.

As he slipped her beneath the covers, she smiled—a dreamy, seductive smile that stole his breath. Then she snuggled into the bed, her hair fanning out over the soft pillow. She was still asleep, still totally unaware.

The epithet Rick uttered was short and pungent. He stripped off his own clothes and left them where they fell. The rush of cold water in the shower did little to soothe away the tension he felt. After five minutes he gave up.

Rick pulled on a pair of pajama bottoms, grabbed a pillow and a blanket from the linen closet, then set about making himself a bed on the couch. The cushions were too soft for comfort. He tried several positions and found none satisfying. Finally he lay still. In the silence of the dark apartment, Rick could hear the quiet rustle of covers as Dani tossed restlessly in his bed. Sighing, he closed his eyes and prayed for sleep. It was going to be a very long night.

Chapter Ten

The coming of dawn bathed the bedroom in its soft, rosy light. Dani awakened gradually, an awareness of her surroundings filtering slowly into her groggy brain. Then, with the realization that she was not in her own bed, memories of the previous day came flooding back.

An image of Charm rose in her mind. Lying very still, Dani waited for the reaction to come. When it did, she found she was still sad but no longer devastated. Malone had seen her through the worst. Now she could begin to heal.

And speaking of Malone, Dani thought, frowning suddenly, where was he? She remembered that he'd brought her home and given her tea. Beyond that everything was blank.

Pushing back the covers, Dani slipped out of bed. As she stood up, the loose folds of her polo shirt slid down over her hips, covering the tops of her thighs. Barefoot, she padded quietly across the room, then paused in the doorway as the object of her search came into view. Looking rumpled, and more than a little the worse for wear, Rick was curled up awkwardly in the middle of the couch.

Dani started toward him, then abruptly stopped, stunned by the sudden wave of tenderness that washed unexpectedly through her. Asleep, the sharp planes of Rick's face seemed to soften. Though the angle of his jaw held the dark shadow of a beard, he looked younger, almost boyishly innocent. Dani smiled as her eyes traveled to his mouth. It was slightly open, his lips relaxed in a pout.

He couldn't possibly be comfortable, Dani realized. The couch was both too narrow and too short to offer him a proper bed. And yet he'd chosen that over sharing the bed with her. Dani shook her head slowly, warmed by the solicitous way he had cared for her, putting her needs above his own.

The evening before, she'd been totally vulnerable. Rick had had every opportunity to take advantage of her. And yet he hadn't, not in any way. Though she'd certainly been in no shape to insist, he had voluntarily sacrificed his own comfort in order to preserve the delicate balance of their relationship. Now Dani found that she was touched, deeply, by his thoughtfulness.

Slowly she walked across the room, then knelt down beside the couch. The blanket had fallen away from Malone's upper body, and Dani's gaze roamed with fascination over the smooth slope of his shoulders and the bronzed muscles of his chest. A light dusting of hair covered his torso. She followed their line downward, lowering her brow as she contemplated the concealing covers.

What, if anything, she wondered, was he wearing under there? There was only one way to find out. Reaching out, Dani grasped the blanket between the tip of her forefinger and her thumb. Gently she began to raise it.

"Dani, what are you doing?"

She gasped softly, raising startled eyes to Rick's. They were open now, as they hadn't been a moment earlier. A delicate blush stole over her cheeks. How long had he been watching her?

Then she saw the amusement in his eyes, and her confidence rallied. There were worse things than being caught trying to ogle a naked man, especially one as glorious as this! "Would you believe I was cold and I wanted another blanket?"

Slowly Rick shook his head. "You make a very poor liar, princess."

"I do not," Dani declared. "Actually when I concentrate, I can be very good at it."

Rick's lips twitched. "I take it you're not concentrating now?"

Before she could stop herself, Dani's gaze had made a telltale sweep of his length. "Not exactly, no."

"I see."

Did he? Dani wondered. Could he possibly have any idea of what she was feeling?

She'd been attracted to Rick from the start, an attraction that had grown with their relationship, sharpening gradually into a pulse-quickening desire. But that was nothing compared to the intensity of emotion she was experiencing now—after waking alone in Rick's bed, tiptoeing in to watch him sleep and realizing just how carefully he'd attended to her needs.

She wanted, no, she *needed* Rick Malone. She could only hope that he felt the same. Slowly Dani reached up to graze the stubble on his cheek with the backs of her fingers. It was rough to her touch. Rick didn't move as her hand explored his face. Only his eyes betrayed what he was feeling. They were dark, watchful and something more—eager.

A shuddering sigh escaped him as her hand trailed lower. She traced the line of his throat, then the sloping curve of his shoulder. When her hand reached his chest, her fingers splayed as she pressed her palm against the warm flesh over his heart. The thundering beat of his pulse pounded along with her own.

And still he made no move toward her. "Rick?" Dani looked up uncertainly. "I don't think I can do this all by myself."

It was the first time ever that she'd used his given name.
Rick heard it, and then realized something within him had
broken free. In the past twenty-four hours something irrevocable had changed between them. Now there was no going
back. "You won't have to, princess," he said softly. "I'll be
there with you every step of the way."

Tossing aside the blanket, Rick rose to his feet. He took
Dani's hand in his and led her into the other room, back to
the bed. He stopped beside it, his hands coming up to encircle Dani's shoulders and pull her to him.

"I need you, Rick," Dani whispered. "I need you very,
very much."

Rick felt a rush of emotion that blotted all else from his
mind. He felt as though he'd waited an eternity to hear her
say the words.

Their first kiss was slow and gentle. Now that the moment had come, Rick intended to savor it. They had all the
time in the world to be together. He was going to use it.
Their tongues met, touching, tasting. Dani's lips were soft
and warm beneath his own. Rick explored their contour
lovingly. He wanted to feel, to know, everything she had to
offer.

Dani's arms reached out to encircle Rick's waist. His kiss
deepened, and she rose on her toes to meet him. Pleasure
flowed through her, heightening her awareness. Her senses
tingled with discovery. Dani's thoughts began to whirl,
leaving her breathless and giddy. And still the kiss went on
and on.

He'd never tasted anything so sweet, thought Rick. He'd
never known that a kiss could offer so much, and at the
same time leave him needing more. Dani's bare legs twined
with his, her fingers caressed the contour of his hips. Desire grew and swelled within him. His hands left her shoulders and traveled downward, then tangled in the soft fabric
of her shirt. Rick uttered an impatient oath.

"Lean back for me, princess." Dani shifted, and in seconds the shirt was up over her head and gone. Her body was sleek and firm, her skin the color of honey. Rick's eyes darkened, caressing her with their gaze.

Then his breath caught as Dani lifted her hands between her breasts and slowly unclasped her bra. The wisp of lacy material fell away, and Rick groaned softly. He'd never seen anyone so lovely in his life. He'd never wanted a woman more.

"Your turn," Dani murmured. She was every bit as impatient as he. Her hands settled on his hips, her thumbs hooking inside the waistband of his pajamas. She started to push them aside, then stopped suddenly, shocked at her own audacity. "Rick, I..."

"Hmm?" He looked up slowly, and was surprised by her expression. She looked hesitant, uncertain, and not at all sure how to proceed. Instinctively his hands went to cover hers. He cupped her palms in his, holding them together as he offered a silent reassurance.

"I'm sorry," Dani whispered raggedly. "I'm not very good at this."

"Shhh." Rick silenced her with a kiss. "You're doing just fine," he murmured, his lips warm against her. "We're doing fine together."

Her hands still clasped beneath his, Rick pushed the pajamas down and stepped out of them. Naked, he was every bit as glorious as Dani had imagined. With a shy smile, she guided his hands to her. In a moment her panties joined his pajamas on the floor. Now there was nothing between them but their own heated flesh.

Rick pushed aside the rumpled covers, and they lay down together on the bed. Dani's hair spilled like molten gold over the dark sheets. Rick's fingers tangled through the soft tresses as his lips took hers once more.

Lying beside him, Dani let her hands run the length of Rick's back from shoulder to buttocks. She reveled in the smooth contours, the hidden muscled strength. Straining closer, she fit her body to his. Skin slid against skin, the friction delicious.

Lost in sensation, Dani felt as though she was being drawn down into a swirling vortex of desire. A wildness rose within her. She didn't stop to question her response, only flowed with it, knowing that it would take her where she'd always wanted to go.

Rick's fingers skimmed over the smooth skin of her breast, his palm curving to cup its weight. Then he lowered his head, his hair dark and gleaming against her creamy skin as he took the rose-colored nipple into his mouth and sucked on it gently.

"Rick . . . ?" Dani's breath escaped with a soft sigh.

He looked up. "Are you ready for me, princess?"

Dani's smile was dreamy. "Very," she said softly.

Slowly, carefully, Rick settled his weight over her. Her thighs parted, her hands reaching to guide him to her. Rick's fingers encircled her buttocks, raising her hips to his. She gasped as he entered her. Rick swallowed the sound with a kiss.

He'd meant to take things slowly, to prolong the pleasure until he was sure he'd carried them both to the peak. But now he found that the intensity of Dani's response chased his own, pushing him farther, and faster, than he would have thought possible. Rick felt his senses begin to reel. Pleasure rose in waves, overwhelming him. He tried to hold back, and found he couldn't. It was too soon. It was too fast. And it was beyond his control. A shudder rippled the length of his body as he lost himself inside her.

For a long moment afterward, Rick lay still. Beneath him, Dani was quiet, although her breathing, like his, was deep and uneven. Absently, it seemed, she stroked the length of

his back with her hand. What was she thinking? he wondered. More than anything, he'd wanted to please her. And
maybe, just maybe, because it had been so important to
him, he'd failed.

"Dani?"

"Mmmm?" Her eyelids fluttered, then slowly opened.
She sent him a lazy smile, knowing it was what he would
want to see. She'd thought this time, with this man, might
be different. He'd attracted her, aroused her, as no other
man had done before. He'd left her breathless with wanting, and all the more frustrated because he'd given her a
glimpse of that elusive brass ring she'd never been able to
grasp.

"That time was for me," Rick said softly. "This time is
all yours."

"What...?" The question ended with a moan as his hand
dropped between her thighs. With sure, steady movement
his fingers awakened her once more. Dani found herself
arching to meet him as tension began to coil within her.

"Rick?" she gasped. "You don't understand. I've
never... That is, I don't know how—"

"Shhh," Rick crooned, his lips pressed against the pulse
point at her throat. Her body signaled a response that was
equal parts pleasure and fear. He knew the source of both.
Slowly he felt her stiffness begin to ease away. "Just let go,
and it will come."

Her eyes, staring up at him, were cloudy with pleasure,
but still guarded. Rick smiled, cupping her face gently in his
palm. "Do you trust me?"

She didn't even have to think about it. Her head dipped
down in a nod.

"Then come with me."

His hand began to move once more, and this time Dani
moved with it. Mists swirled up before her eyes, blocking

out everything save mindless pleasure. She felt control slipping away. Without regret, she let it go. An explosion was building within her, bringing her right to the edge. She shuddered violently, moaning softly with need. This time when he drove inside her she was ready for him. She'd never been more ready for anything in her life.

THEY SLEPT AGAIN, curled into each other as one. This time, when Dani awoke, it was truly morning. The sun was up, the shower running and the bed beside her empty. Flopping back onto her pillow, Dani grinned, then began to laugh out loud. She felt good, no, make that wonderful. And it was about time.

"Good, you're awake."

Dani looked up as Rick emerged from the shower, naked except for a towel slung low around his hips. Another towel encircled his shoulders, and he was using it to dry his hair. Her eyes alight with interest, she pushed herself up to enjoy the view, feasting on details she had missed earlier. Lord, but he was gorgeous!

Rick glanced at the bed where Dani lay, still tangled in the bed covers, then turned quickly away. The last thing he needed right now was the sight of her long, lush body lying naked in his bed. In the past twenty minutes he'd called himself every name in the book. Now, he supposed, it would be her turn.

He'd taken advantage of her that morning, waited until she was wounded and vulnerable, her resistance low. He'd no doubt she'd come out swinging; she always had before. This time he could hardly blame her.

"What's for breakfast?" Dani asked. "I'm starved."

Rick spun around, grabbing at the towel on his hips when it threatened to remain behind. Whatever he'd expected her to say, that was certainly not it. "You want to eat, now?"

Dani chewed on her lower lip, wondering if she'd made some terrible gaffe. Perhaps there was an etiquette to waking up in a man's bed—some rules of correct behavior that she'd never known about or mastered. She looked up, facing him squarely. "Is something wrong with that?"

"No." Rick shook his head quickly. "Of course not."

"Good." Dani threw back the sheet and hopped out of bed, totally unself-conscious of her nudity. "You don't mind if I take a shower first, do you?"

"Be my guest," Rick croaked. It was all the sound that his suddenly dry mouth could offer.

"Thanks." Dani smiled. She padded across the floor, her breasts bobbing lightly with each step she took.

Rick's gaze dropped, caressing the length of her body. He remembered what it felt like to support the weight of her full breasts in his hand, to taste their sweetness with his lips. Rick felt his mouth go dry. He'd expected anger and recriminations; she seemed concerned with neither. If he lived to be a hundred, Rick mused, would he ever understand her?

Dani stopped before him, rising on her toes, her hands braced lightly on the tops of his shoulders. Grinning, she kissed him lightly on the mouth. "Then again," she murmured, her voice edged with laughter, "brunch would be fine, too, if there's something else you'd rather do in the meantime."

Automatically Rick's arms came up to encircle her waist. Was it possible? he wondered, his heart swelling with hope. Yesterday, and again at dawn, Dani had allowed herself to open up, responding to him with a purity of emotion she'd never shown before. Was it possible that her feelings were finally beginning to mirror his?

Rick felt light-headed from the gentle pressure of her nipples rubbing against his chest. He started to lower his mouth to hers, then abruptly stopped. Earlier he'd allowed things to move too fast. This time he wanted to be sure.

"Maybe we'd better talk first." He grasped the tops of Dani's arms and put her firmly, but gently, away.

Why did he always have to be so serious? Dani wondered. The magic interlude at dawn had been one of the best things that had ever happened to her. Malone had made her feel, really feel, what it meant to be a woman. He'd opened the door to possibilities she hadn't even known existed.

This morning she'd awakened happy, giddy with the knowledge that he would be there beside her. Now all she wanted to do was share her happiness. Was that so much to ask?

Dani looked at the implacable expression on Rick's face and sighed. "What do we have to talk about, Malone?"

He wished she wouldn't stand so close, her face tilted up to his as she gazed at him with those wide, wonderful, blue eyes. Even more, he wished that she was dressed, preferably in a turtleneck and long pants. How was he supposed to concentrate when all he could think about was Dani's glorious body and the delights she'd offered him so freely?

"About us," he said. It came out rougher than he'd intended. "You and I."

"What about us?" Dani crossed the room and sat down on the edge of the bed.

There seemed to be nothing to do with her hands. With effort, she forced them to lie still in her lap. Why didn't he say something? she wondered, waiting. His silence was making her crazy. Didn't he realize the effect he was having on her? Last night wasn't enough. It would never be enough. Didn't he know how badly she wanted him again?

Abruptly Dani frowned. She'd never allowed any man to have such power over her before. And now that she had, she wasn't at all sure that she liked it. Earlier there had been no choice. She'd been ruled by emotions, desires, stronger than anything she'd experienced before. But now, in the clear light of day, things suddenly looked very different. And why didn't Malone say something?

On the other side of the room, Rick muttered a quiet oath. One look at the arrogant tilt to her chin, and he knew that the princess was back. Imperiously naked, and utterly splendid. He'd managed to penetrate the facade yesterday. Now he could only pray that he'd be able to do so again.

Swiftly he crossed the room and sat beside her. "Don't shut me out," he said quietly. "I know what you're doing, Dani, and it won't work. I won't let it."

"Oh?" With a swift, angry motion, Dani stood. She strode to the closet and yanked open the door. Rick's bathrobe was hanging on the back. She snatched it off the hook and pulled it on.

Rick watched her draw the sash tight around her waist, and knew instinctively that she was girding herself for battle. The distance she'd placed between them was not only physical but emotional as well. She was slipping away from him again, as she'd done so many times in the past. Even as he watched, he could feel the gulf widening between them.

The knowledge burned inside him like acid. He wouldn't let her go, not again, not now. He wanted to bind her to him so tightly that she would never be able to leave again. Desperation forced him up off the bed and to her side. A thought, an idea, shimmered in his subconscious. Dani had planted it there herself.

"Marry me, Dani," The words came blurting out almost before he realized what he was saying. Immediately he knew it had been a mistake.

"Marry you?" Dani's jaw dropped slightly. Quickly she recovered. "If that's a joke," she snapped, "I think your timing is atrocious."

"It's not a joke, princess."

Dropping her head, Dani turned her face away. To her dismay, she realized that she'd have been better off if he had been kidding. Because now she was going to be forced to examine what had happened between them. He had gotten close, too close. She should have seen it coming. She *had* seen it coming. But at the time, she'd been so sure that she could handle him that she hadn't cared. And now it was too late.

If only he didn't ask so much, Dani thought angrily. If he'd been satisfied to stop at making love with her, things would have been just fine. She could deal with an affair. Yet now she suspected that that would never be enough for him. Why hadn't she realized it sooner?

"I can't marry you, Malone," Dani said quietly. "You know that."

Rick drew in his breath with a sigh. He'd expected the rejection, but that didn't make it any easier to take. Yesterday, last night, he'd been so sure that they'd reached an understanding. But now... Rick shook his head wearily. He wasn't sure of anything anymore.

"It's the money, isn't it?" he said harshly. "You won't marry me because I'm not rich."

"Don't be ridiculous," Dani snapped. "That has nothing to do with it. I have more than enough money for both of us, remember?"

Rick shot her a level glare. "Then what is the matter?"

"I told you before, Malone. I'm not in love with you."

Rick scowled. She had told him before. Then he hadn't liked it. Now, with all that had since passed between them, he couldn't stand it. "How would you know?" he demanded. "In case you don't remember, you also told me that you weren't even sure what love is."

"Maybe not," Dani retorted. "But I'll tell you what love isn't. It's not two people sharing a bed for one night and then declaring an undying commitment to each other in the rosy light of dawn!''

Rick looked at her incredulously. "Are you trying to tell me that what we shared this morning meant nothing to you?''

"Of course not," Dani said hotly, angry at the way he'd twisted her words. "I didn't say that at all. I'm simply trying to make it clear that despite what happened you don't own me, Malone.''

"I don't want to own you, Dani. Maybe that's precisely the problem.''

"What's that supposed to mean?''

Rick shook his head in exasperation. "You look at everything in terms of weakness and strength, winning and losing. But what happens between a man and a woman has nothing to do with that.''

He paused, knowing that the step he was about to take was irrevocable, and knowing too that he was desperate enough to try it anyway. "I'm tired of fighting with you, princess. If you won't at least try and meet me halfway, then maybe it's better if we don't meet at all.''

Dani looked at him for a long moment. The giddy feeling of happiness she'd awakened with was gone. Anger had taken its place first. Now that was beginning to fade. Their relationship had reached an impasse. She knew it just as well as he did. They couldn't simply keep arguing over the same issues, beating their heads against the same impenetrable walls.

It was time for them to go forward. And now, Dani knew, she had only two choices. She could either take a chance and move on with Rick, or stay behind and watch as he moved on without her. When she looked at things that way, there really wasn't much choice at all.

"You know, I warned you, Malone," Dani said softly. Her smile was tremulous, uncertain. "I told you I wasn't going to be very good at this."

Rick's face warmed with sudden emotion. "You said that earlier, too. You were wrong then. I'm willing to bet you're wrong now, too."

"Then, it was easy. All I had to do was follow your lead."

"Now is easy, too," said Rick. He reached out and grasped her hand, pulling her into his arms. "You've already done the hard part, princess. You know how to be strong. Now all you have to do is let me show you how to be soft."

Dani's smile widened as she ran her hands up the column of his throat to tangle in his hair. She was where she'd wanted to be all along—back in Malone's arms. "Does that mean I'm not going to get any breakfast?"

"Later," said Rick. He swept her off her feet and carried her toward the bed. "Much later."

"GOOD MORNING, Danielle." Preston's dulcet tones rang through the front hall as Dani shut the front door behind her. The butler was standing beside the settee, his hands folded discreetly before him. As she looked on, he lifted one and gazed pointedly at his watch.

Another time Dani might have taken issue with his less than subtle gesture. She was no longer fourteen, after all. But now she simply felt too good.

"Good morning, Preston!" she sang out cheerily, breezing past him on her way up the stairs.

"I trust you spent a comfortable night at Mr. Malone's?"

Dani's hand stilled on the banister as she stopped in midstride. Rick had driven her back to Ox Ridge so she could pick up her car, and they'd parted there. So how could Preston possibly know where she had been?

Slowly Dani turned to face him. "Preston, if after all these years you're finally going to confess to having ESP, then all I can say is you should have done it sooner and saved us both a lot of grief."

"Certainly not." Preston gazed at her down the long, narrow bridge of his nose. "I possess the normal faculties, no more, no less."

"Then how did you know where I was?"

"Mr. Malone called last night to say that you were indisposed. It seems he was afraid I might worry."

Dani's eyes twinkled mischievously. "And did you?"

"More to the point," Preston intoned, "should I have?"

Dani bit back a grin. There he went, getting stiff again. He should have realized by now that all that excess dignity only goaded her into being more and more outrageous.

Stroking the side of her jaw, Dani pretended to consider the question. "You know," she said finally, "Rick Malone *is* a very attractive man."

Preston blinked, waiting.

"A bit overbearing perhaps, but with a certain magnetic charm."

He cleared his throat, the sound rumbling deep in his chest.

"And he has the sexiest eyes—"

"In other words," Preston interrupted dryly, "I should have worried."

Dani nodded slowly, her face alight with a smile. "Uh-huh." Laughing, she turned and ran up the stairs then disappeared down the hall.

On the landing below, Preston permitted himself a small smile of his own. "It's about time," he muttered softly before heading to the kitchen to see what the cook was preparing for lunch.

DANI HAD NEVER THOUGHT of herself as being either un-happy or lonely, but as the next few weeks passed, she be-came aware of just how incomplete her life had been before Rick Malone had swaggered into it with his pushy ways and his infuriatingly cocky grin. As always, she was busy; but now there was a difference. Her days took on a new tex-ture, enriched by the knowledge that, though they might not be together, Malone was always there. He was present in her thoughts, and in the warm, satisfied feeling of her body and in the foolish smile she sometimes found herself wearing for no reason at all.

July arrived, and with it, summer's sultry heat settled over Connecticut. With it, too, the time was drawing near for the Silverbrook board to make their selections to the team. Pushing herself mercilessly, Dani crammed activity into every minute of the day. She spent mornings and late after-noons on horseback, taking advantage of the relative cool to hold extra practice sessions both for herself and her string.

Early afternoons found her in the office. The mailing list had been compiled, the solicitation letters mailed out. Now it was up to Dani to follow up, courting the major patrons over the phone, then keeping track of donations as they poured in. With less than two months to go until the an-nual Pegasus Horse Show, the list of things to do seemed to grow daily.

IT WAS IRONIC, Rick decided, that just when things were fi-nally going well between them, he and Dani never seemed to have enough time for themselves. He'd just returned from a three-day trip to Dayton, Ohio, and was sitting outside on his terrace, drinking a beer and watching the sun set. That, and missing Dani. He'd called her the minute he'd gotten in, only to find out from Preston that she was out at the barn, giving round-the-clock care to a pony with a severe case of colic.

Rick frowned, polishing off the last of the brew. Earlier in the summer, the combination of circumstance and his persistence had managed to keep them together almost constantly. Now, just when they should have been able to relax and enjoy each other, outside demands kept pulling them apart. At times, he thought wryly, their schedules seemed to mesh with all the finesse of a Marx Brothers movie.

Abruptly Rick rose to his feet. He'd never been patient in the face of adversity before. He saw no reason to start now.

Stopping only long enough for a quick visit to a local pizza parlor, Rick headed across town toward the Greenfields estate. This time, when he reached the house, he didn't stop, driving instead around the four-car garage. As he'd suspected, the driveway didn't end there. A row of lights was faintly visible in the distance, and Rick turned the Jeep in their direction.

Dani heard the low hum of an engine as the car pulled up outside the barn. Slowly she eased herself up off the straw bedding. Her muscles had stiffened during the past hour she'd spent sitting still, and watchful, in the corner of the stall. The mare was resting quietly now. Dani was almost certain the worst had passed. Still, she had no intention of abandoning her vigil until the vet came back the following morning and pronounced the mare fit.

Hearing a door slam, Dani let herself out of the stall and started down the aisle. She certainly wasn't expecting any visitors, and now she was curious about who might have come. Then her stomach rumbled loudly, reminding her that she'd missed dinner. It had to be Preston, Dani decided. With his appetite, no doubt the butler had realized she'd be hungry and had brought her a snack.

Rick and Dani reached the stable door at the same time. Looking out into the darkened courtyard, it took Dani's eyes a moment to adjust. The pungent aroma of pepperoni pizza, however, was unmistakable.

"Malone delivery service," Rick announced, sweeping through the doorway. "You call, we come."

Delight pierced through her at his unexpected arrival. The feeling was sharp and sweet. "There's only one problem," Dani said, grinning as Rick set the extra large pizza down on top of a tack trunk. "I didn't call."

"No problem." Rick shrugged ingenuously. "You don't call, we come anyway."

"Terrific," Dani murmured, flowing into his arms.

His mouth came down, and hers opened beneath it. Their tongues touched. Pulling lightly, she drew him into her mouth. Dani's arms came up to encircle his neck, holding, just holding. The kiss deepened. It went on and on. Still, it wasn't nearly enough.

"The pizza's getting cold," Rick mentioned, several minutes later.

Dani smiled. "That makes one of us."

"Hmph," Rick grumbled, enjoying her response. "Some nurse you make. I thought you were on watch out here."

"I am." Dani sighed as she stepped back. "The mare in the end stall. She's coming off a bad case of colic, and I don't want to leave her alone. It looks as though I'll probably be out here all night."

Rick nodded. "Think you could do with some company?"

Dani's brow lifted. "You?" she asked teasingly. "Or the pizza?"

"Both," said Rick. He walked over and picked up the box. "We come as a set. Buy one, get the other free."

"Sold," Dani said with a smile.

Chapter Eleven

Heat rose off the asphalt in shimmering waves as Rick climbed out of the Jeep and strode across the parking lot toward the main office of First Fairfield Federal Bank. His suit was made of gray summer-weight wool, and in this heat it made him swelter. Though the bank would be air-conditioned, Rick didn't expect to feel any relief. He was tense, on edge. Asking for money did that to him. Especially since this would be the fifth loan officer he'd spoken to in as many days.

"Mr. Malone?" The receptionist had big brown eyes, glossy hair and a stunning smile. Rick barely spared her a glance. "We're running a little late today. If you'd care to take a seat, Mr. Gleason will be with you shortly."

Nodding, Rick crossed the room and sat in one of the sleek Italian-design leather chairs. In this mood, he'd rather have paced. He settled for flexing his fingers instead. He'd come so close, so close to putting Malone Inc. into the black that he could almost taste it.

But what was that old expression? Close only counted in horseshoes and hand grenades. Certainly not in the landing of major accounts, even one of which could have made all the difference. Rick scowled down at the briefcase he held in his lap. His projections had been a little off, but not by much. Start-up costs in Fairfield County had been higher than he'd anticipated, but he'd managed to cover that. What he couldn't cover for was a lack of large clients.

It wasn't as though he hadn't worked at all, thought Rick. He had. It was just that he was finding himself inundated with small, time-consuming jobs when one large corporate package would have covered everything. He'd counted on bringing in at least one big contract early—the Telecomm project would have done fine. But although Malone Inc. had been among the finalists, in the end Telecomm's board of directors had gone with an established firm that had fifteen years in the business. Now he was back to square one.

He had three more proposals in the works, he mused. Surely one of them was bound to click. It was just a matter of keeping Malone Inc. afloat until they did. But to do that, he was going to need more money. A conservative estimate put the figure at fifty thousand dollars. That was why he had come to see Gleason. Now he could only hope the man would prove more sympathetic to his plight than the other loan officers he'd spoken to.

"Mr. Malone?"

Rick looked up.

"You can go in now."

"Thank you." Rick picked up his briefcase and strode toward the office door. He hoped to hell that Gleason was in a good mood, because he was running out of banks.

"YOU'LL NEVER GUESS who I had dinner with last night," Sabrina said. She lounged back against the cushions of a Louis XVI couch in Dani's library and sipped at a glass of Grand Marnier.

"Who?" Seated opposite her, Dani grinned. Sabrina not only went out with more men than anyone she knew, she also told the best stories about them.

"Terry Gleason. Remember him?"

"Merry Terry? Of course I remember him. He was the fattest boy in high school."

"Yes, well, he's slimmed down since then." Sabrina's finger traced the rim of her glass thoughtfully. "He's also taken a job in his father's bank—quite a good job, in fact. He's a vice president and senior loan officer."

"Good for him." Dani sat back and waited for what was to come. She and Brie had already shared a sumptuous dinner and a thoroughly fattening dessert. Too stuffed to move, Dani was more than happy to while away a pleasant evening with good, old-fashioned girl talk. "Did you have fun?"

"Actually, no." Sabrina frowned. "To tell the truth, he was a terrible bore. The merry Terry of old days was nowhere to be found. All I can say is that losing weight certainly seems to have had an adverse effect on his personality."

"Dieting will do that to you every time," Dani said, sighing. "You know how it is."

"Who me?"

"I know, like you used to tell all the boys—you're just naturally thin, right?" Dani grinned wickedly. "Just like your eyelashes are naturally two inches long."

"Men don't like to think of a woman as an object of artifice," Sabrina sniffed. "I merely tell them what they want to hear."

"Someday one of your dates is going to notice that all you do is push the food around your plate without ever picking any of it up."

"No they won't," Sabrina replied, supremely confident of her appeal. "Not when they've got me to look at instead."

Dani shook her head in exasperation. "You know, you're probably right."

Brie only smiled. "Anyway, darling, to get back to Terry—"

"Do we have to?"

"Of course." Sabrina pulled out a slim gold case and withdrew a long black French cigarette. "I wouldn't have brought him up if there wasn't a good reason."

Dani watched as Brie touched the flame from her lighter to the tip of the cigarette and inhaled deeply. "I thought you gave that up."

"I did." Sabrina glanced around the room for an ashtray and settled for a small crystal plate. "I only smoke now when I have a reason."

Dani's brow lifted. "And Terry Gleason gave you a reason?"

"Not the man, darling, something he said."

Dani watched as Brie tapped the ash of her cigarette delicately onto the plate. "Go on."

"You know how boring some men are. All they want to talk about is themselves, and if not that, then their work."

Dani nodded absently, realizing that Malone didn't fit that mold at all. There'd been times when she'd wished he did.

"Last night, after Terry spent the first two hours rambling on about his sauna, his country club and his new BMW, he must have noticed that my eyes were starting to glaze over. That's when he switched to talking about his job. He knows I belong to Silverbrook, and he seemed to think I'd be interested in hearing about an application he'd had the other day from a man who wanted to use his string of polo ponies as collateral on a small business loan."

"Malone," Dani said softly.

Sabrina nodded. "That's the first thought that crossed my mind, too, although, of course, Terry wouldn't mention any names."

"How many ponies?" asked Dani.

"Three, all top flight."

"What kind of business?"

"Management consulting, with a specialty in finance."

"That's Malone all right. It has to be. Damn!" Dani swore under her breath. "I was afraid something was wrong."

Sabrina looked at her friend curiously. "Just because he's out shopping for a little spare change doesn't mean he's about to go under."

"No, but you have to admit it isn't a good sign. Did he get the loan?"

Slowly Brie shook her head. "Terry went off on some long spiel that was full of jargon like heavily leveraged assets and long-term paybacks, and to tell the truth, I just tuned him out. I figured I'd already heard everything that mattered."

Dani uttered a sound that was part sigh, part scowl. "I wonder what he'll do now."

"Probably visit another bank. At least that's what I'd do if I were in his shoes."

"How he must hate that." Dani set her glass down on the table with a bang as frustration rose within her. "I knew there was something he wasn't telling me. If only he hadn't kept shutting me out. He must have known I'd want to help."

"Maybe he doesn't want your help," Brie said gently.

Dani glanced up, surprised.

"From what I've seen of Rick Malone, he's the kind of man who likes to stand on his own two feet. Besides," Sabrina chided her, "didn't you once tell me that you accused him of being a fortune hunter?"

"Well . . . yes. But I didn't mean it!"

Brie sipped at her drink, waiting patiently.

"All right, maybe I did at the time. But everything's changed since then. And damn Malone for not knowing it!"

"Maybe you ought to try telling him," Sabrina advised.

"I will," Dani muttered, her voice firm with resolve. "I'll make sure Malone gets the message loud and clear."

THE NEXT MORNING Dani raced through her exercises, showered quickly, then dressed in the most austere outfit she could find in her closet—a Chanel suit, silk bow tie blouse and an opera-length strand of pearls. If she was going to talk business with Malone, the least she could do was look the part.

"You look lovely," Preston observed as he poured her a cup of coffee. "Is today a special occasion?"

"No," Dani said distractedly without looking up. The night before she'd been full of bravado about her plans to come to Malone's aid. But now, when it came right down to it, she was rapidly realizing that she had no idea how to convince him to let her. "I just have some business to see to this morning, that's all."

"Business?"

Dani sighed. She recognized the look on Preston's face. He'd never let go now until he'd found out everything he wanted to know. "I'm going to see Malone about a few things, okay?"

"Ah." Preston nodded, looking down over her outfit appreciatively. "Might I say that Mr. Malone seems to be a good influence on your choice of attire?"

"You might," Dani allowed with a level gaze. "But if you did, I'd say you were pressing your luck."

"Indeed." Preston snorted softly. "What else is luck for?"

Seeing her chance, Dani deftly changed the subject. "Have you had any word back yet from Victoria?"

"Not a thing," Preston said with a frown. "I fear this may be a bad sign."

"I'm sure you'll be hearing something soon." Dani finished her coffee and rose from the table. As she strode past the butler, she couldn't resist reaching out and chucking him teasingly under the chin. "After all, no woman with any sense would keep a man like you waiting for long."

"It's been ten years, Danielle."

"All the more reason. Everything's going to work out for you two. Just you wait and see."

She wished she felt as optimistic about her own prospects, Dani thought, half an hour later as she parked her car on the street near Landmark Square. Just because she wanted to help Malone didn't mean that he was going to be at all amenable to the idea. Indeed, his reticence on any topic relating to his job had already made it clear that he had no desire for her to be involved at all.

But that was just plain silly, Dani decided. Obviously Malone's company was having some sort of financial difficulty. And, just as obviously, she had the means to alleviate the problem. Malone would have to be crazy not to accept her offer of assistance.

So why, Dani wondered, did she have a sneaking suspicion that that was exactly what he was going to do?

She'd prepared a small speech, something inane about being in the neighborhood and deciding to drop by, which was intended to carry her through the first awkward moments. But when Dani entered the sixth floor office with the name Malone Inc. neatly stenciled on the door, she promptly forgot everything she'd been about to say.

The office consisted of only two rooms. The outer one, obviously intended to serve as a reception area, was empty save for a tall filing cabinet and a stack of boxes in one corner. From inside the other room she could hear Rick's voice as he spoke on the phone. She'd knocked lightly when she'd entered and gotten no response. Now Dani tried again, louder, as she closed the outer door behind her.

"Be right out," Rick called.

Dani crossed the small room to wait in the doorway. As Malone wrapped up his call, she looked around curiously. To her relief, this office was at least furnished. The oak desk and leather chair, while hardly grand, certainly seemed serviceable. Bookshelves, filled with software manuals, lined one wall; a worn foldout couch took up another. On a low credenza next to the desk sat the showpiece of the room—Malone's computer. From what little Dani knew about such things, the equipment appeared to be state of the art.

"Dani?" Rick rose from behind his desk, his expression chagrined. "I wasn't expecting you."

"I wanted to surprise you," Dani said brightly. There was no reason to mention that she hadn't called because she'd been afraid he'd tell her not to come.

"Well..." Rick cleared his throat uncomfortably. "You certainly did that. Here, come in. Sit down."

It took only a moment for them both to reach the same conclusion—her only choice of seating was the tattered couch. Managing a smile, Dani sank down onto a threadbare cushion, jumping only slightly as a spring pinched her bottom. Across from her, Rick perched on the edge of the desk.

"Sorry," he said. "I'm not really set up for visitors. In my line of work, I tend to go to the client, not the other way around."

"Don't worry about it," Dani said quickly. Now that she was actually there, she found that she hadn't the slightest idea of how to begin. Glancing around the room desperately, her eyes lit on Rick's desk. "I'm not keeping you from anything important, am I?"

"Not at all." Rick tried a smile. It fell flat. Why the hell had she come? he wondered. And why was she dressed in an outfit that looked like something straight out of *Vogue*? He hadn't wanted her to see his office, but it was too late for

that. Now he could only sit there and realize how defini-
tively it pointed up all the differences between them that he
hadn't wanted to think about.

"Look, Malone," Dani began. "I'll tell you why I'm
here." She paused, frowning. Her voice sounded harsh and
strident, as though she'd come to pick a fight, not solve all
his problems.

"Please do." Rick's stance was deceptively casual as he
braced his hands on the edge of the desk and stretched his
long legs out across the rug.

Dani took a deep breath and plunged in. "If Amelie were
here, she'd know just the right thing to say. But she isn't; I
am, and tact has never been my strong suit." She realized
she was rambling, but her mouth seemed to have a will of its
own, quite unconnected to anything her brain wanted to say,
and now she couldn't seem to stop. "I understand that
you're looking for a loan—"

Abruptly Rick rose. He strode around behind his desk
and stood there, glowering. "Just how exactly did you find
that out?"

Dani shrugged. "It doesn't matter—"

"Of course it matters!" Rick shot back. Anger surged
through him. "If you're keeping tabs on my financial deal-
ings, I want to know about it. Or is that something that's
done automatically anytime a man expresses an interest in
Danielle Winslow Hawthorne?"

"Don't be absurd!" Dani snapped, struggling to remain
calm. Somehow things were not going at all the way she'd
planned. "I'm not keeping tabs on you at all. If you must
know, Sabrina's dating Merry Terry Gleason, and the man
has a tendency to talk too much."

"Merry Terry...?" Rick frowned, then comprehension
dawned. "The loan officer from First Fairfield?"

"Exactly. He told her about a man who wanted to put up his polo ponies for collateral, and she put two and two together."

Rick's voice was quiet. "I suppose he also told her that he didn't give me the loan?"

Dani nodded. "That's why I came. I have the money you need, Rick. I'd like you to take it."

Rick turned away. He shoved his hands deep in his pockets and gazed out the window, seeing nothing of the view. Did she have any idea how badly he needed that money, he wondered, or how utterly impossible it would be for him to accept it from her?

In the past few weeks, he'd finally felt as though they were making headway—as though at last Dani was beginning to relax and trust him just a little. But that's all they'd had time for—a good beginning. To take money from her now would only reawaken her suspicions. Not only that, but it was bound to change the timbre of their relationship radically, and for the worse. There were many things he wanted from Dani Hawthorne, Rick reflected, but her money wasn't one of them.

Slowly he turned around to face her. "Thank you for the offer, Dani, but I can't accept."

She'd been expecting his refusal. Now was her chance to offer all the logical, well thought out reasons why he was wrong and she was right. Perversely Dani found herself leaping to her feet instead. "Of course you can!" she cried. "Look, it's very simple. I have more money than I need, and you have less. Perfect, we're made for each other!"

Perhaps if she hadn't phrased it quite that way, the offer wouldn't have struck such a sensitive chord. But suddenly, hearing her equate their finances with other aspects of their relationship, Rick knew exactly what she was doing. He couldn't imagine why he hadn't seen it sooner.

He knew enough about Dani to realize that she liked to be in control, and enough about her past relationships to know that she'd never relinquished that control before. She'd resisted him on many fronts, yet he'd still been foolish enough to believe that some of the barriers had come down. He understood now, with sudden clarity, that she'd never really stopped resisting at all.

"It bothered you when the balance of power shifted, didn't it?" he said quietly.

Immediately, on reflex, Dani's chin came up. "I don't know what you're talking about."

"Don't you?" Rick muttered. "Then let me spell it out for you. As far as you were concerned, everything was fine as long as you were calling the shots. But you gave up some of that precious control of yours two weeks ago when we first made love. I know, because I made it happen. You're not on top in this relationship anymore, but you want to be."

Dani's eyes widened in outrage. "That's not true!"

"Don't try to kid yourself, Dani, or me. I've been in business long enough to recognize a power play when I see one."

"That's not what this is at all!"

"No?" Rick said skeptically. "Let me see then, were you simply planning to give me that money—donate it, perhaps, like you would to a favorite charity?"

"No, of course not," Dani said quickly. She could see the problem with that line of questioning right off.

"Then perhaps you'd rather buy a share in the company?"

That was even worse. Dani drew herself back haughtily, refusing to examine her motives. She had no intention of standing still for an interrogation.

"Well?"

"I was thinking in terms of a loan," she said, her voice clipped.

"Secured?"

"If you wish. It really doesn't matter to me." Dani's angry gaze nailed him. All this time he'd spent talking about how she had to learn to believe in him, and now when it came right down to it, he was the one who wouldn't believe in her! "I trust you, Malone."

The barb struck home, just as it was intended to. Rick winced visibly. "I'm sorry, Dani," he said again. "But I can't take your money."

"Oh," Dani said in a small voice. She gathered her purse and prepared to leave. "Then I guess I'm beginning to understand."

"Understand what?"

Dani wanted to feel anger. Sadness came instead. "This love you profess to feel is a curious thing. It only works one way. It's fine as long as you're the only one doing the giving, right?" Turning away from the wounded look she saw on Rick's face, Dani strode from the room.

"Dani, wait!" Scrambling around the desk, Rick caught her at the door to the outer office. "Let me ask you something."

She stood, her nod barely imperceptible.

"How do you feel every year when those big splashy presents your father sends arrive on your birthday?"

Dani grimaced. "Like I wish I could make him understand that the last thing I want from him is his damn money!"

"Exactly," Rick said quietly.

"But this is different—" Dani began.

Rick shook his head. "Your offer is very generous, princess. I wish I could accept it. But I can't."

"I'm only trying to help," Dani insisted.

"And I'm only trying to keep my sanity," Rick returned. "If you really want to help, then just stay by my side. Everything else will work itself out, believe me."

"If that's what you want..." Dani's voice trailed away uncertainly. Though she still didn't agree with his decision, at least she was beginning to understand what had prompted it.

"It is." Rick lowered his head to hers as he pulled her into his arms for a kiss. When they parted, both were smiling.

"Go on," he said, pushing her toward the door. "Get out of here. I've got work to do. The last thing I need is a distraction like you hanging around the office."

"Okay, I'm going." Dani laughed. "Will I see you tonight?"

"Count on it." Rick's eyes were warm with promise, a promise he intended to keep.

AT THE END OF THE WEEK when Dani learned through an ad in the *Chronicle* that Rick had put Trigger up for sale, she didn't stop to think, she merely acted. The gelding meant a great deal to him, almost as much as Charm had to her; and now she was determined not to let Malone do something he would later regret. Immediately she placed a call to a bloodstock agent she'd dealt with in the past.

"I know the pony," Morey said. "Saw him down in Arizona. He's good, and he's gonna cost you."

"Pay it," Dani said firmly. "Whatever he's asking. I don't want any haggling about the price."

"You don't want to haggle," Morey told her, "you might as well deal direct."

"Not this time, Morey. I want you to make the buy. And make absolutely sure he has no idea who the client is."

"If you say so..." Dani could visualize his shrug. "When do you want to take delivery?"

"I don't."

"Run that by me again, doll. We must have a bad connection."

"Tell him you're buying the pony for a real greenhorn who wants a mount with plenty of high-goal experience. Say you'll only buy on the condition that he play the pony himself for the rest of the year."

"You sure you know what you're doing?" Morey sounded dubious.

"Positive," Dani replied. She hung up the receiver and smiled, glowing with satisfaction. It would have killed Malone to let that pony go; she just knew it. And now he wouldn't have to. Eventually, of course, she'd have to figure out a way to break the news to him about what she'd done. But that came later. For the time being, what Malone didn't know wasn't going to hurt either of them.

Chapter Twelve

The following Thursday Dani had a job to do that she'd been dreading for the past two weeks. That afternoon Missy Johnson would return from her family's annual vacation in the mountains, and Dani would have to tell her about what had happened to Charm.

In the beginning she'd put Missy on the gelding because she trusted him implicitly, and knew that he would never do anything to injure his young rider. As time passed, a bond had grown up between the handicapped little girl and the fuzzy pinto pony—a bond not unlike the one Dani had shared with him herself. She knew how much his death was going to hurt Missy and could only hope that the surprise she'd planned would blunt the edge of that pain.

Dani was standing just inside the barn door, making sure everything was ready, when Celia Johnson found her.

"Missy's waiting in the car," Celia said. "I told her I had to run on ahead for a minute."

Dani nodded, preparing herself for what was to come. She wouldn't have intentionally hurt Missy for anything. Now she had no choice. "I'm all set. If you don't mind, I think I'll go out and talk to her alone."

"Whatever you think is best." Celia looked at the small pinto pony standing in the cross-tie, a large red bow looped around its neck. "Missy will be enthralled," she said softly.

"I hope so."

Celia reached out and laid a comforting hand on Dani's arm. "Don't worry. She'll do better than you think. She may be young, but even at her age she's already had to learn a lot of hard lessons."

"I know. Maybe that's why I want to soften this blow so badly."

Celia ran a hand down the pony's brown-and-white neck. "You're being very generous," she said slowly. "I don't want to sound ungrateful, but I do want you to understand that it isn't really necessary. Missy will be upset about Charm, but in time she'll get over it. This isn't something you have to do."

"It's something I want to do," Dani said quietly. She thought of the shy little girl with the big blue eyes, and then of another shy little girl, so long ago. Though their burdens had been very different, in a way, they also had a lot in common. "For Missy, and also for myself."

Celia smiled. "Go on out to the car, then. She's waiting for you."

Dani crossed the lot to the Johnsons' station wagon. She opened the front door, then crouched down so that she and Missy were at eye level. "Hi," she said brightly, "how are you today?"

"I'm fine," Missy replied. "And I'm ready to go riding." With effort, she angled her brace-covered legs toward the open door, then looked around the stable yard eagerly. "Where's Charm?"

Dani drew a deep, uncomfortable breath. "I'm afraid I have some bad news," she said slowly. "While you were away, Missy, Charm had an accident."

The little girl's eyes grew large. "Was he hurt?"

Dani nodded. "He was hurt very badly," she said gently.

It was a moment before Missy spoke. When she did, her voice was soft, hesitant, as though she already knew the answer to the question she was going to ask. "He's going to be okay, isn't he?"

A lump gathered in Dani's throat as she shook her head. "I'm so sorry, Missy," she whispered, her voice cracking. "We had to put him to sleep."

Dani swallowed heavily as she watched the little girl's lower lip begin to tremble. She reached into the car and gathered Missy into her arms, hugging her close. A month ago she'd have held back, Dani realized; a month ago she'd have been able to. Now she felt Missy's pain as though it were her own.

"Poor Charm," Missy sniffled, her cheeks wet with tears. "He was my very favorite pony in the whole world."

"He was my favorite pony in the whole world, too," Dani agreed. She pulled a handkerchief from the pocket of her jeans and tenderly wiped the little girl's cheeks. "And I'll miss him just as much as you will."

Missy looked up with a child's curiosity. "Did it hurt?"

"I don't think so. It happened very quickly."

"Oh," Missy said solemnly. "I'm glad." Then a sudden thought struck her. "Does that mean I can't go riding anymore?"

"Not at all," Dani said quickly. "In fact, there's a new pony here today, just for you."

"Where?" Missy craned her head, looking around.

"He's in the barn." Dani rose to her feet. "I'll go get him." Then she turned and saw that it wasn't necessary. Rick was standing in the doorway, and now, seeing his cue, he led the pinto pony with the big red bow out to the car.

Missy gasped, clapping her hands in delight. "He looks just like Charm!" she cried.

"And he's very friendly," said Dani, "just like Charm was. He's been waiting here all day just to give you a ride."

Working together, Rick and Dani got Missy out of the car and up into the saddle. "What's his name?" the little girl asked, fingering the big red bow.

Dani grinned. "I'd say that was up to you. After all, he's your pony."

"Mine?" Missy's face lit with wonder. "My very own pony?"

"Uh-huh." Dani didn't trust herself to speak as Missy leaned down and gave the pony a hug, burying her face in his silky mane. When the little girl straightened, her eyes were shining.

"Really?" Missy asked again. "He's really mine?"

"He really is," Celia Johnson confirmed, coming up behind them. "You can ride him as often as you like. And when you're not here, he's going to go home and live at Dani's house with her other ponies."

"Oh, boy!" Missy cried. "My very own pony! Wait until I tell Matilda Grace!"

"What are you going to call him?" asked Rick.

Missy turned to Dani, looking suddenly shy. "Would it be all right if I called him Charm, too?"

Dani fought the urge to sniffle, and lost. "I don't see why not," she said, smiling. "In fact, I think my Charm would be very pleased to know that a namesake of his was looking after you."

Missy rode the pony into the ring, where one of the assistants began the lesson. When she was sure everything was running smoothly, Dani turned back to Rick.

Sunlight washed over him, striking blue highlights in his dark hair. His skin was bronzed from being outdoors, and he looked strong, fit and utterly male. Her gaze lowered, and Dani's eyes were drawn from his muscular forearms to the long-fingered hands that gripped the fence.

Malone's strength was evident; his gentleness less so. Yet both were an integral part of his makeup. Without one, she realized suddenly, the other wouldn't have been nearly so compelling.

"That was a wonderful thing you did," Rick said, breaking into her thoughts. He nodded toward the ring. "That little girl in there is positively glowing."

Dani shrugged, unwilling to show how much his praise meant. "Missy's a wonderful child. She doesn't need my help, but that doesn't stop me from wanting to give it anyway."

"I know just what you mean."

Surprised by his tone, Dani glanced up. "Do you?"

Rick's hand slid across the top of the fence to cover hers. "You don't need my help either, princess. But that doesn't mean I can stay away."

Dani considered that for a moment. "Why did you come here this afternoon, Rick?"

"Actually, there were two reasons."

Dani's brow lifted.

"The first was to provide you with some moral support."

"But how did you know...?"

Rick shrugged. "I watched you teach the class a couple of weeks ago, remember? It wasn't hard to see what Missy meant to you, or to guess that you were going to have a hard time telling her about Charm."

To Dani's surprise she felt a sudden urge to sniffle all over again. How many people did she know who would go out of their way to be there for her without expecting anything in return? She could count the number on the fingers of one hand. The more she knew about him, the more it became obvious that Rick Malone was one of a kind.

"Thank you," she said sincerely. "I appreciate the thought."

Rick nodded. "Although as things turned out, I was superfluous," he said, sounding just the slightest bit disappointed. "You handled everything beautifully."

Dani didn't stop to wonder why she wanted to offer Malone reassurance. What she was about to say was the truth—a truth he deserved to hear. "Maybe I didn't need you," she said slowly, "but still it was nice to know that you were here."

Rick felt a warm glow of pleasure at her words. Slowly but surely, he thought, it was happening. "Why, Dani," he drawled teasingly. "Don't tell me you're getting soft in your old age?"

"Who, me?" Sentimentality vanished; spirit took its place. Rick relished the transformation. "Never! Now quit wasting my time, Malone, and tell me the second reason you're here."

"That's easy. The second reason I came was to provide you with a bit of moral support."

Dani gazed up at him with a frown. "Haven't we covered that already?"

"Yes," said Rick, flashing her a teasing grin. "And no."

"Why do I have the feeling we're about to play twenty questions?"

"Shall I make things easy on you?"

"Try it," Dani advised. "Surprise us both. I'll probably keel over from shock."

"The selection committee made their final decision this morning. Jim Lynch called to tell me that they'd be posting the names of the team members for the Challenge Cup this afternoon."

"This afternoon?" Dani glanced at her watch. "When?"

"They're probably up on the bulletin board right now."

"Now?" Dani cried. "And you let me stand around down here talking?"

Rick knew better than to be surprised by the doubled fist that punched his shoulder. He turned into the blow, and it glanced off harmlessly.

"You louse! How could you not tell me!"

"I'm telling you now," he said calmly. "Shall we go up and see what it says?"

A stroll would have gotten them to the clubhouse in five minutes, a jog in three. Dani and Rick made it in two. Flushed and laughing, they skidded to a halt outside the locker rooms where a cork bulletin board held all important announcements.

Dani's gaze skimmed quickly over the selection. She frowned at a notice saying that a salad bar was now being offered in the Grill, and scowled over a For Sale sign for a used Kawasaki.

"There," Rick said, pointing. His fingers grasped hers and squeezed.

Dani began to read aloud. "This year, the Silverbrook Hunt Club will serve as host for the upcoming Fairfield Challenge Cup. In accordance with this honor, blah, blah, blah..." She skipped through until she came to the section she sought. "After long and careful deliberation, we the Silverbrook Selection Committee have chosen the following players to represent us in this tournament: Rick Malone, Jim Lynch, Trip Malloy, and—" she finished slowly, her voice hushed with awe "—Dani Hawthorne!"

"I did it!" Dani squealed, jumping up in the air. She landed in Rick's arms, and he swung her around in an exuberant circle. "I made the team!"

"Congratulations!" Rick's lips closed over hers, then Dani was pulling away once more.

"That does say Dani Hawthorne, doesn't it?" she asked. Feeling suddenly unsure, she leaned in to peer at the notice closely.

Rick leaned in with her. "It certainly does."

Together they read the fine print. The four players named had been chosen as a starting team. Harley Greer had been named as an alternate player in case any of the first string should fail to play well.

"I can't believe it." Dani exhaled softly. "I can't believe it really happened."

"I, of course," Rick said smugly, "never doubted you for a minute."

"Not even *one* minute?" Dani teased. Now that the weeks of waiting were over, she felt giddy with relief. "Not even when that wide pass of mine during the Boulder Brook game got picked off for the winning goal?"

Staunchly Rick shook his head.

"Or that time a few weeks ago when I was looking back over my shoulder, rode Ringo straight into the goalpost and nearly knocked myself silly?"

His lips began to twitch.

"Or maybe that day when I hooked Harley's waistband with my stick and pulled him right out of the saddle?"

"All right," Rick allowed. "Maybe once or twice you did manage to shake my faith, just a little."

"There's nothing like an honest man," Dani said with a sigh. She slid an arm around Malone's waist as they strolled down the corridor.

"Speaking of honesty..."

She glanced up.

"Just where exactly was that stick of yours aiming when it pulled Harley off his pony and dumped him on the ground?"

Dani grinned wickedly. "Why, straight for Harley, of course."

OVER THE WEEKEND, vans began to arrive carrying the teams of polo ponies from all up and down the East Coast. Excitement filled the air, and with it, a heady sense of expectation. Dani had thought she'd relax after the team selections had been made. Now she found that the tension was only beginning. And nobody, from the players to the Silverbrook officials, to the lowliest hotwalkers, was immune.

Even Malone, who was normally unflappable, seemed on edge. The realization puzzled Dani. She knew most of the players who would be in attendance, and he possessed more experience in this sort of match play than any of them. It couldn't be the tournament that was getting to him, she decided. But if not that, then what else could possibly be the matter?

On Sunday afternoon, the day before the first round was due to begin, she found him in the Grill, sitting uncharacteristically by himself. "Mind if I join you?" Dani asked. Taking his acceptance for granted, she slipped into the booth beside him and plunked her bottle of cold beer down on the table.

"I'm glad you're here," said Rick. His tone was flat, devoid of emotion. Despite his words, he sounded anything but glad to see her. "Actually I was just about to come and find you."

"Really?" Dani asked, feeling suddenly wary. "Why?"

"I had an interesting phone call the other day from Joe Matlock. You remember him, don't you?"

Cautiously Dani nodded. She'd seen the look on Malone's face when he'd glanced up, and it had been every bit as remote as his voice. She'd never seen him when he was really angry before, but she'd always figured he was the type to blow cold rather than hot. And the feeling coming from him now was positively chilling.

"We had a nice chat about some information he found out, but I asked him for a few more facts. He got back to me this morning. Of course you remember that cash flow problem I was having?"

"Uh-huh." Prudence told her not to say a word until she saw where the conversation was going.

"And, of course, you were aware that I put Trigger up for sale to cover it?"

Dani started to nod, then quickly thought better of it. They'd never discussed Trigger's sale before. Maybe she was better off feigning ignorance. Undecided, she settled for a noncommittal grunt.

"Come on, Dani, you can do better than that," Rick growled. "Especially for a horse you paid fifty thousand dollars for."

Dani's head snapped up. So much for ignorance, she thought, swallowing heavily. "How did you find out?"

Rick's brows drew together in a frown. Even though the evidence had pointed overwhelmingly in Dani's direction, he'd still nurtured the hope that Joe was wrong. Now, even that small prospect was gone.

"When Joe saw the ad I'd placed, apparently his first thought was to buy Trigger for himself. Imagine his surprise when he found out that the horse had been sold the very same day it went on the market, to a woman who paid full price, yet never even asked to see him, much less have him vetted out!"

That had been a mistake, Dani realized belatedly. Of course handling the transaction that way would be bound to cause questions. At the time she'd been so anxious to make sure that nobody else got the gelding before she did that she hadn't stopped to think things through. Now obviously it was time to pay for the omission.

"I'll say one thing for Joe," Rick continued. "When something gets his curiosity up, there's no holding him back. And this time he didn't stop asking questions until he had enough answers to figure out exactly what was going on. When he did, Joe—being Joe—called me up to congratulate me on just how well I had you wrapped around my little finger. Except that I didn't have the slightest idea what he was talking about!''

Rick's glare was hard, flat, undeniably angry. ''Bu. I bet you would've, wouldn't you, princess? Because you're a master at tying people up in knots and getting them to do exactly what you want.''

''Wait a minute!'' Dani cried. ''It wasn't like that at all!''

''Oh, no?'' Rick's frown was skeptical. ''I told you I didn't want your money, Dani, and I meant it. I'm willing to give you the benefit of the doubt. If you weren't trying to interfere in my life, then I'd like to know just what exactly was going on.''

She'd known it would come to this, sooner or later. It was just that she hadn't expected a confrontation so soon, or so suddenly. She'd thought she'd have time to prepare. Yet now, looking at the implacable expression on Rick's face, she sensed he wasn't going to want to hear anything about her good intentions.

''How do you know I wasn't just trying to buy a good polo pony?'' she asked, throwing out the first idea that came to mind.

Rick's gaze narrowed. ''If that's so, why didn't you approach me directly?''

This question, at least, she could answer. ''Because I didn't think you'd sell to me.''

''You're right,'' Rick said shortly. ''I wouldn't have.''

''You see!'' cried Dani. ''I was right to let Morey make the deal.''

''What you really mean,'' Rick said harshly, ''is that you think you were right in trying to manipulate my life!''

''Don't put words in my mouth!''

''Princess, I don't have to. You're doing a fine job of it all by yourself.''

Dani felt a fury building inside her. She'd only been trying to help. Why couldn't he understand that? ''I wasn't trying to manipulate you, Malone. I don't give a damn what you do with the money. For all I care, you can throw it out the nearest window.''

"You really don't understand, do you?" Rick asked quietly. "You haven't the slightest idea what I'm talking about."

Stubbornly Dani remained silent. She'd known he was bound to be upset, but she hadn't envisioned anything like this. Malone looked ready to chew nails.

For a long moment Rick was silent as well. Finally he sighed softly. "You're tough, all right, princess, I'll give you that. But one day you'll realize that sometimes it takes more courage to give in gracefully than it does to insist on always having your own way. I only hope I'm still around by the time you figure that out."

"Malone, listen to me—"

"No," Rick said firmly, "I've done enough listening. Now it's your turn. I won't kowtow to you, Dani. Either you accept me for what I am, an equal partner in this relationship, or else . . ."

Dani glared at him incredulously. "Or else what?" she pushed.

Rick's expression was grim as he rose from the table. "Or else I guess I'll just have to accept the fact that the differences between us are greater than our ability to overcome them."

Damn it! thought Dani, watching him leave. Why did he have to be so pigheaded? Talk about manipulation! He was the one who had twisted it all—her actions, her words, everything!

She snorted softly in frustration. Was it her fault she had a tendency to take charge? She'd seen something that needed doing, and she'd done it. Was that so awful?

A minute passed, and then another. With a small sigh, Dani glanced over at the empty doorway. Maybe what she'd done wasn't so awful, but now that she stopped and thought about it, it didn't seem terribly admirable either. Whether she'd meant to or not, she'd found Malone's weakness and exploited it. He'd threatened the calm, orderly tenor of her life, and she'd retaliated by using his own needs against him.

Malone had told her he hadn't wanted her help, but she'd refused to listen. She was so used to being in control that she'd never given his rights a moment's thought. He was right to demand equality, because she'd been guilty of treating him like a child.

Dani rose from the table quickly. If there was one thing she hated, it was admitting she'd been wrong. But this time she had no choice. She'd pushed Malone too far. In his place, she'd have reacted every bit as strongly. He was an adult, he could make his own decisions. And if he wanted to sell one of his ponies, that was his business. She had no right to interfere. It was time to offer an apology.

BY THE TIME DANI headed over to Rick's condominium late that afternoon, she had planned her mission with care. A grocery bag on the seat beside her held two thick filet mignons, several ears of fresh picked corn and all the makings for a salad. Nestled near the top was a container holding her secret weapon—a pint of the cook's incredible béarnaise sauce. Malone might be able to resist her, but Dani would bet anything that he wouldn't be able to turn down the meal she was going to prepare.

She carried the heavy bag up the steps, rang Rick's doorbell, then waited. And waited. When he finally appeared several minutes later, he didn't seem the slightest bit pleased to see her. "I'm working," he said shortly. The sheaf of papers he held in his hand bore testimony to his claim. "What do you want?"

"I came to apologize," Dani announced. "But first I came to cook. I always grovel better on a full stomach." She breezed past him and headed toward the kitchen. "Don't let me disturb your work. I'll call you when dinner's ready."

Rick frowned after her. "I thought you told me you didn't know how to cook."

Dani smiled back over her shoulder. "This is an easy meal. A child could do it."

"And I'd have thought for damn sure that Danielle Winslow Hawthorne didn't grovel!"

This time she threw him a wink. "I guess you'll just have to wait till after dinner to find out, won't you?" She'd expected him to go back to his study, but to Dani's surprise Rick followed her to the kitchen.

He watched as she unpacked the bag, lining up her supplies on the counter. She looked perfectly at home in his kitchen, he realized, just as she did on the back of a polo pony or dressed to kill in silk and diamonds. For the time being he decided not to question why she was there; it was enough that she had come.

"If you're going to stand around," Dani said, "you may as well make yourself useful. How are you at shucking corn?"

"Ah, shucks, ma'am," Rick drawled. "I'm the best."

Laughing, Dani threw him an ear. "I should have known."

They worked together to prepare the meal, swapping utensils and trading gibes. When it was ready to eat, the companionable mood persisted, helped along by a bottle of Bordeaux and a desire on both their parts to put the morning's unpleasantness behind them. But when the food was gone, and the kitchen cleaned up, Dani knew it was time to get down to the business that had brought her to Rick's in the first place.

"Have I lulled you into a receptive frame of mind?" she asked as he sat down on the couch beside her.

"That depends." Rick's arm rested along the back of the cushion, his fingers tangling in her hair. "What did you have in mind?"

"This is serious," Dani said firmly. Clearly unimpressed, the fingers began to massage the back of her neck. "I came over here this evening to apologize."

"I'm ready." Rick's eyes twinkled. "Any time."

"You were right this afternoon. I never should have interfered."

"And?"

Dani looked at him in surprise. "And what?"

"You've admitted I was right. Now aren't you going to tell me you were wrong?"

Dani frowned at the way he'd cut straight to the heart of the matter. He knew her entirely too well. "I wasn't really wrong," she hedged.

"Oh?"

"Maybe just a little misguided."

"Keep going," said Rick. "You're getting warmer."

"Give me a break! I don't have much practice at this sort of thing, all right?"

"I'll just bet you don't."

Dani growled softly in frustration. "All right, here it is. I was wrong, okay? You're a grown man. If you want to do something stupid, you have every right."

"Forget what I said about getting warmer. If that's the apology, I think I'd have just as soon gone without it."

"Your choice." Dani smiled sweetly.

Like hell, thought Rick. When, since meeting Dani, had he ever had any choices? When had he wanted any? It was time, he decided, for a confession of his own.

"When I found out this morning what you'd done," he said, "my first response was to be angry as hell."

"So I noticed," Dani muttered. She leaned into the hand that was now insinuating its way inside her blouse to trace the line of her collarbone.

"But my second," Rick continued, "was pure relief that Trigger hadn't actually been sold to some greenhorn. I'm very pleased he went to you, princess. I know you'll treat him every bit as well as he treats you."

"Maybe," Dani murmured noncommittally. "If I choose to take delivery."

"Why wouldn't you?"

Dani shrugged. "You know how it is, Malone. Those extra mouths add up. Plenty of things could happen by the end of the season. Who knows? I may decide I don't need an extra polo pony, after all."

Rick's expression warmed. "Why you little devil!"

"Name-calling, Malone?" Dani smiled. She held up one hand, her forefinger beckoning. "I dare you to come over here and say that."

"A dare is a dangerous thing," Rick muttered, moving to close the space between them. "It could get you into trouble."

"I certainly hope so." Dani sighed. She held open her arms, and Rick moved into them.

Dani's eyelids fluttered shut as Rick's mouth lowered to hers. The touch of his lips was warm and firm. Their mouths moved together as Rick shifted his weight to settle her across his thighs. Dani's lips parted, and his tongue slipped inside, probing then retreating with a seductive intimacy that stole her breath away.

Dani moaned softly. Her body felt suffused with warmth. A tremor of urgency, of awakening need, rippled through her. Her hands dropped to the front of his shirt, reaching for the top button.

Rick drew back to gaze down upon her. He caught her fingers in his, holding them still. "We'll be more comfortable in bed," he said.

"Don't you know I'd follow you anywhere?" Dani asked. Her voice was light, teasing, then all at once a lump gathered in her throat as she realized the truth of what she had said. "At least," she amended quickly, nuzzling his neck, "anywhere I wanted to go."

She felt Rick's quiet laughter as a rumble in his chest. "That's what I thought," he said.

Cradling her in his arms, he rose from the couch and strode down the hall to his bedroom. He lowered her to her feet beside the bed. Dani reached for Rick's shirt and slid it off his shoulders. Her own followed it to the floor. Their gazes locked, eyes watching each other avidly as the hunger built between them. Quickly Rick pulled off the rest of his clothes, then reached to help Dani with hers.

The moment he touched her, Dani felt desire soar. His hands cupped her hips, easing her pants downward. His fingers teased the length of her thighs. "Hurry," Dani whispered, consumed with yearning. The feeling was hot and heavy and beyond her control. She flew with the sensation, reveling in it.

Dani lay down on the bed, then held out a hand for Rick. For a moment he didn't move at all, but simply stood, gazing down upon her. Even lying still she was a picture of grace. Her body was long and lean but in no way boyish. The muted light in the bedroom drew delectable shadows on the lush curve of her breasts, the gentle swell of her hips.

His love, Rick thought, smiling. His woman. He reached for her hand and grasped it warmly. Dani's gaze drifted upward. Her smile met his own. He lay down beside her on the bed.

Rick folded her into his embrace, their bodies touching from shoulder to thigh. At once, the tempo began to spiral.

Dani's senses were filled with Rick: the taste, the feel, the scent of him. His hands stroked a tingling trail down the smooth skin of her body; his lips followed. His mouth closed over the taut peak of her breast, sucking gently, and Dani cried out, arching toward him. His fingers drifted lower, tracing the jutting bone of her hip, then closed over the nest of silky blond curls below.

With the gentle movement of his fingers, Dani felt herself sliding toward oblivion. Drawing a ragged breath, she brought herself back. She lifted her hand, then drew her tongue slowly down its length, moistening it. Then she reached for him.

Rick shuddered as her fingers closed around him. He growled something inaudible, and Dani smiled. This time, she vowed, was for both of them.

For a long time afterward she lay spent, her body warm, glowing, pulsing with tiny tremors. If only, Dani mused, this was all there was. If only they didn't have to think, to fight, to want such very different things.

"I could be happy," she murmured contentedly, "if I never left this bed again."

"No you couldn't," Rick said with a laugh.

Dani raised herself on her arms to look down into his face. "You don't think you could keep me satisfied?" she asked lightly.

Rick shook his head. "I know you too well to even try. You'd never be satisfied with less than everything life has to offer."

"I don't know." Dani shook her head, frowning. When she spoke, her voice was soft. "For a while I thought maybe I could be."

"And now?"

Dani looked down into Rick's eyes. "Now sometimes I don't know what to think."

"That's a start," Rick said quietly.

"Is it?" Dani asked. "Sometimes I wonder if I wasn't better off before."

Rick sighed. Part of him wanted to lie back, to be content simply to bask in the afterglow of what they had shared. But another part demanded that he speak up. Because the more they shared, the greedier he became. He had Dani's body. It only made him want her heart and mind all the more. His hands came up, his palms shaping the sides of her face. What he was about to say wouldn't be easy. Not for either of them.

"I know you've been hurt. And I'm sorry. But it happens," he said slowly. "It happens to everyone. I was barely a teenager when my father died. Irrational as it was, I felt as though he'd deserted me. I hurt so badly I thought I'd never trust anyone that way again. Maybe that's why when Ben died the pain was even greater. Because that time I knew better. I could have avoided it if I'd wanted to. But as bad as the hurt was, I was never sorry. Ben enriched my life, just as my father had, just as you do."

"You don't understand," Dani said raggedly. "My parents didn't leave me because they had to. I might have understood that. But they had a choice, and they chose not to care. After a while..." Her voice faded away, then came back stronger. "After a while, so did I."

"But you do care, Dani." Rick's gaze came up, hard and determined. "You can't tell me that you don't."

"I—"

"Coward," Rick breathed softly.

Dani's breath drew inward on a gasp; her eyes were haunted. "All right," she said finally, "I care about you, Malone. Is that what you wanted to hear? But I don't love you."

"Yes, you do, princess," Rick said quietly. He gathered her into his arms. "You're just too stubborn to admit it."

Dani lay nestled against his hard chest until the steady cadence of Rick's breathing told her that he had fallen asleep. Then she sighed quietly. What were the chances, she wondered, that he could possibly be right?

Chapter Thirteen

The next morning the Fairfield Challenge Cup began. Eighteen teams had entered the two-week-long competition, with the excitement building until a week from Saturday when the finals would be played before a large audience. With the addition of Rick to the roster, Silverbrook fielded one of the strongest teams. As expected, they breezed through the first week, besting their competition in the early rounds by a comfortable margin.

Immersed in the competition, Dani found that she was spending nearly every waking moment at the club. She rose at dawn, dressed quietly and slipped out of the house, often not returning until well after dark. It wasn't surprising, therefore, that she hadn't seen Preston for almost a week, when she slept late one morning and ran into him over breakfast. Once again, to her dismay, he was sulking.

"Coffee, miss?" Preston asked distractedly. He sighed loudly as he delivered the cup to the table. "Cream? Sugar?"

Dani frowned up at him. "Preston, you know very well I take my coffee black."

"Yes, miss." Another sigh heaved through his large frame. "Perhaps I might join you in a cup?"

"Of course." Dani jumped up and pulled out a chair. "In fact, why don't you sit down and I'll pour?" Fiddling with the coffeepot, she watched as the butler settled his bulk into a miserable heap on the chair. It was a sure sign of trouble when Preston went so far as to forget all about the basic tenets of good posture.

"There." Dani handed him his coffee and sat beside him. "Now why don't you tell me all about it?"

"There isn't much to tell." Preston measured four teaspoons of sugar into the cup, then added a generous dollop of cream. "Victoria said no."

"No, what?" Remembering how he'd muffed his last shot at proposing, Dani realized there was a distinct possibility that the butler still hadn't tendered a recognizable offer.

"She won't come. I wrote to her just like you said, but she turned me down cold."

Dani's brow furrowed. She hadn't even considered that possibility. "Why would she do something like that?"

Preston shrugged heavily. "Victoria said that what we had years ago was wonderful, but that love was for youngsters and starry-eyed romantics. She seemed to think that she was much too old to be getting involved in all that nonsense again."

So Victoria was the practical type. Dani certainly couldn't fault her for that. But that didn't mean that she was going to stand by and watch while Preston got hurt.

"I'm so sorry." She reached out and put an arm around the butler's shoulder. "Is there anything I can do?"

Dani had thought this latest setback would have left Preston beaten. It took only a moment, however, for her to see how wrong she was. Rather than giving in to it, the adversity seemed to have strengthened the butler's resolve.

"Actually," he said, brightening, "I did have an idea."

"Go on." Dani grinned with relish. At that point she'd have agreed to just about anything, including booking seats for both of them on British Airways.

"Suppose I were to write and tell Victoria that you were getting married. I could imply that there'd been an...um, indiscretion committed and say that you'd be requiring her services shortly. I've told her so much about you, you see. I'm sure she'd be tickled by the opportunity."

Dani's mouth fell open in shock. "You mean, you want to lie to Victoria?"

The butler's expression was pained. "It's only a very small lie."

"Small, my foot!" Dani snorted. "How would you explain what you'd done when she arrived and saw that things were not at all what she'd been led to believe?"

"By that time it wouldn't make any difference," Preston said earnestly. Clearly he'd given the matter a great deal of thought. "As soon as we see each other again, I'm sure she'll remember how good things were for us once. After that—" he paused, clearing his throat delicately "—we'll simply let nature take its course."

Dani took a deep breath, and then another. "Tell me something, Preston," she said finally. "It *has* been a long time. Are you absolutely certain about your feelings for Victoria?"

"Yes." The butler's nod was firm. "And I'm certain of her feelings, too. No woman would write two letters a month to a man for ten years if she didn't care about him."

Dani frowned thoughtfully. How could he be so sure of what he felt? she wondered. Just like Malone, Preston claimed to be in love and to have no doubts at all about the matter. Whereas she, who wasn't in love, was plagued by qualms and confusion. She envied them both for the strength of their convictions. It seemed so easy for them to believe. Why was it so impossible for her?

"Am I to understand from your silence that you don't want to help?"

Looking up, Dani shook her head slowly. "I don't think you should start off a relationship with a lie," she said, and watched the butler's face fall. "But, yes, I do want very much to help. There must be another way to get Victoria to come. Just give me a little time to think about it, I'm sure we'll be able to come up with something."

"I sincerely hope so," Preston said with a sigh. He picked up his coffee and downed it in a gulp. "If this keeps up much longer, I won't be able to fit into any of my clothes at all."

"Good to see you, Rick. Glad you could make it."

"Bill." Rick held out his hand as Bill Walters rose from a mahogany desk and strode across his plushly carpeted office to greet him.

It was Tuesday of the second week of the Challenge Cup, and match play had moved into the quarterfinals. Still, Rick wouldn't have missed this meeting for anything. He'd submitted a proposal to UNICORP's board two weeks earlier. If they'd wanted to turn him down, he reflected, they could have done it over the phone. Instead, he'd been invited to meet with the company's chief financial officer. It had to be a good sign.

"Please, have a seat."

Rick sat in one of two burgundy leather wing chairs that faced the CFO's desk. He settled his briefcase on the floor beside his chair where his papers would be handy for easy reference.

"I've reviewed your proposal with my staff," Bill began. "We think it makes a lot of sense. Your suggestions for investment planning in our pension fund are excellent."

Rick nodded silently, waiting for the older man to continue. He realized he was sitting on the edge of his seat. With effort, he willed himself to sit back and cross his legs.

Bill Walters began to smile. "We'd like you to get started on the project as soon as possible. Congratulations, Rick, and welcome to the team."

"Thank you very much." Rick was amazed by how calm his voice sounded, betraying no hint of the excitement he felt inside. Emotions washed through him too quickly to count: relief, determination, gratitude, and finally, sheer exhilaration. "I look forward to working with you."

"We're sure you'll do a fine job. How soon can you get started?"

Rick pulled out his calendar and consulted it. There was no reason the CFO had to know that its pages were empty. "Would Monday be all right?"

"Fine. I'll have my people ready." Bill Walters rose and held out his hand. "We'll set up an office for you here."

"Good." Rick nodded as he grasped Bill's hand in his. "I'd like to be as close to the investment group as possible."

"No problem," Bill said heartily, walking Rick to the door. "We're prepared to offer you all the support you need."

Rick held his shoulders stiff, his back straight as he walked away down the hallway filled with executive offices. Riding the elevator downward, he permitted himself a small smile. By the time he crossed the reception lobby on the ground floor, it had turned into a broad grin. But it wasn't until he'd climbed into the Jeep and pulled the door securely shut behind him that he finally relaxed. A loud whoop of joy reverberated through the small compartment. Then he threw back his head and laughed out loud.

He'd done it, Rick thought. At last he'd landed the big one. Malone Inc. was finally on its way. Then all at once his mood sobered. Now there was only one thing standing between him and Dani, Rick realized. And that was Dani herself.

THAT AFTERNOON, when Rick told her about his new contract, Dani was every bit as thrilled as he had been. She knew how much the project meant to Malone, how badly he'd wanted to prove that he could make it on his own. Now she was genuinely pleased by his success. They spent Tuesday night celebrating, then Wednesday morning gearing up for the semifinal match Silverbrook was scheduled to play that afternoon.

Rick had watched their upcoming opponents in several of their earlier games, and now he knew what to expect. Only one of the players on the Blue Birch team was American. Of the remaining three, two were Argentine, and one French. Their ponies were Argentine-bred and pampas-trained. They were quick, wiry and tough as nails. The team had gotten as far as it had on a combination of lightning-fast play and a penchant for rough-and-tumble brawling. They would be tough to beat, and Rick knew it.

Determined not to let their opponents race off with an early advantage, the Silverbrook team went on the field for the first toss-in and came out fighting. The surprise worked in their favor. The first goal, scored at the end of the chukker, went to Jim.

That, however, only redoubled Blue Birch's efforts. By the time the game broke for halftime, two injured ponies had been led from the field; Trip Malloy had taken a ball in the ribs and been replaced by Harley; and Dani sported a bruise on the side of her calf where she'd received a rather vicious kick. The score was still one to zero.

During the next two chukkers, little changed. For once Dani found she was grateful for Harley's hair-raising style of play. Now that his aggression was channeled against a worthy opponent, she could almost appreciate the way he attacked the game as though it were a personal enemy he had to overcome.

The last chukker opened with Silverbrook still ahead.
Aware that they had only seven and a half minutes in which
to score, the Blue Birch team let loose with an attack that
made their earlier efforts seem tame. As the match hurtled
toward its conclusion, the Silverbrook players found their
talents strained to the limit. Rick, in particular, had his
hands full trying to contain the opposing number three
player, a hotheaded Argentine named Paulo.

Time and again Paulo marshaled his team, driving the
ball and his lathered pony toward the goal. And time and
again the four tired Silverbrook players were able to push
them back. Less than thirty seconds remained in the game
when Paulo made his last desperate attempt.

Rick was off to the other side, too far away to be of any
assistance when he saw the Argentine player pick off a pass
and send the ball flying downfield. Paulo's spurs gouged his
pony's sides, and the animal flattened to the ground in its
attempt to outrun the Silverbrook pursuers. Inch by inch,
it pulled away.

Even as Rick raced to block the goal, he knew he was too
late. He saw Paulo's teeth flash in a triumphant grin as the
Argentine swung his mallet upward. Then, incredibly, his
pony misjudged its footing. Rather than galloping alongside the ball, it overran, forcing Paulo to make a difficult
shot between its front hooves. The hit was neither clean nor
accurate. It sliced wide, flying harmlessly past the goal only
seconds before the horn blasted and the game was over.

On the other side of the field, Dani watched the wooden
ball roll to a stop, then slumped wearily in her saddle. Elation would come later. For now she needed all her strength
just to trot across the field and turn her tired pony over to
the hotwalkers. On the sidelines she dismounted, considered her options, then simply dropped where she stood—
beneath the tall, shady tree where the extra ponies were
tethered. For the time being she had neither the desire nor

the energy to move any farther. Working slowly, she pulled off her gloves, followed by her helmet and pads.

Moments passed while Dani closed her eyes and waited for the rejuvenation she knew would come. When eventually it did, she stood up and smiled. It was time to celebrate. She gathered up her equipment and was about to head off in search of the rest of the team when a flurry of furtive whispering among the hotwalkers caught her attention.

"It's Paulo's pony that's missing," she heard one of them say. "He didn't turn it in."

Another gave a nasty laugh. "He said it was to blame for making him miss the last shot. He's going to teach it a lesson."

Dani felt a chill that rippled the length of her spine. There was no mistaking what the hotwalkers had meant. Quickly she spun around to confront the boys who'd been speaking. "Where?" she demanded, her eyes hardening. "Where did Paulo go?"

One boy shrugged, but the other, the one who had laughed, now grinned broadly. If there was going to be trouble, he intended to be in on it. "Out behind the barns. He was carrying a big whip. I wouldn't want to be in that pony's shoes for anything."

I wouldn't either, Dani thought as she hurried around the clubhouse toward the barns. She didn't stop to consider the wisdom of what she was doing. She only knew that she had to act. Happy, Paulo possessed all the controlled energy of a firecracker about to explode. Angry, he was a menace she didn't even want to think about.

She'd topped the hill when she heard the sound of a high-pitched whinny that ended on a frightened squeal. Her fatigue forgotten, Dani began to run. It wasn't until she'd reached the back side of the last barn that she found them. The sight that awaited her made her blood boil.

Paulo's pony was rearing back wildly. Its ears were pinned, lying flat along its head; its eyes were rimmed with white. Paulo held the reins in one hand and a large leather whip in the other. His face was dark, contorted with rage. He was yelling, his voice harsh and guttural, in a language Dani didn't understand. As she watched, he raised his hand to strike.

"No!" Dani cried out. She ran toward them. "No, leave him alone!"

Paulo glanced back over his shoulder and swore viciously. Fury coursed through Dani's veins, and with it, adrenaline. "Damn you, Paulo!" she yelled, grabbing for the whip. "Stop it!"

Roughly he shook her off. "This is not your business," he snapped. "Do not interfere with things that are none of your concern."

"This does concern me," Dani shot back. "I refuse to let you abuse that horse!"

"Oh, no?" His teeth bared in a nasty grin. "And how do you propose to stop me?"

Paulo raised his arm once more. Dani didn't think, only reacted, as she thrust herself between the man and the horse. Surprise, then anger, flickered across the Argentine's face as she raised her arm to deflect the blow. She succeeded, but only partly. The thick leather thong slithered out of Dani's grasp, landing her a glancing blow across the cheek.

Automatically her hands came up. Quickly, defiantly, Dani struck back. She caught Paulo off guard, and he made no defense against her sharp punch and the flat-handed chop that followed. His face blanched, then grew slack as the combination sent him sprawling in the dirt.

The pony jerked back, wrenching the reins from Paulo's grasp. Immediately the animal galloped off down the road. Scowling murderously, the Argentine leaped to his feet.

Dani eyed him warily, ready, if need be, to finish what she had started.

Before he could retaliate, however, the rest of the players came streaming around the end of the barn. Two of his Blue Birch teammates leaped on Paulo, holding him back. The other took off after the fleeing pony.

"Dani!"

She heard the anguish in Rick's voice, and knew what she'd see before she even turned around. When she did, he was so close that she was enfolded directly into his arms.

For a long moment Rick was simply content to hold her, to reassure himself that she was all right. He'd never been so frightened in his entire life as he had been seconds before when he'd raced around the barn and seen Dani standing up to Paulo. Nor had he ever felt so helpless as when he realized he was too far away to prevent whatever was going to happen.

Now he should have been relieved that everything had turned out all right. Instead he was angry as hell. She was crazy, Rick decided. She had to be. Only a madwoman would take on Paulo Garcia; only a wonder woman would live to tell about it.

Aware of the curious glances from the other players, Dani disentangled herself gently from Rick's arms. She was glowing, flushed with satisfaction. "It's all right," she said, looking up at him. "I'm fine, really."

Letting her go, Rick stepped back. In the aftermath his body shook with reaction. He fought a battle to control his temper, and lost.

"It is not all right," he said furiously. "How could you have done such a stupid thing? Paulo is a maniac. Everybody knows that. Don't you realize what could have happened?"

"There was nothing else I could have done," Dani said quietly. Her eyes followed his to the bruise on her cheek. She knew he was hurting for her, perhaps even more than she hurt for herself. "You know what he would have done to that pony."

"I know what he could have done to you!"

"I had no choice," Dani stated firmly. "Besides, I knew what I was doing. I'm not a child."

"No, but that doesn't stop you from acting like one sometimes. Didn't it ever occur to you to go for help?"

"No," Dani said, because it hadn't. She was used to fighting her own battles. She'd seen nothing unusual in handling this one. "Anyway, there wasn't time."

"Dani." Her name slipped out with a quiet sigh. "When are you going to realize that you don't always have to take on the world alone? There are plenty of people who are willing to be on your side."

"People come and go, Malone."

Rick reached out and grasped her shoulders. His eyes met hers in a level stare. "I'm not going anywhere, princess."

The words washed over Dani like a warm wave. Deep inside, she felt a tiny wellspring of trust begin to grow. Rick's gaze was direct and unflinchingly honest. He offered her everything, holding back nothing at all. And she wanted so badly to believe him.

"We all need someone every now and then," he said softly. "It's nothing to be ashamed of."

Need? Dani thought wildly. That wasn't what she felt, nor what she wanted to feel. She might not be sure what love was, but she did know one thing: her love, when it came, would spring from strength, not weakness. An equal partner, wasn't that what Malone had said he wanted? Well, that was exactly what he was going to get!

"I don't need you, Malone," Dani said firmly. Immediately she saw by the look on his face that he'd misunderstood.

"The hell you don't!"

Then Rick looked at her, standing so tall and strong before him, and realized for the first time that he was wrong. She didn't need him, because everything she wanted was already hers. There was simply nothing more he could offer her. The knowledge burned inside his gut like fire.

Dani reached out to him. "Rick, you don't understand—"

He shrugged her hand away. "Yes, I do," he said grimly. "Finally I think I understand it all. It's just no good, Dani. No matter how hard I try, I can't make it work. We can never get past the fact that you can't offer me your love, and I can't offer you anything less."

Dani's mouth opened, then shut without saying a word. Much as she wanted to, she couldn't refute what he had said. Rick spun on his heel and strode away. She swore softly in frustration before flinging one last challenge into the air.

"I thought you said you weren't going anywhere, Malone!"

He stopped, then slowly turned. "There's a big difference between wanting to leave, and having to. Think about it. I'm sure you'll figure it out."

After that Dani was in no mood to hang around the club. Quickly she showered, changed and packed up her things. When she got home an hour later, Preston was waiting.

"Good," he said, nodding to himself as she came through the front door. "You're all right."

"Of course I'm all right, Preston," Dani said shortly. "Why wouldn't I be?"

"Mr. Malone called and asked me to look out for you." The butler eyed her with disapproval. "He mentioned something about an altercation with one of the other players, and said he wanted to be sure you got home safely."

Dani's brow rose faintly in surprise as she filed the information away for future consideration. "As you can see, I'm here and I'm all in one piece."

"Nothing short of a miracle, from what I hear."

"Oh?"

It was all the opening the butler needed. "Danielle, you know I don't like to interfere—"

Dani snorted under her breath.

"But I'm afraid I really must protest this untoward behavior of yours. I understand from Mr. Malone that you were involved in a brawl this afternoon."

"It wasn't my fault."

"Of course not. Nevertheless—"

"I know, Preston." Dani sighed. "Under the same circumstances, you probably would have reacted with the utmost decorum. But somehow it just didn't occur to me."

"Does it ever?" Preston asked dryly.

Dani considered for a moment. "No."

The butler's stance was rigid with reproach. "No matter what the provocation, a lady does not resolve her problems with her fists."

"Yes, Preston," Dani said meekly. She turned and started up the stairs.

"Nor her feet!"

"I'll try to keep that in mind."

"See that you do."

Nodding and muttering, Dani continued down the hall to her room. When she got there, she saw that Preston had been in to turn down the covers on her bed. All at once the idea seemed like just the thing for the weariness that assailed her.

Dani pulled off her clothes and tossed them over the back of a chair. Naked, she slipped between the cool covers. Her head lay cushioned in the soft pillow as she stared at the ceiling thoughtfully. So Malone had called to check on her?

The gesture was as charming as it was unexpected, and for some reason, she felt ridiculously touched.

When she'd last seen Malone, he'd been furious. And considering how he'd misunderstood what she'd been trying to say, she couldn't really blame him. Yet even blazingly angry, he'd still cared enough to look out for her welfare.

Slowly a feeling of warmth and contentment stole over her. Dani felt as she had when she was a tiny child, waiting for her mother to come up and tuck her into bed. It had been so long that, for a moment, she didn't recognize the emotion. Then all at once it came to her. She felt cherished. Yes, that was it.

Her face warmed with a radiant smile. She'd been given back another piece of her lost childhood, Dani realized. And Rick Malone was the man who had given it to her.

Chapter Fourteen

On Thursday afternoon, while Black Rock played in the other semifinal match, the Pegasus Program went on as usual. Though Dani could have handed the class over to an assistant, she chose not to. Staying busy served two purposes. First it kept her from worrying about Saturday's match. And second, it kept her from wondering what Malone was up to.

She'd spent the past twenty-four hours mulling over what he'd said. *You can't offer me your love, and I can't offer you anything less.* The words, and the sad acceptance in his voice when he'd said them, left an aching void deep inside. The worst part, Dani mused, was that he was right.

"Hey, cut it out!"

The angry cry brought Dani's thoughts back to the present with a jolt. Two of the ponies had managed to get themselves boxed into a corner of the ring, and one of their riders, a large boy named Ralph, was laughing as he shoved the other rider playfully.

"That's enough, Ralph!" Dani called as she hurried over to extricate them. "Come on, join the rest of the group."

By the time order was restored, it was almost time for the class to end. One by one, the children filed from the ring to hand their ponies over to the grooms. As usual, Missy hung back, waiting at the end of the line for Dani. Now, as Dani sauntered over to where Charm stood by the gate, she could hear the little girl talking with animation.

"Just you wait until we're done," she was saying. "I brought you a carrot, and an apple, too. I wanted to bring some sugar, but Mommy said it was bad for your teeth. That's what I told Matilda Grace, but I think she may have slipped some in anyway."

Dani's steps slowed, then stopped all together as Missy leaned down to give Charm an exuberant hug. The little girl's eyes were bright, her face flushed with happiness. The love she offered her new pony was unconditional, and in no way tarnished by the memory of the other pony she'd lost.

Enlightenment pierced through Dani like a shaft of golden light. Self-reproach followed close behind. Rick was right, she realized suddenly. She *was* a coward. Even Missy, whom fate had dealt with so unfairly, wasn't afraid to open her heart and try again. And if that little girl could still trust in the basic goodness of life, who was she to lack faith in the power of love?

"Come on, Dani, hurry up!" Missy called out. "Charm wants his carrot."

"Hold your horses, I'm coming."

"You mean, hold your pony," Missy corrected delightedly.

"Yes." Dani laughed. "You're absolutely right."

She helped the little girl to dismount, then settled her in her wheelchair. Missy held Charm's reins while Dani ran up the stirrups and pulled off his saddle. Then Dani went and fetched a halter, and the pony lowered his head so that Missy was able to slip the bridle off from behind his ears and ease the bit from his mouth.

"Can I give him his treat now?" Missy asked.

"Sure." Dani handed the little girl the end of the pony's lead rope. "And after that, if you like, you can help with his bath."

"Goody!" cried Missy, clapping her hands. She took the bag of carrots her mother held out to her and fed one to Charm.

"You're good for her," Celia said quietly. The two women walked together to the tack room to hang up Charm's saddle and bridle. "Most people talk down to Missy, or else they assume that because she has to sit in a wheelchair she can't possibly be any help at all."

"I don't see why," Dani said matter-of-factly. "Missy is one of the most self-reliant children I know. She doesn't seem to let anything get in her way. Look how she's bounced back from Charm's death. I was afraid she'd be devastated. Yet, looking at her now—" she nodded over to where Missy was feeding the pinto his third carrot "—you'd never guess that anything had gone wrong at all."

Celia straightened the leather reins, then looped them over the hook. "Missy is a very loving child, but I want her to be realistic about life, too. Because of the CP, she'll have to be. People aren't perfect—they just do the best they can. And sometimes you have to pick up the slack yourself."

Celia's words echoed through Dani's thoughts later as she sat in the quiet Silverbrook office. After the Johnsons had left, she'd watched the end of the polo match—seeing Black Rock go down in defeat to the Rivercrest team from Long Island—before heading back to the clubhouse to put in an hour of work. Now she was supposed to be typing up the prize list for the Pegasus Horse Show. Instead, she stared thoughtfully out the window.

People do the best they can, she thought. Even her parents had done what they could. It was just that their best hadn't been nearly good enough. They were cold, uncaring people. And she had allowed their behavior to shade her view of the entire world.

Dani thought about Preston, trying so desperately to woo Victoria to his side; and about Missy, who had lost Charm,

yet still gave her love wholeheartedly to her new pony.
Everyone got hurt; everyone felt pain. It was part of being
alive. By shutting people out, she may have saved herself
some anguish, but she had also deprived herself of much,
much more—the warmth, the caring, the sharing, without
which life wasn't complete.

"People do the best they can," she repeated softly. And
she'd be willing to bet anything that Malone's best was
pretty damn good. She might not be sure what love was, but
one thing was becoming increasingly clear: if ever she could
love a man, if ever she was capable of feeling that depth of
emotion, he would be the one.

The phone on the desk began to ring, and Dani reached
for it automatically. Frowning at the intrusion, she fit the
receiver to her ear. "Hello, Pegasus," she said. "May I help
you?"

Then, as her gaze drifted over the cluttered desk, she was
struck by an idea so simple, so perfect, that she was amazed
she hadn't thought of it sooner. Preston had helped her to
dream again. Now it was up to her to do the same for him.

SATURDAY DAWNED bright and clear. The weather was
warm, but not oppressive; a brisk breeze turned the flags
surrounding the polo field into strips of flying color. Dani
awoke early. Like a child on Christmas, her body tingled
with a wondrous sense of expectation.

Though the match wasn't until two, she decided to leave
for the club immediately. She was nervous enough as it was,
without having to deal with Preston's solicitous hovering. To
Dani's surprise, when she left the house, Sabrina's Mercedes was just coming up the drive. She waited by the steps,
grinning as the little convertible executed a sliding stop that
sent a shower of gravel flying into the bushes.

"You're up early," Dani said by way of a greeting.

Sabrina leaned her crossed arms on top of the open window and smiled. "That's one way of looking at it."

"What's the other?"

"Let's just say that with all these polo-playing hunks in town it seems a shame to waste any time sleeping."

Dani looked at her friend incredulously. Brie's eyes were clear, her hair shining, her face artfully made up. In short, she looked gorgeous. "You mean you didn't go to bed last night?"

Brie chuckled wickedly. "I didn't say that."

"Sabrina, you're one of a kind." Dani shook her head in admiration. "If I were you, I'd probably have stale breath, lank hair and big black circles under my eyes."

"Really?" Sabrina's brow rose. "Well, in your place, I'd be positively glowing."

Dani looked at her in surprise. "What do you mean?"

"Simple," Brie said with a shrug. "I always glow when I fall in love."

Sabrina took one look at Dani's dumbfounded expression and laughed heartily. "Come on," she said. "Get in. I figured you could probably use some moral support this morning, so I've come to drive you to the club."

Dani had walked around the car, climbed in and fastened her seat belt before she finally found her voice. "You're wrong, you know," she said finally.

"Maybe." Brie darted a glance out of the corner of her eye. "Maybe not." She started the car and its powerful engine hummed quietly. Then she floored the accelerator, and with a roar they were off. "Let's just say that I've done it enough times that I know what to look for."

"Then I wish you'd explain it to me," Dani said with a sigh. "Because I don't understand how it works at all."

"I can't imagine why." Sabrina steered the car with one hand. With the other, she slipped a heavy-metal cassette into the tape player. "Falling in love is the easiest thing in the world."

"For you, maybe."

Sabrina's laugh was gay. "I have to admit, I am unusually gifted."

Dani grinned. Doubtless there were men all over the world who would agree with her. "Who was it last night?"

"Bob Mercer from Boulder Brook. Have you met him?"

Dani shook her head. "I don't think so."

"Believe me, if you had, you'd know it. Blond hair, shoulders like a linebacker, rides like a dream."

"So," said Dani, turning in the seat to face her. "Are you in love with him?"

"Heavens, no! I only met the man yesterday. Even I can't work that fast."

"But how do you know?"

Sabrina's brow lifted. "Know what?"

"When you fall in love," Dani said slowly, "how do you know that's really it? What does it feel like?"

Brie glanced at her balefully. "If I could answer that, I'd be famous. People have won the Nobel Prize for less."

Dani uttered a small, frustrated growl. "I know I care for Rick...a lot," she added after a pause. "But I always thought that love would be something more, something magical."

"It is." Sabrina's red-tipped fingers spun the wheel, and the Mercedes whipped around a turn. "The magic is there with you and Rick. You just haven't allowed yourself to feel it."

"That's what he says." Dani frowned. "He also says he's in love with me."

"If I were you, I'd be singing on rooftops." Brie glanced at Dani's morose expression. "Obviously you don't feel the same. So what's the problem?"

"I don't know." Dani shook her head. "It's just that I don't want to make any mistakes."

Sabrina reached out and placed a hand on Dani's arm. "Don't push it," she said. "It'll come. When you decide you're in love with Rick, you'll know."

"But how?"

Sabrina looked at Dani and laughed. "For all those flip remarks you like to throw around, you don't take things lightly. Knowing you, you'll probably feel as though you've been hit over the head by a ton of bricks."

"But what if it doesn't happen?"

"Trust me," Sabrina said wisely. "It will."

BY TWO O'CLOCK, Dani felt as though an entire chorus line of butterflies was doing high kicks in her stomach. She'd chosen the ponies she was going to ride, checked and re-checked her equipment, then finally gone into the locker room and pulled on her yellow jersey, white breeches and high brown boots. Now there was nothing left to do but go out and play.

She'd chosen Melody for the first chukker. The mare would give her confidence in the beginning when she needed it most. As she waited for the game to begin, Dani trotted a series of slow circles at the end of the field and mentally re-viewed everything she knew about the Rivercrest team.

Blue Birch, Silverbrook's last rivals, had been fast and flashy. By contrast, the Rivercrest team was smooth and fluid. Their technical skills were excellent, but that wasn't what set them apart. Watching them in a match earlier in the week, Dani had been mesmerized by the sheer poetic beauty of their play. They were so good they made even the hard-est shots look easy.

So good, in fact, that the odds were running two to one in their favor. Dani grinned at the thought. She'd always thrived on a challenge. This time, it seemed, she was going to get one.

After all the mental preparation she'd done, Dani was shocked to discover that the first two chukkers were almost boringly routine. Both teams used the time to take measure of the other. Most of the play centered in the middle of the field, and although several attacks were launched on each goal, there hadn't been a single score.

By the third chukker, the spectators were beginning to grow restless. Their mood carried out to the field, affecting the players as well. Passes became faster and more accurate, hits harder and more determined. Dani was riding well, and she knew it. As she'd hoped, her level of play had risen to match those around her. Although nothing had been said, she knew that the Rivercrest team had expected to find her to be the weak link. From the increasing respect with which they treated her, it was clear they had not.

Still, despite Silverbrook's efforts, it was Rivercrest that scored the first goal. A pass pulled the defender, Trip Malloy, wide, and the red-shirted Rivercrest forward dribbled the ball between the goalposts. A burst of applause rippled through the stands. Only moments later, the horn sounded. The first half of the game was over.

During the halftime break, Rick called the members of the team together for an impromptu strategy session. "We're handing it to them on a platter," he announced. "They're controlling the game, and we're letting them. If we intend to win, it's got to stop, and the sooner the better."

"I disagree," Trip broke in. "It seems to me that we've had the ball just as much as they have."

Impatiently Rick shook his head. "That isn't what I meant. We've all watched them play. Stylistically they ride a very different match than we do. They're slower and calmer. They can afford to be—they have so much control out there that they make every movement count. We're good, but we're not that good. Yet we've let them slow us down to play at their pace. It's hurting us now, and it's only going to get worse.''

Jim and Trip went off to change their shirts, leaving Rick and Dani by themselves. Was he still angry at her? Dani wondered. She wanted to make amends, but she wasn't quite sure how to begin. Tentatively, she offered Rick a smile. He didn't return it. His expression was tense, preoccupied. When he spoke finally, his tone was all business.

''They're playing you hard because you're a woman,'' he said. ''You're bearing the brunt of their attack, and I just wanted you to know I think you're doing a damn fine job.''

''Thank you,'' Dani said softly. Had he given her an opening, she might have told him how much his praise meant. He didn't.

''Don't thank me,'' Rick said gruffly. ''Just keep playing the way you have been.'' He turned away as the warning bell sounded. Then abruptly, he spun back. ''Give 'em hell, Dani,'' he growled. ''If anyone can do it, you can.''

In the fifth chukker, Rick scored Silverbrook's first goal. It was a triumph of brute strength and determination to succeed as he survived one rough hit, then muscled aside another before deftly stroking the ball between the posts. Almost immediately, he pulled Trigger to a stop. The bay stood on three legs, favoring the fourth.

Dani watched Rick quickly dismount. Though he tried to hide it, she saw his wince as he leaned over to check the bay's leg. Obviously the pony wasn't the only one suffering from the aftereffects of the hit. Spinning Ringo around she trotted to the sidelines and grabbed Melody's reins.

''Here,'' she said, leading the mare to Rick. ''Take her.''

Rick frowned sharply. ''They're bringing Silver out.''

''She's already had two hard chukkers,'' Dani pointed out. ''She'll never make it through the end of the game.''

''Then I'll ride Scout.''

Dani scowled down at him. "He hasn't got the experience to carry you through the last chukker, and we both know it."

For a moment Rick was silent. "Give me another pony, then," he said finally. "Not Melody. You should be riding her. She's your best."

Yes, thought Dani. Melody was her best. And for just that reason Melody was the only one that would do. He might not admit it, but Rick was hurting. Dani longed to take him in her arms and soothe his pain away. For now, that just wasn't possible. But if she couldn't take care of Rick, then her best polo pony would. Dani knew Melody. She'd trained the mare herself. She would keep him safe.

As the sixth chukker opened, tension crackled in the air. Even the Rivercrest team, normally so controlled, were playing on edge. The tempo of the game picked up. As minutes passed, the play became fast and furious. Each team strove to find that extra edge, that small advantage that would enable them to score.

Usually by that point in a match, Dani was exhausted. Now she was exhilarated. She'd pushed herself to the limit and found that she was equal to the challenge. In the closing minutes of the match, that knowledge added an extra sparkle of confidence to her play. When she saw the ball fly downfield toward the Rivercrest goal, Dani sent Trumpet racing after it. The shot was hers. She was sure of it.

Then, as she galloped after the ball, Dani saw Rick take off, riding a line on the shot as well. Since he was the superior player, immediately three members of the Rivercrest team moved to head him off. She had two choices, Dani realized suddenly. She could take the shot, and perhaps score the winning goal—a feat she'd once thought meant more to her than anything in the world. Or she could ride to Rick's aid.

All at once something moved within Dani as the world seemed to shift into a brighter focus—one that was clearer, more perfect than she'd ever known before. It would hit her like a ton of bricks, Brie had said, and suddenly Dani knew her friend hadn't been far off. Because in that split second she finally knew what love meant. It was caring for someone so much that his well-being meant everything to her. More than the shot, the game, the winning or the losing. More than anything else in the whole world.

Angling Trumpet away from the ball, Dani set a course toward the opposing players. Determinedly she steered the gelding into their path. They had to either give ground or crash, and for a heart-stopping moment she was afraid they would choose the latter. Then abruptly the Rivercrest players veered away.

Just ahead of them, Rick reached the ball. His mallet connected cleanly, and a loud crack echoed the length of the field. Dani held her breath as the white sphere hurtled toward the goal, then expelled it in one long sigh as the ball flew between the posts.

"I love you, Rick Malone," Dani said softly. She glanced across the field to where he was galloping Melody back for the next toss-in. Her heart swelled with emotion until her senses reeled with the fullness of it. "I love you."

Though there was still more than a minute to play, the game was over, and both teams seemed to know it. The last sixty seconds passed without incident. When the horn sounded, signaling the end, Dani stood in her stirrups and cheered. They'd done it! The Silverbrook team had finally won the Challenge Cup.

As she trotted from the field, Dani found herself grinning like an idiot. Not only that, but she was powerless to stop. Elation bubbled within her, heady like fine champagne. Even better was the feeling of rightness that the discovery of her love for Rick had brought with it. Confusion slipped away, and harmony took its place. For the first time, Dani realized, she felt truly at peace, both with herself and her emotions.

After handing Trumpet over to the hotwalkers, she scanned the sidelines eagerly. When she finally spotted Rick, he was heading in her direction. From the stormy expression on his face, Dani could tell that he was none too pleased. It was par for the course, she thought. Nothing had ever been easy between them. Why had she ever imagined anything would change now?

Rick's long, angry strides carried him straight to her. Quickly Dani moved to forestall the argument she knew was coming. "Congratulations on your goal," she said, flashing him a cheeky grin. "Your playing was superb!"

Her praise didn't appease him in the slightest. "It wasn't easy," he snapped, "considering that you played the game like my mother."

Dani felt so good it was an effort to keep from laughing. She settled for lifting her brow. "I didn't know your mother played polo."

Rick was not amused. "You know what I mean! You were riding shotgun for me out there, and I didn't like it one bit."

Dani's grin widened. The fact that she and Rick were sparring again didn't bother her in the slightest. By now they were old hands at it.

"As I recall," she said placidly, "the last time something like this came up, you yelled at me for taking your shot. This time I figured I was better off staying out of your way."

Rick glared at her furiously. Perversely, the calmer Dani looked, the angrier he felt. "Staying out of my way, hell! That wasn't all you were doing. Ask the Rivercrest team. In your own, inimitable way you managed to keep three-quarters of them out of my way as well!"

"Well, it worked, didn't it? You scored the goal, and we won the game." Dani propped her hands on her hips. "In case you haven't realized, that's what was supposed to happen."

Rick muttered an obscenity under his breath. With a frown, he glanced at the crowd of players and spectators that was beginning to gather around them. They were standing no more than twenty feet from the officials' box, and it was almost time for the presentation ceremony to begin. Obviously they were bound to attract attention. He had no desire to make a spectacle of himself, Rick decided. He'd make one final point, and then leave it at that.

"Next time," he said, swinging back to Dani, "try staying on your own side of the field. You're not my guardian angel, Dani. You had no right to interfere."

"That's where you're wrong!" Dani snapped, oblivious to the growing crowd. "I had every right, Malone, and do you want to know why?"

Rick's sigh was resigned. "All right, Dani, I give up. Why?"

"Oh, for Pete's sake." Dani shook her head fiercely as her eyes clouded with sudden tears. "Because I love you, Malone." Her voice dropped to a whisper. "That's why."

Rick realized his mouth was open, and quickly pulled it shut. In all the time he'd known her, Dani had never ceased to surprise him. Obviously she wasn't about to start now. Then, all at once, the truth of what she'd said sank in, and exhilaration soared within him. He gazed downward into her eyes. They were filled with enough warmth, enough caring, enough love, to last him a lifetime.

His breath caught in his throat. "Are you sure?"

"Of course," Dani said blithely. Now that she was beginning to get used to the idea of being in love, she found she rather liked it. "And I'll tell you something else," she added, eyes twinkling. "You better believe it's in my best interests to look out for you, because I want that body of yours in perfect working order for our wedding night!"

At that, a cacophony of hoots and catcalls erupted around them as the assembled players broke into a loud cheer. Realizing abruptly what she had done, Dani felt her face grow hot. Now, however, Rick was the one who seemed oblivious to their audience as he dropped his pads and mallet on the ground and pulled her into his arms.

"Dani," he murmured into her ear, "are you saying what I think you are?"

Tremulously Dani nodded. Then Rick lowered his mouth to hers as he drew them together for a hard, stirring kiss—an act that only prompted more cheers from the delighted spectators.

It wasn't until much later, long after the presentation of the trophy and the riotous champagne toasts, and after the players had been interviewed and the ponies bedded down, that Rick and Dani finally had a chance to be alone. Sitting on the love seat in the library at Greenfields, Dani drew her legs up onto the cushion and rested her head on Rick's shoulder.

"When did you know for sure?" he asked.

"The end of the last chukker," Dani replied with a smile. "Although by the time I realized what was going on, it seemed so perfectly obvious that I was amazed I hadn't figured it out sooner. I knew I cared about you. But despite what you said, or maybe because of it, I didn't want to believe that what I felt was love. I thought love made people weak. It was frightening for me to accept the way I was coming to depend on you, terrifying to think that I could need someone so much."

Rick nodded. He'd known the demons she was fighting. Now he wanted to hear everything, to understand fully how she'd managed to win. "What changed your mind?"

Dani's fingers came up to play with the placket of Rick's shirt. "Today during the polo match, I finally realized that it wasn't a one-way street. You needed me just as much as I

needed you. I remembered what you said about being part-
ners, equal in every way, and for the first time I really
understood what you meant.'' She shrugged lightly. ''After
that, there didn't seem nearly so much to be frightened of
anymore.''

In spite of himself, Rick laughed, his head shaking in
wonderment. ''You've got to be the only person in the world
who could run off three galloping horses, not to mention
three very determined men with big sticks, and still manage
to think of it as the least frightening of your options.''

''Well, you know me,'' Dani said, laughing with him. ''I
never have done things the easy way.''

''Are you sorry?'' Rick asked when they'd grown quiet
once more. ''I know how much scoring that goal would have
meant to you.''

Dani raised her head, looking up into his eyes. ''Not at
all,'' she said truthfully. ''The victory was a team effort as
it should have been.'' Her arm wound around the back of
his neck, drawing him closer. ''And if I do say so myself,
Malone,'' she whispered against his lips, ''you and I make
one hell of a fine team.''

Epilogue

Mr. Charles Hawthorne of Chicago, Illinois, and the Countess Amelie Barazini of Westport, Connecticut, and Florence, Italy, are pleased to announce the marriage of their daughter, Danielle Winslow Hawthorne, to Richard Malone. The wedding will take place at Greenfields, the bride's home in Westport. The future Mrs. Malone, a graduate of Miss Porter's and Yale University, is a director of the Pegasus Program, and a polo player with the Silverbrook Hunt Club. Mr. Malone, who is a graduate of UCLA and Stanford School of Business, is President and Chief Executive Officer of Malone Inc. He, too, is a member of the Silverbrook polo team. Following a wedding trip to Bora Bora, Mr. and Mrs. Malone will reside in Westport.

THE SCENE IN THE LIBRARY was chaos. It was there that the bridal party had gathered to await their cue—the stirring chords of music that would send the procession out the French doors and across the terrace to the flower-decked grotto where the ceremony would take place.

Charles Hawthorne was perched on the edge of the desk. With one hand he held the telephone receiver to his ear, and with the other he filled the notepad at his side with pages of tall, slanted script. Brie, as maid of honor, was dressed in a long blue-and-white off-the-shoulder gown. At the moment she was searching frantically for a hairbrush. A door flew open, and Amelie breezed through. Resplendent in emerald silk and gems to match, she glanced around the room, waved vaguely in her daughter's direction, then was gone just as quickly as she'd come. The florist was making last-minute adjustments to the bridal bouquet, while the caterer was moaning loudly about a shipment of melted ice.

In the midst of all the confusion stood an oasis of calm. Dressed and ready, Dani waited patiently for the ceremony to begin.

"Stop hovering, Preston," she said, looking back over her shoulder at the butler, who was straightening her veil. "It makes me nervous just to look at you."

"Brides are supposed to be nervous, miss."

"Well, I'm not," Dani said firmly. "I know exactly what I'm doing."

Preston permitted himself a small smile. "There were times when I doubted I'd live to see the day."

"The same might be said of you and Victoria," Dani pointed out. "The way you beat around the bush, you're lucky she ever agreed to come."

"That was your doing." Preston plucked at the beaded edging one last time. "The idea you had to offer her the post of administrative head of the Pegasus Program was sheer genius. It made all the difference."

"It made all the difference to me, too," Dani agreed, remembering how the British nanny's capable manner and no-nonsense approach had turned the office around. "Victoria is a wonder. I don't know how we ever managed to get along without her. And, of course, after all her years of experience she's terrific with the children, too."

Preston smiled innocently. "I'm sure she could be persuaded to go back into private service if the right opportunity arose."

"Don't start with me, Preston," Dani warned, laughing in spite of herself.

"No, miss," Preston said solemnly. "Of course not."

"Dani, do I look okay?"

She glanced down to find Missy standing beside her, the little girl's arms braced in a pair of metal crutches. Missy's blue lace dress fell to the floor, and a spray of white baby roses were woven through her dark curls. Dani pushed her gown aside carefully and crouched down. "You look lovely," she said. "You're the most beautiful flower girl that I've ever seen."

Missy preened happily. "When I grow up, I'm going to have a big wedding just like this one. And I bet I won't have to use crutches anymore either. When they play the music, I'm going to skip down the aisle."

"I bet you will, sweetheart," Dani said, smiling softly. "I just bet you will."

Outside on the terrace, Rick took his place at the edge of the grotto. Beside him, similarly dressed in a gray morning suit, stood Billy Matlock.

"You know," Billy said slowly, "I envy you, Rick. You finally found what you really wanted."

Rick's answering smile was wry. "As it turned out, finding her wasn't half as hard as catching her."

"Tell me about it."

Rick glanced over, surprised by Billy's tone.

"I guess I forgot to mention that I have a date with Sabrina for later?"

"Yes." Rick chuckled softly, remembering the night the four of them had spent out together. "As a matter of fact, you did. Good luck."

"Thanks," Billy growled. "I'll probably need it."

"Try being patient," Rick advised. "It works wonders."

Billy snorted under his breath. "I've never been the patient type."

"Trust me." Rick smiled as a faraway look came into his eyes. "You'll learn."

Inside the library, Dani crossed the room to peek out through the French doors. The guests were seated, the musicians ready. It was time for the wedding to begin.

"All right," said Brie, appearing beside them. "I'm all set. What's holding this show up?"

Silently Dani nodded toward the end of the room where her father was still talking on the phone.

"Is that all?"

Dani watched as the brunette walked behind the mahogany bar, stooped and began to fiddle with the phone jack. She stifled a laugh when her father frowned suddenly, then reached down to jiggle the button on the phone. Finally, giving the connection up for lost, he slammed down the receiver and crossed the room to where she stood.

Balefully Charles Hawthorne eyed Missy's crutches and the braces, which were covered but not quite hidden by the long, frilly dress. "This is going to be a damned slow procession," he growled.

"What's the hurry?" Dani raised one eyebrow coolly. "Do you have a plane to catch?"

For the first time in her life, Dani saw her father look flustered. He cleared his throat uncomfortably. "No, I'm not going anywhere."

"Then we wait," Dani said firmly, glad that Missy hadn't overheard the exchange. "As long as it takes."

Another time she'd have been furious at her father for his insensitive attitude, Dani realized as the music finally began to play. But not now, and not ever again; because it simply didn't matter anymore. She'd made peace with her parents when she'd found peace with Rick.

Her father took her arm, and they stepped slowly out onto the terrace. Dani lifted her head, thrust out her chin and looked down toward the end of the long blue carpet where Rick stood waiting. At last her past was truly behind her. In his eyes, she saw all the promise her future held.

ATTRACTIVE, SPACE SAVING BOOK RACK

Display your most prized novels on this handsome and sturdy book rack. The hand-rubbed walnut finish will blend into your library decor with quiet elegance, providing a practical organizer for your favorite hard-or soft-covered books.

Only $9.95

Approximately 16" x 8" when assembled

Assembles in seconds!

To order, rush your name, address and zip code, along with a check or money order for $10.70* ($9.95 plus 75¢ postage and handling) payable to *Harlequin Reader Service*:

Harlequin Reader Service
Book Rack Offer
901 Fuhrmann Blvd.
P.O. Box 1396
Buffalo, NY 14269-1396

Offer not available in Canada.

BKR-1A

*New York and Iowa residents add appropriate sales tax.

Take 4 best-selling love stories FREE
Plus get a FREE surprise gift!

Keeping the Faith

by
Judith Arnold

It renewed old friendships, kindled new relationships, but the fifteen-year reunion of *The Dream*'s college staff affected all six of the Columbia-Barnard graduates: Laura, Seth, Kimberly, Andrew, Julianne and Troy.

Follow the continuing story of these courageous, vital men and women who find themselves at a crossroads—as their idealism of the sixties clashes with the reality of life in the eighties.

You may laugh, you may cry, but you will find a piece of yourself in *Keeping the Faith*.

Don't miss American Romance #201 *Promises* in June, #205 *Commitments* in July and #209 *Dreams* in August.

KFaith-gen